WHO AM I?

Other Fictive Press Titles by Carol Matas

Tucson Jo

When I Die: A Meditation on Death for Children & Their Families

WHO AM I?

Carol Matas

FICTIVE PRESS

A FICTIVE PRESS Book

Copyright © 2016 by Carol Matas.
All rights reserved. This book or any portion thereof may not be reproduced or used in any manner whatsoever without the express written permission of the publisher, except for brief quotations in a book review or scholarly journal.

Who Am I? is a work of fiction. Names, characters, places and incidents are the product of the author's imagination or are used fictitiously. Any resemblance to actual events or persons, living or dead, is entirely coincidental.

A First Fictive Press Edition. *Who Am I?* was previously published by Scholastic Canada as a trilogy: *Cloning Miranda, The Second Clone* and *The Dark Clone.*

Fictive Press is a division of BizNet Communications (2815699 Canada Inc.), British Columbia, Canada.
fictivepress.com
"Fictive Press" and "fictivepress.com" are trademarks of 2815699 Canada Inc.

Cover design by Fictive Press.
Author photo by Bonnie Brask.

Library and Archives Canada Cataloguing in Publication

Matas, Carol, 1949-
[Novels. Selections]

Who am I? / Carol Matas. -- First Fictive Press edition.

Previously published separately under titles: Cloning Miranda, The second clone and The dark clone.

Issued in print and electronic formats.
ISBN 978-1-927663-37-0 (paperback).
--ISBN 978-1-927663-38-7 (kindle).
--ISBN 978-1-927663-39-4 (epub).--ISBN 978-1-927663-40-0 (pdf)

I. Title. II. Title: Novels. Selections.

PS8576.A7994A6 2016   jC813'.54   C2016-900290-X
C2016-900291-8

For my grandchildren,
Zevi, Naomi,
Lucille, Davis, Nora,
Kai and Meira.
With love,
Tata/Safta

Part One

WHO

Chapter 1

"Miranda, why do you always have to be so good? You drive me crazy!"

Emma's words echo in my mind as I sit in English class, going over our conversation from last night.

Emma stood, hands on hips, face flushed, black curly hair swinging as she shook her head.

"Don't get so mad!" I answered.

"I'm *not* mad."

"Yes, you are."

"I'm just ... frustrated. You never do anything fun."

"Why is it fun to stay out after our curfew? Our parents will just worry."

"So?"

"So, don't you care?"

"No!"

"Not at all?"

"No! They're my *parents*. They're *supposed* to worry. That's their job. My job is to be a teenager. Stay out late. Have fun. Come on. Bob'll drive us out to the Art Smith Trail. Hiking at night. It'll be awesome."

"No," I said stubbornly. "My parents trust me. They'd be frantic." I got onto my bike. The two of us were standing just outside Sue's house in Palm Desert. Sue's older brother Bob had suddenly got this idea for a hike. Sue begged him to take us along. He was just humoring us anyway. I could tell. He didn't want a bunch of kids with him and his friends.

"We're not wanted anyway," I said to Emma. "Bob's just teasing us. Now, are you coming or not?"

"No, you go ahead," Emma sulked.

"You want to ride home alone?"

"No."

"Then come on."

"You make me so mad!" Reluctantly she got onto her bike.

As we rode to her house, where my mom had agreed to pick me up, I tried to calm her down. "I have an important rehearsal tomorrow," I reminded her.

She sighed. "I know. But you'll be great at the recital."

"Great isn't good enough," I muttered. "I have to be perfect. And that means practice, practice, practice."

It was dark so I couldn't see her rolling her eyes but I knew she was doing it. Still, I did feel I had to be perfect. Nothing less would do. It was expected. I had the lead for my dance recital. What if I tripped? What if I lost a count?

"Listen to yourself," Emma chided me. "'I have to be home on time, I have to get "A"s in everything, I have to be perfect' ... No one's *perfect*!"

She was right, of course. That's why I loved having her as my best friend. She was the only one around me who didn't want me to be perfect. For a split second I wondered if she was right and I was too much of a goody-goody. But I didn't like to dwell on that too much.

"It's no wonder my mom loves you so much," Emma complained. "'Miranda's such a good influence on you' ..."

"See how reasonable *my* parents are?" I grinned. "They like you because *I* do. And they've never said you're a *bad*

10

influence on me even though you are."

"I *try* to be," Emma corrected me. "I never succeed."

So as I sit here, paying no attention to what's going on in class, I can't help but think about what she said. And I can't help but wonder about it. I mean, Emma's parents are pretty reasonable—but that doesn't matter to Emma. She does the opposite of what they want just to make them mad. And when she *really* believes they're wrong and she's right, she'll lie or cheat to get her way. So, I wonder—why is Emma the way she is, and why am I the way I am? I guess what I really wonder is, why am I so good? Is it bad to be good? Am I a real teenager or just some kind of fake? Maybe I should practice saying no to Mom and Dad just so I can be more normal. I have to admit I'm starting to see myself as a little weird.

"Miranda? Are you with us?"

I just about jump out of my skin. Mrs. Dromboski is talking to me.

"Yes. Yes."

"Could you share your thoughts?"

Tell everyone in class what was going through my mind? I don't think so.

"Your thoughts, Miranda. After all, we are discussing your namesake from *The Tempest*. What does Miranda mean when she says, 'How beauteous mankind is! O brave new world, / That has such people in't'?"

"Well," I blurt out, "she thinks those guys are hot. And it's cool that there are so many of them."

The entire class breaks out laughing.

"Hot," Mrs. Dromboski repeats. "You're right, Miranda, as

usual. That's *exactly* what she means."

See what I'm saying? I can't even get into trouble in class.

School finally over, Emma and I hurry out the front door.

"That must be my mom." I grimace. I can barely see the car through the mob of boys surrounding her new Mercedes convertible.

They step aside as I walk up and I slip into the front seat. "Let's go, Mom," I say, under my breath.

She waves at the mob, rather like a queen waving to her subjects, then burns rubber as we leave the crush. I roll my eyes. "Honestly!"

"You can be a terrible stick-in-the-mud," Mom chides me. She smiles, her long hair whipping in the wind. We're often mistaken for sisters—tall, slim, and blonde with blue eyes. We even dress similarly: tailored jackets, cuffed, slim cut pants, freshly ironed shirts and, of course, penny loafers. I don't see why she had to buy such a flashy car. But she says she likes it and that I shouldn't be so self-conscious.

We arrive at the dance studio and I hurry into the dressing room to put on my costume. Most of the girls are there already in various states of undress. I'm not best friends with any of them but they don't hate me either. Well, maybe Cally hates me. She's so awkward and big and lumpy. I suppose her parents forced her to take ballet in the hope that it would make her more graceful, slim her down. But it's been a disaster for her.

She tries to make up for her clumsiness with a sense of humor, though. She starts to tell a joke as soon as I walk in. She looks like she hasn't noticed me but as soon as I hear the beginning of the joke I know she has.

"What do you call it when a blonde dyes her hair brown?

Artificial intelligence."

I laugh along with everyone else even though I know she meant it for me.

My costume is a long black skirt over a deep red leotard. I play the scheming queen in a piece our teacher, Ms. Leonard, choreographed. She's very happy with my technique but not with my interpretation. She tells me over and over that I have to reach down inside myself and find the dark places. But I'd like to know what rulebook on life has decided that we all have dark places? Maybe we don't—well, I can't seem to find mine, anyway.

As we troop into the rehearsal room Ms. Leonard greets us all in that way she has, like she sees you but she doesn't. She always seems to be in two places at once and I have no idea where the second place is.

"Ahh, girls, wonderful, let me check your costumes. Angie, that's a bit loose on you. Marlene, that's perfect. Michael, you look just right ..."

There are two boys in our class, and one of them, Peter, is very talented. He plays the king.

"Now, Miranda," she instructs me, "I want you to take a moment before we start. Think of the cruelest thing anyone has ever said to you."

I rack my brains but those stupid blonde jokes are pretty close to the worst. I shake my head.

"Miranda!" Ms. Leonard says, exasperated. "Everyone has had cruel experiences in their lives. A schoolyard bully, a girlfriend who hurt your feelings. Come now. You need this to get into your character. You're still far too nice."

I think back quickly. All my memories are good ones. If anything awful did happen to me, I can't remember. I shake my head. "Sorry, Ms. Leonard. I had a pretty happy childhood, I guess."

She throws her arms in the air in a dramatic gesture. "Then you must use your *imagination*. Imagine what it would feel like to be so angry, to hate someone so much that you had to plot to hurt them. You must *feel* it."

"I'll try," I promise.

"Fine, let's begin." She glides away in order to turn on her iPod, which is connected to a pretty powerful sound system.

"Places, please!" She claps her hands.

We all take our places. She taps the iPod and music blasts out. The princess, Rachel, and the prince, Michael, open the first scene. I wait on the side, poised, trying to make myself angry.

That blonde joke was nasty, I tell myself. I feel a small jab of anger. On the other hand, I think, imagine the taunts poor Cally must endure every day. She wants to lash out but she's probably afraid to do it to someone who'll lash back. She knows I won't. So ... And then I'm not mad anymore. I sigh. Mom calls me her little psychologist. Ever since I was small I was able to tell why people were doing what they were doing. When I was five my parents had a party and Uncle Rob got drunk, and I had to explain to my dad that Uncle Rob felt bad when he came to our house because he wasn't rich and successful like his brother. I remember them looking at me all astonished and my mom saying, "Meet Ms. Freud." I didn't understand her so I demanded that she tell me who Freud was—and of course, that's when they started saying how brilliant I was.

My entrance is about to come up and I'm no farther ahead with feeling mad. I start to count down to my first jeté, watching Rachel closely since I must jeté over to her, when suddenly she goes all blurry. I blink my eyes. It doesn't help. Everything is blurry.

"Miranda!" Ms. Leonard stops the music. "You missed your entrance."

"I know," I whisper, "but … but …"

"What is it?"

"I can't see properly."

And *now* I feel something real. Fear. No matter how much I blink or shake my head it won't go away—everything around me is fuzzy and blurred.

Ms. Leonard takes me over to a chair and sits me down. "I'll go find your mother," she says, obviously worried.

"Hurry," I urge her. "It's getting worse."

Chapter 2

Mom thinks there's something in my eyes, like an eyelash or a piece of grit. She pulls my lower lids down but she can't see anything.

"I'd better take her to the doctor," she tells Ms. Leonard, and she hustles me into the dressing room, helps me change and has me in the car in minutes. "You can't fool around with your eyes," she says. "If there's something in there it could scratch the cornea."

Meanwhile, I am trying not to panic. The thing is, I'm never sick. When I say never, I mean never. I'll get an occasional sniffle or a mild sore throat sometimes but it's not enough to slow me down. Once I had a stomach flu and it was horrible—but it was only once. Emma calls me Superwoman because no matter what is going around the school, I don't catch it, and she does.

"Mom," I say in a small voice, "what is it?"

The blurring won't go away. It's like being in the steam room of our country club. Everything's misty.

"Did it happen all of a sudden?" she asks.

"Yes."

"I don't know, Mira," she says. She only calls me that at certain times, if she's worried or if we're having a special moment. Obviously, she's worried.

I still go to a pediatrician and we have to walk through a

16

jumble of toys and screaming babies when we get to his waiting room. I'm rushed into his office almost immediately because Mom and Dad own this clinic. In fact, they own health clinics right across the country—the Coburn Conglomerate—named after my grandmother because it was her money Dad used to build this empire of his.

Dr. Corne greets me gravely, as always. The other pediatricians in the practice are full of jokes and seem to have perpetual smiles on their faces, but not Dr. Corne. I don't think I've ever seen him smile. He's not mean or grumpy. He's just serious.

"Let's have a look at you, Miranda," he says. "Is there something in your eye?"

"I don't know," I reply. "I was waiting for my cue at dance rehearsal and suddenly everything went blurry. It's still blurry."

He peers into both my eyes with his small light. Then he checks my chart. "You were last here just under a year ago and you were in perfect health."

"That's right," Mom nods.

He examines my eyes again. "Miranda, I'm going to order some tests."

Then, just as suddenly as it happened, it disappears.

"My eyes are fine again, Dr. Corne!" I exclaim. "It's gone away."

"Wait here for a minute, Miranda," Dr. Corne says and he motions my mom to follow him out of the room. They shut the door but it doesn't catch and it slides open just a bit. I can hear snatches of their conversation. "Tests, something there ... impossible, I'm afraid ... can't be ... wait, be patient ..."

The door opens. Mom walks back in, the color drained out

17

of her face.

"What is it?" I say, alarmed.

"We're not sure, Miranda," Dr. Corne says. "But I can see something in your eyes, something that shouldn't be there."

"What? It's gone now. I'm fine."

"The cloudy vision is gone for the moment, but we still need to do some tests. All right? They won't hurt."

I guess I don't have any choice so I agree. Since it's my parents' clinic I don't have to wait—they do all the tests right away. First a nurse takes some blood, then she gives me a slew of tests: CAT, EEG, MRI—who knows what any of it is—why can't medical people speak English?

It gets very, very late and I start to get hungry and grumpy. My dad shows up about halfway through the whole thing and, of course, he's holding a new teddy bear that he's managed to buy before getting here. Anytime I've been bothered about anything, a new teddy has appeared almost immediately. This is a big brown one with very cute eyes and a really soft cuddly body. He gives it to me as I come out of the MRI.

"Thanks, Daddy." I throw my arms around him and he squeezes me in a big hug.

"You all right, Mimi?" That's what he calls me when he's upset. They can pretend there's nothing wrong as much as they want but as long as they are calling me nicknames, I know I'm in trouble.

"I feel fine. My eyes went all funny but they're back to normal. I'm glad I've never minded being stuck in small spaces," I add, looking back at the MRI machine.

"Some people go crazy after a minute in one of them," Daddy grins, "but you aren't afraid of anything."

How can I admit to him how scared I got when my eyes

18

went blurry like that? I smile.

"That's my girl," he says. "I'm sure it's nothing. They just have to take precautions."

It's after eight by the time all the tests are finished and we go home. It's not a long drive from the clinic in Palm Desert to the outskirts of La Quinta where we live, maybe ten, fifteen minutes.

When we get home, Mom grills us some steaks and I make the salad, trying to pretend it's a normal supper. We sit down to dinner around nine, in the kitchen. By that time I'm almost faint from hunger. About halfway through the meal the doorbell rings. When Mom comes back from the door it's with Dr. Corne. He looks serious, but he always looks serious so I try not to get worried. He often comes to the house to discuss the clinic with my mom and dad, so it's not all that strange to see him here. Still, my mouth goes dry and although I was shoveling my food in a minute ago, now I can't even swallow. I reach for a glass of water.

"Miranda," Dr. Corne says, "please finish your dinner. Your parents and I must talk for a few minutes."

Mom grabs onto the back of a chair. Daddy drops his knife and it clatters to the floor. What is going on? Do I have some fatal disease?

"What is it?" I say, my voice coming out squeaky and high.

"I'll tell you, Miranda, I promise. Just let me speak to your parents first."

He follows them into Daddy's study, on the other side of the house. I sit and stare at my food. I notice my phone sticking out from under some bills on the side table. If only I'd had it at the clinic I could have texted Emma. Well, at least I can FaceTime her now.

19

"Emma?"

"Hi. How was rehearsal?"

"Something really weird happened. My eyes went all funny and my mom rushed me to the clinic and they did all these tests and now Dr. Corne is over here talking to my parents."

"Wow," she says, her brow furrowing with worry. "You're not sick are you? You *never* get sick."

"I feel fine."

"Good." She pauses. "So why's Dr. Corne over there?"

"That's what I'd like to know. He said he saw something in my eyes that shouldn't be there."

"What?"

"I don't *know*!"

"Okay, okay, let's not panic," Emma says. "It's probably some sort of stupid cyst or something. Amy Horowitz had one on her eye. They did this little operation and that was that."

"This is *in* my eye, not on it."

"Right. Well. Let's not panic."

Every time she says that I feel more panicky.

Mom's voice interrupting us startles me so much I almost drop the phone. "Mira, could you come into the study please? We have to speak with you." She's white, almost green. Now I'm really nervous.

"Emma, gotta go."

"Call me back!" Emma shouts.

"I will."

I follow Mom to the study. She takes my hand. Hers is ice cold and trembling. I sit down in one of the big overstuffed leather chairs. Mom lets go of my hand and I wonder why.

Dr. Corne is standing by the fireplace. "Miranda, I'm afraid I have some bad news."

Daddy kneels down beside me, and takes my hand. Mom has edged back towards the doorway. She stands just inside the door as if she's afraid to come all the way into the room.

"Miranda," Dr. Corne continues, "the tests showed that you have a tumor growing behind your eyes."

"A tumor?" I repeat. "Like cancer?"

"No, actually it's not cancer. It's a rare and pervasive disorder. Something is wrong with your blood vessels. They aren't growing right. They are producing tumors—you also have them in your liver and we can see the beginnings of more in your kidneys and in your lungs."

I don't speak. I don't understand.

"We're going to do everything we can to make you better," Dr. Corne assures me.

"But," I object, "I'm fine. I feel fine."

I look at Daddy. Maybe he can make Dr. Corne take his words back. "It's all right, Mimi. We can help you. We know we can." He pauses. "Your mom and I ... well, we can't believe it. You've always been so healthy we never thought we'd have to help you but we're ready. We've always been ready."

"Allan!" My mom takes a step forward and her voice is sharp with reproof.

"I didn't say anything," he defends himself. "I just mean, you don't have to worry ..."

I gaze at Dr. Corne. "Will you have to operate?"

"That will only buy us a little time. The tumors will still return."

"I don't understand," I protest. "Daddy says I'll be fine. But you're saying ..."

"I'm just saying that operating on these tumors isn't a cure. But your parents have connections to the top researchers, the

21

best specialists—in fact they tell me they know someone who can help. Let's see what he says before we jump to any conclusions."

"You see?" Daddy encourages me. "You'll be fine. I promise."

Mom walks over to me then and takes my hand. "Nothing is going to happen to you, Mira. *Nothing*." Her gaze is so fierce she almost scares me.

I am trying to take this all in. What they seem to be saying is that I have some horrible, fatal disease, and somehow they're going to save me. But you can't save someone from a fatal disease. So they must just be trying to make me feel better. My eyes fill with tears.

"I'm going to die, aren't I?"

"No!" Mom and Dad exclaim at the same time.

Dr. Corne pats my shoulder. "I know this is a terrible shock, Miranda. But the Coburn Clinics are the best in the state. They'll try everything." He pats my shoulder again and then he leaves.

"Dr. Corne doesn't know the man we've been working with," Daddy says. "You mustn't worry. Your mom and I were just shocked at first. But you'll be fine. I promise."

Daddy has never made a promise he can't keep. But how is he going to cure me of an incurable disease?

22

Chapter 3

Out of habit, I get up and go to school, although I hardly slept a wink all night. I lay in bed and stared into the dark. I couldn't even call Emma back although I know she must have been worried sick.

It's hard to imagine *not* being. At one point I felt a terror so deep, so overwhelming, that I snuck outside and sat under the lemon trees in the dark. I breathed in their sweet fragrance and gazed at the stars and tried not to think at all.

In the car, as Mom drives, I keep getting this image of tumors growing all through my body, taking it over. Mom, oddly enough, is in good spirits.

"I just spoke to the specialist," she chatters on. "Everything is going to be fine. When you get home from school your father and I will tell you all the details. I'm sorry we behaved so badly yesterday—it was a shock. We thought ..."

"You thought what?" I ask. I have the distinct feeling she isn't telling me everything.

"Nothing."

"What causes this disease anyway? Why have I got it?"

She practically squirms then. "We'll explain everything after school, Miranda," she assures me.

"Is there a name for it?"

"Von Hippel-Lindau," Mom answers.

"That's my disease? It sounds like some bad dubbed movie.

23

Everyone will laugh at me!"

We arrive at school. Mom puts her hand on mine. "You mustn't worry. It'll be okay."

I shake my head and get out of the car. I think Mom and Dad are kidding themselves. They can't face the truth. Last night when I couldn't sleep, I wished I could have had all those colds and flus I never got. Maybe this is my payment for never being sick. Getting really sick all at once. I wondered if I should pray except we've never discussed God or praying or anything in our house—if there is a God wouldn't he/she get mad at me for just starting to pay attention now? Yesterday, I was worried about being too good. I'd happily go back to that worry now. I just don't want to be dead.

Emma can tell something is wrong the minute I walk into class. She pulls me aside.

"It's bad," I say.

"You could have called me last night!" she accuses.

"I didn't want to tell you," I admit. "It would have made it seem too real."

She puts her hand on my arm. "Tell me. That's what friends are for."

"It's some sort of tumor."

Emma gasps. "What sort?"

"I'm not sure. Mom just told me the name on the way to school."

"We'll look it up during lunch hour," Emma says. "They can cure anything nowadays," she continues, trying to reassure me.

"That's what my parents say."

"Okay then, lets not panic," Emma says. And unlike last night, this time I know she's panicking.

24

Finally lunch hour arrives. Emma and I go to the library where we are allowed to use our phones if it's for research. I'm not sure exactly who came up with that idea because Ms. Lain never checks to see what anyone is doing as long as we are quiet about it. We get Sue to come too, because she's a good friend. I google Von Hippel-Lindau with Sue sitting on one side of me, and Emma on the other. But what it says upsets me even more, although I didn't think that was possible. Blindness. That's what the eye tumors lead to. And a cure? None, unless all the organs can be transplanted. The one good thing is it's not contagious. That's a relief. Emma, who gets freaked out by any kind of sickness, even the common cold, was already starting to worry about being close to me. Turns out it's genetic.

"Genetic," Sue muses. "That means you've had it since you were born."

"What do you mean?" I ask.

"It's in your DNA. It's part of you. Sue takes my phone and does a search. "Look, here's the definition of DNA, or deoxyribonucleic acid. According to the *Merriam-Webster* dictionary, *DNA is a substance that carries genetic information in the cells of plants and animals.* See the helix? That's what it looks like."

I glance at the colorful twisty strands as Sue taps to enlarge them on the screen.

This is in the category of too much information. I just want to know what is happening to me and why.

"But why didn't I get sick when I was born?" I ask.

"Look," Sue says, pointing to a paragraph further down the screen. "It says here that it usually doesn't present until puberty. Sort of like a time bomb, ticking away."

25

"But I'm fourteen," I object. "I should have gotten sick years ago."

"Maybe it started then," Sue says. "Or maybe the timer didn't work right away. What I can't figure out is why your parents are so surprised—one of them must have it too, right? That's what genetic means. Inherited."

"But they're both *totally* healthy," I say, puzzled.

"This might explain it," she says after a moment. "*Five percent are spontaneous mutations*," she quotes.

"Which means, I suppose, that my genes just went wonky completely on their own—and mutated into this weird thing. But why?"

"Who knows," Sue says with a sigh. "Your mom could have been exposed to something when she was carrying you—or maybe it's just a fluke." She shakes her head. "Sorry, Miranda. It sounds bad, really bad."

"Sue, you have to swear not to tell anyone," I say. "I don't want everyone at school feeling sorry for me."

"Or afraid they'll catch it," Emma grimaces. "People can react that way, even though it's stupid."

Then she pauses, at a loss for words. I can see she has tears in her eyes but she doesn't want to let me see how upset she is. I *am* her best friend, after all.

"You guys go to lunch," I say. "I'm going to read this over again."

Reluctantly they both leave, Sue giving me a pitying look on her way out the door.

No known cure. No known cure. I keep reading it over and over. Mom and Dad must be grasping at straws. There's nothing anyone can do. But why did my genes have to go out of control like that? Why? It makes me feel so helpless. I've

26

always been able to control everything, with hard work, practice, focus; I've always kept my life in order. Now it's spinning, spinning ...

I push up from the desk and go to my locker. I get my knapsack and head out of the school. I can't be here anymore. I need some fresh air.

It's a beautiful day. Spring is still more than a month away but it's already getting hot. I look up at the palm trees as I stand on the corner and realize I don't know how to take the bus home. I've never done it. And I can't walk. It's miles to our house. Even when I'm bad, trying to skip school, I can't do it right. I reach into my knapsack, grab my phone and call Mom.

"Can you come and get me? I'm on the corner of Palm Drive, right near the school."

She doesn't ask why. "I'll be right there."

The sun beats down on my face. For a minute I worry that I forgot to put on my moisturizer with sunscreen in it this morning. Then I laugh out loud. What does it matter? I'll be dead long before I have to worry about skin cancer.

When Mom picks me up she seems almost cheerful. "I told you not to worry," she scolds me, "and I meant it."

I don't answer her. She's obviously lost her mind, from the stress and everything. I'm dying and she can't accept it. I put on the radio, loud, so she won't talk to me. When we get home Daddy is there, on the phone. When he sees me he hangs up and comes over to me.

"Listen, Mimi," he says, "you mustn't be so upset. We have everything under control."

None of us is in control anymore. They've *both* lost their minds.

"Come out by the pool," he says. "Lorna's made us all a late

27

lunch."

We go outside and sit down at a table shaded by a large yellow umbrella. Lorna has fixed my favorite, spinach salad with grilled chicken, and she's made fresh corn bread. I can't eat. I feel sick inside. Mom tucks into her food as if she doesn't have a care in the world.

"We've spoken to Dr. Mullen," Daddy says. "He works at a special clinic we own here in town."

"What special clinic?" I ask.

"It's not far from here," he says. "Actually it's only a few miles away. It's called the G.R.F."

"I didn't know you had another clinic here in town," I say, puzzled.

"Well, it's not open to the public. It's really a research facility," Daddy explains. "They've been doing a lot of work on transplants. And other things."

"You're going to give me transplants?" I ask. "But my liver? My *lungs*? You can't do that, can you?"

"You'd need a perfect match," Daddy admits. "But the doctor is sure he can find one."

I shake my head. I can't believe any of this. No one can have their lungs taken out and live normally. And Dr. Corne said the tumors would grow back, anyway. Something is wrong with my blood or my blood vessels ...

"We'll take you over there soon for some tests. Now finish your lunch."

We sit in silence for a few minutes as I pick at my lunch. Then I say, "I looked the disease up online. I know it's genetic. But neither of you has ever had it, have you?"

Mom and Dad stare at me.

"Genetic?" Dad repeats. "But that would mean we—or one

28

of us—passed it down to you. And I know we haven't. After all, one of us would be sick by now, right?"

Why is he asking *me*? He's the one who's head of one of the biggest health groups in the country! I seem to know more about this disease than he does. Then I realize that he's probably been so busy trying to organize my treatment with this special doctor that he hasn't had time to really think it through.

"There's a small percentage of kids who develop it spontaneously," I say. "Maybe I'm just lucky."

Suddenly Mom gets up from the table.

"Genetic," she mutters. She turns to go back into the house but her gait is so unsteady she almost stumbles as she walks. Dad shrugs at me and pats my hand.

"Let me go talk to her," he says.

I sit by myself for a moment but then can't stand being left here alone, worrying. I get up and follow them into the house.

Mom and Dad are standing in the kitchen arguing! I've never heard them argue before. And then I'm struck by how odd that is. Don't all families argue? Emma's certainly does and so does Sue's. I've heard them myself. I've been told about it. And yet this is the first time I've ever heard my parents fight.

"There must have been a way he could have prevented this!" Mom is furious.

"I'll fire him," Daddy fumes.

"You can't fire him now. We need him!

"She must have had it from birth," Mom continues. "And he *missed* it. He's checked her since. Why didn't he catch it earlier?"

Who is she talking about? Not Dr. Corne—I don't think.

29

And how could he have caught it earlier? I'm not following this at all. Then Mom explodes.

"I can't do this again. I can't! This wasn't supposed to happen!"

"Supposed to happen?" Dad challenges her. "We're way beyond that now, aren't we?"

"Are you blaming me?"

"Did I say that?"

"It sounds like you are," Mom hisses at him. "You blame me, don't you?"

"How could I?" Daddy explodes. "When we have Miranda ...," and then he sees me. "Oh, oh, oh, Miranda, have you been listening?"

I nod.

They both rush over to me. Mom glares at Daddy.

"You shouldn't have listened to us, Miranda. We're upset, naturally."

"What were you talking about?" I ask. "Who checked me?"

"Nothing," Daddy says, "nothing. Don't you have dance rehearsal soon?"

"Yes. Can I go?"

"Of course you can. Dr. Corne says there's no reason you shouldn't perform tomorrow. I keep telling you, you're going to be fine."

As Daddy drives me over to my rehearsal I ask him again what they were talking about. They've always been so honest and open with me but now when it really matters they seem to have actually stopped talking to me. I say that to Daddy.

"You're right, Miranda, of course you are. Honesty has always been our policy." He pauses and looks like he's searching for what to say.

30

"We had you checked out very thoroughly by a specialist at the G.R.F. clinic when you were a baby. They screened you for every possible disease and well, they do genetic research, too, so they checked out your genetic health. And they didn't find this. So either they missed it or you're right and it developed later. Mom thinks they somehow should have found it."

"It all sounds pretty sci-fi," I say.

He smiles. "Not at all. It's common to screen for genetic disease these days. Our tests are just a little more sophisticated."

"Not quite sophisticated enough, though," I say, thinking out loud. Dad's face falls. He looks crushed.

"You're right," he agrees.

We are nearing the dance studio.

"What should I tell Ms. Leonard when she asks how I am?"

"Tell her that it's complicated, but you'll be fine. She doesn't need all the details."

Ms. Leonard doesn't want to hear the details. She's delighted I'm back and the show can go on. She tells me to stop immediately if my blurry vision returns. The girls all ask me if I'm all right. I say I am. I really don't want anyone to know.

I change into my costume silently, unable to make small talk—I barely even register the other girls. Yesterday I was in perfect health, going for a perfect performance. Or so I thought. Today I feel dirty and ruined.

Ms. Leonard starts the music. I make my entrance. And I find I'm angry. I'm jealous of Rachel and the fact that she'll live and I'll die. I'm jealous of all of them. I *hate* all of them!

When we finish Ms. Leonard claps her hands in glee.

"You've found it, Miranda. That dark place inside you.

31

You've reached it. Good for you."

Good for me, I feel like saying. I have a fatal disease but I guess it's worth it if it makes my performance more believable. Instead, like the good girl I am, I smile and say, "Thank you, Ms. Leonard."

It's not fair. It's just not fair. What did I ever do to deserve this?

Chapter 4

I lie in bed and stare at the ceiling. The conversation I overheard today keeps going through my mind. Dad explained everything, but not *quite* everything. What could Mom have meant when she said, "I can't do this again!" I asked her about it when I got home but she said that I must've misheard. I'm sure I heard it correctly—and why won't she explain it to me? So I asked Dad again. He said he didn't remember her saying that and even if she did she was so upset she wasn't making sense. It's their answers now that aren't making sense.

I can't sleep. I get up and creep down the hall so my parents won't hear me. Our house is ranch style, the bedrooms and Dad's study in one wing, the kitchen in the center, then the dining room, a formal living room and finally, the family room with the pool and tennis court off that. We can also access the pool from the kitchen, convenient for me and my friends. Everything is done in wood, pale colors, southwestern style. It's a beautiful house.

I wander into the family room and go for the picture albums. I love to sit at night and look through the photos of all our vacations, and think about the fun we've had. We went to London last year and saw *Twelfth Night* and *The Tempest* done by the Royal Shakespeare Company. I laughed so hard in *Twelfth Night* I almost fell out of my seat. Maybe I'll be an

33

actress, I think. And then I can hardly breathe, because suddenly I remember that I can't make plans. I don't have a future. It doesn't matter what my mom and dad say. The article said that there is no cure.

I flip through the pictures: me in front of the Tower of London, me in front of the British Museum. A loose photo drops out. I pick it up. Me in front of ... that's odd. I look closer at the picture. How did that get in here? It's me all right, in front of some big castle, but it couldn't be from the London trip. I look about ten years old. Where was it taken? Funny. I can't remember being there at all. And those clothes. Ugh. Did I really like to dress like that? Overalls? I don't remember ever owning a pair of overalls, even at that age.

I take the picture out and put it in my bathrobe pocket so I can ask Mom about it in the morning. I look at my watch. It's almost 1 a.m. I turn the TV on quietly so Mom and Dad won't hear it—not that they would, if they stay in their bedroom. I choose Netflix and settle on an old *Buffie The Vampire Slayer* episode.

My body is inside out, blood vessels, muscles, red and white, and everywhere are large black growths, they multiply, they expand, they are covering everything. I start to scream but where is my voice coming from? Where am I? Where am I?

I wake up gasping. I get up and stagger back to my room. I'm pouring sweat but I'm cold too. I head for my bathroom, get into the shower, and stand under the hot water, letting it wash over me, my mind, finally, a blank. Warmed through, I towel off, put on my flannel pajamas, and crawl under the sheets. I'm afraid to dream again and I can't fall asleep for ages.

"Miranda. Miranda." I open my eyes. It's Lorna.

"Up you get. Your mother told me to make sure you're ready. You have to go to the doctor's this morning. You'll miss just your first class. What do you want to wear? The blue pants and blue jacket? It's a little cooler today. Or what about your new brown top?"

"You choose," I mutter. Lorna has been dressing me since I was little.

She bustles around the room, picking out clothes for me. "Tonight's the big night. Are you nervous?"

"Funny how when you know you're about to die, a stupid dance recital doesn't mean all that much."

Lorna drops the clothes on the floor. "What?"

"They didn't tell you?"

"They told me you were sick. But that you'd get better. *For sure*, you'd get better."

"They're lying."

I can't believe these words are coming out of my mouth. Neither can Lorna.

"Miranda, what's gotten into you? I've never heard you speak disrespectfully of your parents. And let me tell you, they don't deserve it." She is picking up the clothes as she talks. "If they say you'll get better, you will. Not once have they—" and then she stops, frozen. "Where'd you get this picture?" She is holding up the photo that I found last night. It must have dropped onto the floor when I threw my bathrobe off last night.

"It was in the album from our London trip. It's a mistake. Obviously, it's from years earlier. I was going to ask Mom or

35

Dad."

"No, no," she says, "I'll put it back where it belongs. You just get dressed now."

And she's gone. Why is everyone around here acting so strangely? I didn't even get a chance to ask her which trip that was from. I get out of bed, go into my bathroom, wash my face and brush my teeth, then put on the pants, brown top and loafers Lorna left out.

When I get to the kitchen she has yoghurt and fruit waiting for me. I eat it standing. Mom hurries in.

"Let's go, darling."

"Where are we going?"

"To the G.R.F. clinic we told you about. Dr. Mullen is expecting us."

"More tests?" I ask.

"Just a couple. He can use the results of the other tests. He needs a little more blood, and he wants to check you over himself. He's scheduling the operation for next week."

"What? What operation? It's *incurable.* I'm not going through some big horrible operation just so I can die later."

"Mira," Mom says, "don't be silly. We wouldn't let you do that. Come on. He'll explain everything. You're going to be cured, I've told you."

I shake my head, grab my knapsack, make sure I have my phone this time in case the tests take longer than Mom thinks, and follow her out. Once in the car I text Emma and tell her I'll just be missing our first class. She texts back asking why. I tell her more tests. I know her phone will be off soon when classes start but at least this way she shouldn't worry *too* much.

I've gotten horribly behind in English over the last two

36

days. I'm supposed to be writing an essay comparing Ariel and Caliban. I pull out my Shakespeare and read as we drive. Why I'm bothering I don't know. If I'm going to die I guess I don't have to worry about English assignments. On the other hand, if Mom is right and I'm not going to die, I'd better get cracking on it.

I laugh out loud. Mom looks at me.

"Nothing," I say. "Everything just seems a little funny to me. Not really 'ha ha' funny, but 'so weird you have to laugh' funny. Never mind."

"Mira," Mom says, "this has been an awful shock for all of us—most of all for you, of course. I think you're handling it remarkably well. No tears, no hysterics. Sensible, like always. But Daddy and I would have expected no less."

If only I knew how to go hysterical it would probably be a relief. But this is the only way I seem to be able to react. So I return to my book and read until Mom pulls the car up in front of the clinic.

The clinic turns out to be a large three-story building on Canyon Drive, set well back from the street, date palms lining the driveway. Red bougainvillea surround the front and a lemon tree just beginning to blossom stands in the small grassy area to the left.

Mom leaves the car in the drive and we don't even have to knock—a nurse opens the door as we reach it. She is tall and very thin, with brown hair tied in a bun on top of her head. She smiles and I can tell she smokes. Her teeth are all yellow.

"Follow me, please," she says.

A middle-aged man in a white coat bustles down the hallway toward us. "Ahh, look at you. This *must* be Miranda. Come in. Come in."

37

He has one of those posh British accents, which makes him sound very smart. His eyes are a watery blue and his thinning hair is the color of wheat. He seems delighted to see me. Somehow I can't feel the same way. After all, I wouldn't be here if I weren't sick. Really sick.

"How's your vision?" he asks.

"All right."

"No more blurring?"

"No."

"Good. Good. Jean here will take your blood while we talk."

He ushers me into an examining room, sits me on the table. Jean rolls up my sleeve while he chatters on.

"You mustn't worry, Miranda. It's serious, but we can cure you. *Cure* you."

"But at school … online it said—"

"Oh!" He laughs. "That's all old information. We're going to get rid of all this with a brand new gene therapy. You may need a new liver. That's where the tumors are worst, which is a little unusual—normally they appear other places first. But you aren't yellow so your liver function is still good, considering … At any rate, not to worry! We have a liver for you! And the rest we can shrink away to nothing."

"But …"

"No buts. If we need to replace your lungs and kidneys we can do that too. You've probably seen lots of doctor shows on TV—and you're going to ask me how I've found a perfect match. Well, that's my little secret. But in no time you won't even know you've had this disease."

The nurse has taken my blood while he's been talking. He peers into my eyes with his light. "No, not to worry. It's unexpected, this, but we're prepared. Now off you go to

38

school. Can't afford to get behind."

Before I know it, Mom and I are back in the car heading for school.

"Wow!" I say. "Isn't he a little too much like a mad scientist? Someone should give him some calm-down pills."

Mom laughs, the first time she's done that since we got the news. "You heard him," she says. "You're going to be fine!"

"But when did he find a perfect match for me? And don't you have to take drugs forever?"

"No, he means a *perfect* match," Mom says. "So your body won't reject it. No drugs. You'll be as good as new."

"But *how* could he find such a perfect match?"

"He just *has*," Mom says, her voice sounding a little irritated. "Don't keep asking, Miranda. Just be thankful."

"Is it because of Daddy? Did he find it in one of his hospitals? Someone who died? But don't they have to use the organ right away? Like right after the person dies?"

"Your father *did* help," she says quickly. "You know, with all his clinics and connections. I guess they figured out a way to preserve those organs for you ... I didn't ask. Dr. Mullen is the expert."

"I didn't know you *could* get such a perfect match," I persist. "Unless you have a twin or something."

"Drop it!" Mom explodes suddenly. "There is no need for these questions!"

I am so startled by her reaction I literally flinch. She's always explained things to me, we've always talked everything out. She's *never* snapped at me like that, she's always *encouraged* me to ask questions.

I stare at her. What is going on?

I reach into my bag, grab my phone and text Emma

everything even though I know her phone will be turned off in class. At least it gives me something to do as my mom and I sit side by side in an unnatural silence.

Chapter 5

I arrive at school in the middle of second period English. Mrs. Dromboski is talking about Caliban.

"Shakespeare describes him as a 'savage and deformed slave,'" she says, as I take my seat. "Shakespeare is obviously not afraid of creating a loutish, ugly monster. Is there anything about Caliban to like?"

"I feel sorry for him," Emma says.

"He tried to attack Miranda," Sue says, her voice severe. "There's nothing to feel sorry for."

"He says he'll be wise," Emma counters. "He's growing. He's changing."

"A monster's a monster," Sue states flatly.

"Miranda?" Mrs. Dromboski asks. "What do you think?"

If it weren't for the three of us Mrs. Dromboski wouldn't have a class, I think. No one else participates. I glance around the room. Everyone is in their own world—Selena is engrossed in one of her murder mysteries, hidden behind her Shakespeare, Tod is sleeping, Juan is doing math homework, Michelle and Lara are sending notes back and forth to each other old school since we can't use our phones, Jason is staring off into space ... If it weren't for the three of us, the rest of the kids might actually have to pay attention. No wonder they're always complimenting us after class. It's not that they respect us, or even like us necessarily. We're *useful* to them.

41

Why did I never realize this before?

"Miranda? Are you with us?"

"The world needs monsters," I respond, "so we can hurt and despise them."

Like me, I think to myself. That's what I am now. If people could see inside my body, all filled with tumors, totally disgusting, everyone would hate me, too.

Mrs. Dromboski raises an eyebrow. "Perhaps, Miranda, but that's a bit harsh, don't you think?"

I shrug.

After class Sue and Emma join me in the hallway on the way to math.

"I just realized something," I say.

"What?" Emma asks.

"The rest of the kids in class—"

"Good work in there," Michelle calls out as she rushes to her locker.

"Yeah, great," Tod agrees as he catches up with us.

"What?" Emma asks me, as I haven't finished my sentence.

I glance at Tod and decide not to tell Emma and Sue my theory until we are alone.

"Nothing, never mind," I say.

"Where were you?" Tod asks. "You're never late."

I can't think of a good reason—I can't tell him the truth but I can't lie either.

"Her mom's car broke down," Emma volunteers.

"Jeez. Really? It's so awesome. What happened?"

Tod is much more concerned about my mom's car than he'd probably be about me if I told him what is really going on.

"Nothing, just a part gone wrong," Emma continues. "The

42

computer picked it up and signaled it had to go into the garage right away. It happens sometimes with a new car." Emma is so good at lying—but then, she's had lots of practice with her parents.

As the day drags on I find myself in the oddest mental state. One minute I forget about being sick and everything seems normal. The next minute I remember and everything seems so horrible I want to cry. In fact I do start crying every once in a while and I have to hide from everyone. And then I start to worry about the recital. Maybe it'll be my last chance to dance, and I don't want to disappoint myself or my parents.

After school Mom picks me up and takes me straight home so I can eat and get ready for tonight. I go to my room to pack my makeup, but can't find my mascara. Emma again, probably. Not that she would ever steal. She just uses my stuff and then throws everything in her makeup case without realizing it. I go to Mom's room to borrow her mascara. As I walk down the hallway, I can hear Mom talking to Lorna in the bedroom.

"What did she say?" It is Mom's voice.

"She was curious, of course. She didn't remember being there."

I stop outside the door.

"I'd been looking through the other albums." Mom again. "I was so upset. I must have had that one in my hand and when I looked through Miranda's albums I left it there."

"You should lock those albums up," Lorna says.

"Oh, surely that's not necessary. Miranda never goes through my things."

"She's going to start to wonder. Don't take any chances. Let me put them in your wardrobe, in the drawer we can lock."

43

Mom sighs. "All right."

"It'll be easier. They'll be right in your room," Lorna says, "where you can look at them. I'll go get them."

She turns toward the door. I don't know what to do. Obviously I wasn't supposed to hear any of that. Instinctively I take a few steps back. Lorna comes out of the room and I suppose she assumes I've just gotten there. I hurry past her into Mom's room.

"Mom!"

"Yes, dear?"

I want to ask her about what I just heard but somehow I can't.

"I need some mascara."

Mom gets her mascara and gives it to me. "Are you all packed up?"

"No." I pause searching for what to say. "I saw this picture last night in the photo album. Me, in overalls, in front of an old castle. Where was that? I don't remember it at all."

"Oh!" Mom's face turns bright red. What is going on? "That!" She pauses. "That!" she repeats. "Oh, it was so silly," she says in a rush. "Don't you remember? It's not a real castle. It was a picture we had taken of you, by a photographer. The castle is just a backdrop. The overalls were put on for fun, for the picture."

"Really?" I say, trying to think back. "I don't remember it."

"No, well, why should you? You wouldn't forget a real vacation to a real castle, would you? But why should you remember that silly old photo? Now go get ready."

I carry the mascara back to my room and sit down on my bed not knowing what to think. I need Emma. I fish my phone out of my back pocket.

44

"Emma, want to stay over here tonight after the recital? We can sleep in tomorrow, then go hiking in the canyons. What about it?"

"Yeah, I'd love to. Did you ask your parents?"

"Like they're going to say no. Look, I just overheard the weirdest conversation. I'll tell you when we get back here, okay?"

"Okay. I'll go ask Mom."

Why are there photo albums I can't see? Ever since they found out I was sick Mom and Dad have been acting stranger and stranger. Especially my mom.

"Miranda! Are you ready? Come and eat." It is Mom calling me.

"Be right there."

I finish packing and go to the kitchen. Lorna has made some soup, which is perfect since I can't eat anything heavy. Maybe Emma and I can have pizza after the recital. My stomach is a mass of butterflies. I eat, all the while tempted to confront Mom, but I just don't know what to say. Mom asks Lorna to drive me so she can get dressed and ready.

The dance studio has rented a small theatre at the junior college for the evening. There are no dressing rooms, so when I get there Ms. Leonard directs me to the classroom where everyone is changing. We have to use the women's washroom to put on our makeup. Everyone is nervous and excited. I'm terrified. I decide to pretend that nothing has changed. I resolve to concentrate only on my dancing.

Ms. Leonard lets each group walk through their number so we can get used to the stage. I go over the steps in my head as I wait in the wings. I can hear the audience laughing and talking on the other side of the closed curtain—I'm so nervous

45

I can barely remember my steps when our turn comes. Then we go back to our classroom and wait as the younger children from the school begin the program. Finally Peter knocks on the door, imitating Ms. Leonard's voice as he calls "Places please."

We run up the back stairs to the wings. Ms. Leonard nods. The music starts. Rachel makes her entrance. I count. And then I enter. Everything is working perfectly, I can feel it. My body moves in time to the music; I know the evil queen's anger. Everyone around me is in sync too—no one trips or loses a beat. There is a hush in the theatre, no one coughing or talking, no babies crying, as if time is suspended. I dance, I soar, I fly and then ... it's over. The applause crashes all around us—I look up from my curtsy to see that the entire crowd is on their feet.

Ms. Leonard bustles on to the stage and takes a bow. Then she grabs me, Rachel, Peter and Michael, and pulls us out for a special bow. I blush, but it feels wonderful. And then I think, if only I could know for sure that one day I'd be able to do this again. Tears spring to my eyes and for the first time since all this happened I feel sorry for myself. Really sorry. But I hate that feeling. I'll fight it, I vow to myself. Dr. Mullen says I can get better and so do Mom and Dad. So I *will* get better. I won't give up.

We run offstage, laughing and talking and congratulating each other. We change quickly and hurry to meet our families in the lobby. It is pandemonium. There's a crush of people talking at the top of their lungs. Kids are trying to find their families, babies are crying, girls are shrieking congratulations to their friends. Everyone's parents, and sisters, and brothers, come up to tell me how wonderful I was. I can hardly take it

46

all in. I've danced before at recitals and always had a good response but this is overwhelming.

Dad offers to take the entire group out for pizza and about half of our class, along with their families, agrees. We head over to California Pizza. By the time we get there, two huge tables have been set up for us at the back. We order drinks and tacos and dip while we wait. Emma and her family come along too. Everyone talks and laughs. I feel so happy. Everything has to be all right, I tell myself. Everything *will* be all right.

Chapter 6

My parents are so proud of me. But they always are. A little voice inside of me wonders how they would have reacted had I fallen on my face. Well, fortunately I won't have to find out. When we get home I thank Daddy for taking everyone out, then Emma and I go to my room.

Emma isn't jealous of my dancing because she's got her own talent. She has an amazing voice. She's taking lessons now and is considering being an opera singer. She's very petite, not your typical diva, but her voice is *gigantic*.

"You were great," she says as we change into our PJs.

"You really should start to dance, Emma," I reply. She's heard this from me before. "If you could dance, and the way you sing, Broadway would bow down before you."

She grins. "I'll take dance lessons if you take acting. I know you want to!"

"And you know how my parents feel about it. Living in California, *everyone* takes acting. They say all it amounts to is waitress training and they want better for me."

"Do you *always* have to do what they say?"

"How could I even get to acting class," I counter, "if my mom wouldn't drive me?"

"You'd have to walk to the nearest bus," Emma says.

"And how would I afford it?"

"Get a job."

48

"They'd never let me get a job. 'School must come first.'"

"You're hopeless!" Emma exclaims, throwing a pillow at me.

"I know," I sigh, holding the pillow to my chest. "I can't seem to help it." I pause. "But listen, there's something funny going on here." I tell her about the photo and about the conversation I overheard between Lorna and my mom.

"That is sort of weird," Emma agrees. "Are you tired?"

"Not at all."

"Okay. Let's go and look through your photo albums. The ones that aren't hidden. Maybe we'll find another picture that isn't supposed to be there. Unless you want to break into your mom's locked drawer."

I grimace. "I don't. But why should I have to? What are they hiding?"

"You know parents," Emma scoffs. "They think the stupidest things are important and they try to 'protect' us. It's probably *nothing*."

"Yeah," I agree, "you're probably right."

"Come on," she says. "I'm wide awake anyway. This'll be fun."

Mom and Dad are sitting in the kitchen talking. Emma and I grab drinks and some popcorn.

"Watching a movie?" Daddy asks.

"Yes," says Emma without a moment's pause. And that sets us both off giggling.

"It's not a movie you shouldn't be watching, is it?" Mom asks, looking at us suspiciously.

"It's a Goofy movie," Emma grins. "We're going to try to decide, once and for all, what Goofy really is."

"Why," says Daddy, "that's easy. He's a dog."

49

"I don't think so, Mr. Martin," Emma replies shaking her head. "It needs some scientific investigation. There may have been a mix-up in the lab when he was made."

Dad smiles but Mom gets up abruptly and hurries out of the room.

"Did I say something?" Emma asks.

"Not at all, no," Daddy reassures her. "Lynda is just easily upset these days."

"Thanks a lot," I say, suddenly upset too. "I'd almost managed to forget this whole thing tonight." I sit down on a chair with a thud, the entire nasty business rushing back to me.

Daddy raises his eyebrows. He's never heard me snap at him like that before. Emma gets her drink and the popcorn.

"Come on, Miranda."

I push up and follow her to the family room. We shut the double doors.

"Boy, you're a good liar," I say.

"Practice, practice, practice," she smiles.

I know Emma would never *really* cheat or lie—except to her parents and she feels that's a different case altogether. "And I only do it when they're being stupid," she often assures me. "Like when they ask me what movie we're going to watch. They must think I live on nothing but Disney movies!" But Emma would never cheat on an exam or lie to a friend, for instance. Then I wouldn't be her friend. I couldn't.

I pull out the albums and we start to look through them. There are lots and lots of cute baby pictures, Mom holding me, Daddy lifting me into the air, that sort of thing. And as I get older, the trips, me on horseback, me at my first dance recital ...

50

"Ooh, look at this," Emma exclaims, "our first picture together. It was my birthday party, the year I turned nine. Remember? We had Mr. Cook that year at school and we made friends because he just loved both of us and was always putting us together to do projects?"

"We did that great one on the planets," I say. "Oh. Here it is. Look. My dad took a picture of it."

"I don't see anything odd here," she comments. "No overalls, for instance."

"Do you ever remember me wearing overalls?" I ask.

"You? I don't think so!"

"That's what I mean. But it's not that so much—it's what I overheard. How upset they were. I mean, why would they have to hide these other albums? And my mom really looked like she was making up the whole thing about the photographer. I've *never* seen her lie but this sure looked like her first. She was beet red!"

"Why don't we find out?"

"What do you mean?"

"Why don't we look at the other albums?"

"Emma!"

"Well, if they won't tell you—I mean—you *did* ask. You gave her a chance to be honest. And from what you've described, I don't think she was. So, you'll have to find out. After all, it's to do with *you*."

"But Lorna said she was going to lock the photos up," I protest.

"Yes. And where would your mom keep the key?"

"I don't know."

"We'd have to search her room."

"I couldn't. How could I? She'd kill me if she found out. I

51

mean, she's never searched *my* room. It wouldn't be right."

"You've never lied to her," Emma points out. "A fact," she adds, "that your parents don't appreciate enough. A teenager who never lies to her parents. They should give you a medal."

"I've never had to!"

"Until now."

I feel really confused. In a way, she's right—I've tried the honest approach. I asked Mom what that photo was about. If her answer were true, why would she want to hide the albums from me? But Mom has *never* lied to me, so why start now? None of it makes any sense.

My dad walks into the family room. "I thought you two were going to watch a movie."

"We are," I reply, "but we started to look through these albums."

Then I have an idea. Maybe Mom hasn't mentioned the picture to Daddy. Maybe if I ask him about it he'll give me a straight answer. Or he might confirm what Mom said about the photographer. Maybe she was turning red like that not because she was lying but for a completely different reason— like maybe she was just hot.

I hate Emma's idea of sneaking around Mom's room.

"Daddy," I begin, "when I was looking at these albums the other night I found a picture of me standing in front of a castle. But I don't remember that trip at all." I don't tell him Mom's version of me in front of a fake backdrop.

He repeats what I've said. "You, standing in front of a castle. Really? Gee, honey, I'm not sure ... How old were you in the photo, do you think?"

"I don't know. It looked like I was around ten. And I was wearing overalls. I've never worn overalls in my life. There's not one other picture of me in overalls in all those albums."

"I suppose that's true. Gee," he says again, "I'm not sure. I don't remember exactly. Maybe it was that trip we took to England."

"Daddy, when I was ten we went to Greece."

"Well, it must be that. There are lots of old castles there. You obviously wore overalls and you just don't remember."

My heart sinks—he doesn't say the same thing as Mom. Why?

"Then," I ask, "why did Mom say it was a fake backdrop and she had that picture taken of me right here?"

Daddy pauses and stares at me. "Miranda, if your mom already told you where the photo was from, why ask me?"

I don't answer.

"Miranda!"

"Because I'm not sure she's telling me the truth," I blurt out.

"Miranda! When have we ever lied to you?"

At this point Emma gets up and slips past Dad.

"I need something more to drink," she says. Which isn't true but I guess it must be pretty uncomfortable for her to sit and listen to this.

"Well, you never have," I admit. "But now you're all mysterious about everything. Like how you're miraculously going to cure me of an incurable disease, for instance. And I'm worried Mom wasn't telling the truth about the photo because you're right, she never lies, but when she was telling me about it her face went all red, and it looked like she was making it all up. And anyway, why wouldn't I remember it?" I finally stop, almost gasping for breath.

Daddy shakes his head. "We're all under way too much

53

stress, honey. You're probably reading something into your mother's reaction that isn't even there."

"Then why didn't *you* remember where that picture is from?"

"Miranda. I haven't even seen the picture. It's from years ago. Why *should* I remember? Why should you?" He sits down beside me and takes my hands in his. "I think you're blowing everything way out of proportion. You're really worried about your illness and the operation and instead you're focusing on this silly photo."

Before I can stop myself I say, "If it's so silly, why does Lorna want it locked up so I can't see it?"

"What?" Daddy's face goes white and he drops my hands.

"I overheard her talking to Mom," I hurry on, unable to let it drop. "They were so worried about it they were going to lock it and some others up in your bedroom." I realize I'm holding my breath, hoping he has a good answer.

He looks at the floor for a minute. Then he gets up.

"I'll get Mom. I don't know what this is all about but I suggest we deal with this together."

"What about Emma?"

"Emma can stay in your room and watch TV there until we've talked. I'm sure she won't mind. I'll go and tell her."

He walks out of the room, his shoulders drooping, as if he's suddenly very tired.

I know Emma will be mad at me. I think she was actually looking forward to searching my parents' room. But I couldn't. This is better. We'll talk it out. Daddy is right. They've never lied to me. There must be some logical explanation.

54

Chapter 7

I sit and wait for Mom and Dad to return. How are they going to explain themselves? I flip through the albums. I've been lucky. Really lucky. I've gotten on so well with my parents. I've had all the advantages money can buy—great clothes, trips, lessons. Yeah, I've been pretty lucky, I guess, up until now.

It takes a long time before they both come back to the family room. At least ten or fifteen minutes. I begin to get suspicious again—I have to wonder if they aren't deciding on the same story. Otherwise, why not come directly back?

"Sorry, darling," Mom says, as they come in, "I was in the shower." Her hair is still damp.

You're really paranoid, I say to myself. Stop it. Listen to what they have to say, it's bound to make sense.

"Your father tells me that you've become suspicious," Mom begins without waiting for me to speak.

"Wouldn't you be?" I shoot back.

"Yes, yes, I suppose I would," she admits. "But really, Miranda, you mustn't get worked up. It won't help your health."

"Just tell me what's going on, then," I demand, exasperated.

"The conversation you overheard was, well, it was about some ... silly pictures your father and I took ... ridiculous ones ... one day we dressed up in outrageous costumes and

55

hammed it up … it's nothing. Parents don't have to share every silly moment with their children."

I look at her and then at Daddy. They both certainly seem embarrassed enough. And it's true, if they want to act like children I guess they wouldn't appreciate me seeing that. And yet, it still doesn't quite fit with how secretive she and Lorna had sounded. I mean, why lock up silly pictures?

"Why lock them up?" I ask, watching her closely.

She doesn't turn a funny color but she does take a deep breath before she answers.

"You know the crazy world we live in. Your father has a reputation as a serious businessman. What if you found them and thought they were so funny you took some to school and, for instance, Jason took one and showed it to his dad and it ended up all over CNN?"

"What's in the pictures?" I'm still unconvinced. "Can I see them?"

"Yes, I've brought a couple to show you."

She reaches into her thick white bathrobe and draws out some photos. Mom is dressed like Cleopatra, Daddy is dressed like Hercules.

"These look like Halloween pictures," I say. "I don't get it. What's wrong with this?"

"Nothing," she replies. "But if we're going to be silly we don't need the entire world knowing about it. So you see you jumped to all the wrong conclusions."

"What about me in the overalls?"

"Same thing. You dressed up with us that day, like I told you!"

"But Daddy didn't remember!" I object.

"I forgot, Mimi," he says. "I forgot all about this. We got

56

giddy one weekend and tried on every costume we could get from an agency, took pictures, made up movies, acted out the parts. Do you remember now?"

I try. It sounds like so much fun. How can I have forgotten? Finally I shake my head. "I don't remember."

"You will," Daddy assures me. "The brain's a funny thing, what we can remember and what we can't. It'll probably come back to you. Or maybe it won't. It doesn't matter."

"Can I see the rest of the photos?"

"Some other time," Mom says. "It's late now."

I look at the pictures she's given me. There is actually something a little odd about one but I can't put my finger on what it is. "Can I keep just one?"

"All right," Mom agrees. "Now why don't you go to your room. It's late. We're tired." She shakes her head. "And stop worrying. It's pointless. There is nothing odd going on." She bends over and gives me a kiss. Daddy does the same.

I take the photo with me and head for my room.

Maybe these tumors are affecting me in more ways than I'd like to admit. That thought makes me shudder. The explanation they offered is perfectly reasonable. They've never lied to me. I have to stop being so suspicious—and I have to stop Emma from egging me on.

Emma is sitting on my bed when I get there, eyes wide to the point of goggling. She grabs me as I come in and shuts the door.

"I have to tell you …," she says, her voice a squeak.

"Emma," I interrupt, before she's finished. "They had a perfectly good explanation. Kind of stupid but it must be true. Why would they make up something like that?"

"What did they tell you?"

57

I tell her their story then show her the picture. She stares at it. "There's something weird about this picture," she mutters. "Is it your mom's hair?"

I look closely at it. I'd also felt there was something odd—and then it hits me. "Her hair is short. But it's been long ever since I can remember. If you look at all the other photos, since I was a baby, she has long hair in them."

"A wig," Emma suggests.

"Yeah, of course!" I exclaim. "Well, that's an easy one. Although it looks so real."

Emma moves to the bed and pulls a photo out from behind the covers. "This won't be so simple to explain."

"What's that?" I ask.

"You tell me."

I look at it. It is me, a younger me, standing in front of a school. Madison Elementary, it says over the door.

Madison?

"But I went to LaJolla Elementary and then to Juniper Middle," I say. "And now we're at Desert High so ..." Then I stop and stare at Emma. "Where did you get this?"

"I heard your dad come get your mom. They were talking like crazy for ages but I couldn't hear what they said. When they left their room I came out into the hallway too, so I could ask what I should do. Like, were they finished talking to you? Your dad told me to watch some TV.

"They went to talk to you and after a while I got thirsty. I only said I was thirsty before because I wanted to get out of the room while you and your dad talked. So when I went back into the hallway I noticed your parents' door was open. I thought I'd just peek in—and then I saw this album open on the bed."

58

"You didn't?" I interrupt.

"I couldn't help myself! I had to wonder if it was one of those secret albums Lorna was talking about. And I didn't have to look for the key or anything. So I snuck in and looked through it really fast. There are all these pictures of you but with different friends and it is not here because there is snow in some of them."

"Snow?"

"Yeah, snow."

I shake my head and sit down on the bed, staring at the picture.

"What does it mean, do you think?" I ask Emma.

"What do you think?"

"Well," I say slowly, "maybe this isn't the first time I've been sick. Maybe I've been sick before. Maybe I was so sick I've lost some of my memories. I've heard of that happening. Amnesia. That would explain my parents lying because you aren't supposed to push an amnesia victim to remember. I saw that on a Sunday Night Movie once. Or maybe there is a tumor in my brain pressing on something and I'm losing part of my memory and they don't want to tell me and upset me."

"Yeah," Emma says, looking very downcast. "I guess ..."

It *is* an awful thought—your brain checking out like that, maybe slowly being destroyed.

I stare at the picture, but it suddenly starts to go out of focus. "Emma!" I cry, grasping her hand. "My eyes. They're going blurry again."

"I'll go get your parents," she says, as she leaps up. She starts out the door then hurries back and puts the picture we've been looking at in my top drawer. "Plenty of time to deal with this later. You have to think about getting better. Don't

59

say anything to your parents now." And she runs out of the room.

Say anything? Why would I? I couldn't care less anymore. I'm too terrified. Blindness—that's what the internet said. Will I be blind before morning comes? And what do any of these details matter anyway? Somehow Mom and Dad have figured out a way to save me. I should be thankful for that and not question what they are doing.

Mom hurries into the room, followed by Emma. "Mira, come on, dear. Dr. Mullen wants to see you right away."

"Now?"

"Now. He's going to admit you to the clinic for the weekend and you'll have the operation on Monday. Come on, I'll help you get dressed."

"I'm scared," I whisper.

"Don't be, sweetheart. I promised you everything would be fine, didn't I?"

"What about Emma?"

"Daddy will drive her home and he'll meet us at the clinic."

Emma hurries into the bathroom to change into her clothes. Mom helps me get dressed.

"Can I come to visit her, Mrs. Martin?" Emma asks as she packs up her bag.

"We'll see, Emma," Mom says. "Miranda will have her phone and I promise I'll get her to call you first thing tomorrow."

Emma comes over and gives me a big hug.

I can tell she doesn't know what to say. I can barely see her.

"Good luck," she says fervently.

"Thanks." I hug her back.

Daddy comes in. He hugs me too. "You'll be fine, Mimi. I'll

60

see you soon. Dr. Mullen isn't at all worried. He said it was to be expected. Are you ready, Emma?"

"Yes," she says.

"Then let's go."

Mom finishes getting me packed. On our way out she asks if I have my phone.

I check and I do. All my music is on it so that's something.

"And I've packed your Kindle," Mom assures me, "so you won't be bored."

Not that I could read a word right now.

Then we leave the house to go to the clinic.

Chapter 8

It's a lonely, spooky drive to the clinic. The streets are dark and mostly empty. Every once in a while other headlights flash past us—to me they look like blurry white orbs suddenly materializing out of the gloom, then disappearing again. And inside those cars are people—probably healthy people, going to a party or returning home from a movie. People who will live their lives out, unlike me.

I feel completely isolated from everyone and everything. I start to think about what it might be like to die. Will it hurt? Will it be horribly scary? Is there anything after death or will it be a blackness, a blank, like being unconscious? I turn on the radio so this unbearable silence is broken. Finally, we pull up at the clinic door.

Ms. Yellow Teeth is standing outside waiting for us. She takes my arm and helps me down the hall, Mom hanging onto my other arm. Instead of an examining room, I'm led into some kind of bedroom but since my vision is so blurry, I can't see any details. I can make out a bed, and some kind of table by the bed, and I see an inner door, which probably leads to a bathroom.

"It's lovely," Mom says. "Can you see any of it, Mira?"

"I can see it, but as if there's a fog around everything."

"Your eyes may improve again," the nurse says, her voice much more pleasant than her looks. "Now let's get you settled.

My name is Jean, by the way, in case you've forgotten."

Jean and Mom help me get into my PJs and settle me into the bed. Jean pats the pillows and shows me where the buzzer is, should I need to reach her. "I'm going to give her something so she can sleep," she advises Mom. "She needs her rest."

"Hey!" I say. "I'm right here. You can talk to me."

"Miranda!" Mom is worried that I'm not being my usual polite self. Doesn't she realize that good manners are not what's important here?

"I'll sit with her until she falls asleep," Mom tells Jean, as the nurse puts a pill in one of my hands and a glass of water in the other. I down the pill without question. I don't want to be sitting up all night thinking of every terrible thing that could happen. I settle back against the pillows and close my eyes. It's easier to have them closed than to try to see through the blur.

"Daddy and I will come back first thing in the morning," Mom says. And that's the last thing I remember.

When I wake up, everything is quiet. The lights are dimmed. I can see perfectly again. Maybe I'm still dreaming. I push myself up and look around. The room is covered in blue wallpaper decorated with small yellow flowers. It's very pretty. In one corner sits a vanity table with a mirror over it. The bed is in the center of the room. The pillowcases are bright yellow, the quilt a deep blue. A vase of fresh flowers sits on a table beside my bed, roses, freesias and lilies sending out a sweet scent. I push the button. I should tell the nurse I can see again.

I lie and wait for her to appear but she doesn't. I push the button again. No one comes. What time is it? I grab my phone. 3:11 a.m. I get out of the bed and put on the slippers that sit neatly on the pale-blue tiled floor. I go to the door, open it and peer down the corridor. No one is there. I decide to try to find someone. I pad silently down the long corridor, past door after door, all of them closed. I wonder if I'm the only patient here. Didn't Dad say that this was mainly a research clinic? At the end of the corridor, the far wall seems to be open a crack, as if it's a door not a wall. That's odd. Then I hear someone crying. I stop dead. It sounds like a young girl or child and he or she is right behind this wall. Where is everyone? Why doesn't anyone come and help? Tentatively, I push against the wall, which swings back easily. It opens onto a huge space, all dimly lit but bright enough that I can make out just about everything. At first I'm not sure what I'm looking at, it's all so strange.

The left-hand side of the room looks like a playroom with toys, climbing equipment, exercise machines, big chairs, and a bookshelf. On the other side of the room is a small kitchen. In the center is a kind of bedroom, that is, there's a bed and a nightstand but none of it is separated from the rest so the effect is very unusual. Stranger still, there's someone in the bed. The child I heard crying.

I walk softly over and clear my throat.

"Are you all right? I'm trying to find someone here to help but ..."

The figure in the bed stops crying abruptly at the sound of my voice. A shape rises from the covers, throws them off, and turns toward me. Time seems to stop. I am looking at a girl, perhaps ten years old, with long straight blonde hair, blue eyes, a high forehead, a little dimple in her chin ... I am

64

looking at the spitting image of myself when I was ten years old. She stares at me, speechless. Slowly, slowly, now I'm sure I'm dreaming, I walk over to her. I reach out and touch her. She jumps back, as if my touch might be electric.

"Who are you?" I ask, somehow finding my voice.

Her eyes are wide as saucers as she stares at me. She gulps for air. Then she grabs my hand and starts to kiss it.

"I will make you better," she says, her eyes fervent. "Thank you. Thank you. Thank you."

"What are you talking about?" I ask.

"Oh my heavens!" Jean runs up to me. "How did you get here? Oh, heavens. Come with me, Miranda. Back to bed. Back to bed." She pulls on me and drags me out of the room. I glance back over my shoulder and see the child shaking with emotion.

"Who is that? I want to know! Call my mother."

"I will, Miranda. Don't worry. I'll call her. Let's just get you back in bed."

"I pressed the button for you," I accuse her. "Why didn't you come?"

"I hadn't realized that my beeper battery was low. I didn't hear your page. I went to check on you and then I saw ..."

By now we're back in my room. She gets me into bed.

"I want to call my mom."

"Of course. You go right ahead. I'll get Dr. Mullen."

My mom's sleepy voice answers the phone. "Yes?"

"Mom! Get over here. There's a girl, she's like another me. What's going on? Is she my sister? Is she sick too?" And then I have another thought. "Is she the girl in the overalls?"

"Oh dear God," Mom mutters. "Allan, wake up." I can hear her shaking my dad. "Wake up. It's Miranda. She's found

65

number ten."

"What?" I can hear my dad's voice.

Just then Dr. Mullen bustles in.

"Ah, Miranda, aren't dreams funny?" he says. "They seem so real." He takes a syringe from behind his back, rubs my arm with a little alcohol, and sticks me!

"What are you doing?" I exclaim, dropping my phone.

❧

"Miranda? Miranda?"

I open my eyes. Everything is blurry again but not quite as bad as it was before I went to sleep, the first time. I can see Dr. Mullen pretty clearly. He is smiling at me. Mom's just behind him.

I bolt up in bed. I stare around disoriented. Is it still night? With no windows, there is no way to tell. I grab my phone and check. 8:17 a.m.

"Why did you do that to me?" I accuse Dr. Mullen.

"Do what, Miranda?" Dr. Mullen asks, looking genuinely puzzled.

"Give me a needle! I want to know what is going on here? Who was that girl?"

"Miranda, this is the first time I've been in to see you," Dr. Mullen assures me.

"You were here last night," I insist. "You stuck me with a needle after I'd seen her—a ten-year-old version of myself." I glare at my mom. "I called you. You know it's true."

"You didn't call me, Mira," she says gently.

I pick up my phone. "I did too," I say, "and I can prove it."

But when I check my "Recents" list there is no call to my mom in the middle of the night.

66

"That's not possible," I protest.

"It's the medication we gave you before you went to sleep, Miranda," Dr. Mullen says. "You sleep so soundly on it that your dreams are bound to be very lucid. It's normal. What did you dream?"

"It wasn't a dream!" I say. "It wasn't. I saw her! I'll show you her room!"

Mom looks at Dr. Mullen.

"Of course you can verify what you saw," he agrees, nodding at me. "But first let me check you over. Then you and your mother can explore the entire clinic."

He peers into my eyes with his light, takes my blood pressure, holds up three fingers and asks me how many I see, has me follow them with my eyes, and on and on. When he's finished he rubs his hands with pleasure.

"Excellent, excellent," he says. "Miranda, we're going to spend the rest of the weekend getting you rested and ready for the operation. We are going to give you a new liver. You're very lucky. We're sure the tumors in your kidneys, in your lungs, and even the tumor in your eyes, can be shrunk by our new gene therapy. Maybe we could shrink them in your liver, too, but it's beginning to fail and we're not sure the gene therapy will work quickly enough—so that's the organ we're going to transplant. Once you have recovered from that you'll start the gene therapy and I expect you to be back at school, good as new, in no time."

He leaves the room, as cheerful-looking as one of those little smiley emoticons.

"Come on, Mom," I urge her. "You have to see this."

She follows me out of my room. I am in the long corridor but it looks different in the bright light of day. There is no door

67

at the end of the hall, just a wall. I turn back to look at my bedroom. My vision is fuzzy again but I can make out blue wallpaper. Instead of a vanity table in the corner of the room, I notice a large chair.

"Are there flowers on the wallpaper in my room?" I ask Mom.

"No, dear," she answers.

"No yellow flowers?"

"No, dear."

I walk across the hall and open the door. It's a small office. I look around bewildered.

"I don't understand," I say in a small voice.

Mom puts her arm around me. "Tell me about your dream," she says. "Was it scary?"

"Yes!" I exclaim.

"You had a nightmare."

Slowly I walk back to my room. "I guess I did," I admit. "But it felt so real."

"Those are the scariest kind," Mom says. "Come on, back to bed. You need to eat a good breakfast. While you eat you can tell me the whole thing."

I take one last look around and shake my head. And then I remember the photo, and what Emma and I had been doing. That would explain the dream.

"Mom, could these tumors be affecting my brain? Is that why I don't remember the overalls or anything?"

Mom looks very sad. "I'm afraid so, dear," she says, "but you mustn't worry. It's temporary. Dr. Mullen assures us there will be no permanent brain damage."

"I wouldn't mind being able to forget that dream."

"I know, honey. Come on. Let's get you back to bed."

Chapter 9

I still feel woozy from the pill Jean gave me last night so I'm not very hungry. I drink some orange juice, begin to listen to one of the books I downloaded to my Kindle, and then doze off again. When I wake up mom isn't here. Probably went out for one of the zillion coffees she drinks every day. I grab my phone from the nightstand—it's just 10 a.m. I call Emma.

"Hi," I say.

"Miranda! Are you okay?"

"Yeah, sort of. My eyes are a little better this morning. But I had such a weird dream last night."

I tell Emma everything that happened and how real it felt. When I finish Emma is silent. "Funny, huh?" I say. "Must be all that stuff you and I were talking about, you know, that photo of me in the overalls. Mom thinks maybe this tumor is affecting my memory." Again silence.

"Emma?"

"Yeah."

"What are you thinking?"

"Maybe I shouldn't say anything. You've got enough to cope with."

"Say."

"I don't know."

"Emma!"

"Okay. Here's the deal. We've been best friends since we

69

were nine, right?"

"Right."

"You've always told me everything, right?"

"Right."

"You never told me about some silly weekend dressing up with your parents. And we used to spend almost every weekend together."

"Well," I answer, "I must have just forgotten to tell you this one thing."

"That's kinda weird, don't you think?"

"What?"

"The one thing you forgot to tell me is the one thing that conveniently explains all those pictures."

Now I'm silent.

"Miranda?"

"Yeah?"

"What are *you* thinking?"

"You're right. It *is* weird."

"And last night," she continues, "what if you *weren't* dreaming. It would explain the photos. Maybe you have a sister or something but she's, I don't know, mentally ill, so they have to keep her locked away in the clinic. She sounds pretty unhinged from what you said.

"That would make sense," I muse. "But it wouldn't explain why my mom has different hair in the other picture—unless you're right and it's a wig."

I pause again to think.

"What?" asks Emma.

"Except we look like twins, not sisters. She's *exactly* like me."

"Well, that can happen. Look at Tracy Lind and her sister.

70

They really look almost identical. Like twins. But they're a year apart."

"True."

"You need to see if you can find her again."

"But I told you, it *must* be a dream, the corridor is different, my room is different ... oh."

"Oh?"

"What if ...? No, Emma, we're getting completely stupid here. Maybe Mom is right. The tumor is affecting my brain."

"Just tell me," she urges. "I won't laugh."

"What if they changed my room while I was out. Drugged. The corridor is different because now I'm in a different room."

"Yikes."

"Yeah," I say, "yikes."

"It's possible," she agrees. "There's only one way to find out."

"Don't say it."

"You'll have to explore the clinic."

"But Dr. Mullen said I could. So they couldn't have anything to hide."

"Tonight, when everyone is asleep. Pretend to take your pill. You know, like in the movies, put it under your tongue and swallow. And then go exploring."

"Not alone. I couldn't."

"Invite me."

"How?"

"Tell your mom you want me to stay over there with you tonight. Make a big deal out of it."

"There's no room for you."

"Like they couldn't find a cot or something. Come on. It's a private clinic. Even public hospitals let family members sleep

71

over."

"Family members."

"Well, I'm like your family. At least *try* it. The worst they can say is no and then you'll have to do it alone."

"Let me see if I can convince my mom."

"Okay. Talk to you later."

"Right. Bye."

"Bye."

Could Emma be right? Is it possible?

When Mom comes back, sipping her coffee (how did I guess?), I ask her to take me on a tour.

"Sure, honey. How are your eyes?"

"Actually, better."

I hadn't noticed, I was so involved with talking to Emma, but they have improved. My sight is just a little fuzzy now.

I put on my slippers and robe and she takes me on a tour. My room is on the main floor along with offices and examining rooms. There are one or two locked doors, probably labs, Mom tells me. The second floor also has a couple of nice bedrooms and a number of labs, again, some of which we can't enter. The third floor is off limits.

"Why?" I ask Mom.

"That's where they do the experiments and everything."

Maybe that's where I was last night, I think. But no, I'm sure I didn't climb any stairs when I first got here. I must have been on the main floor.

"Can Emma come for a visit tonight?" I ask.

"Well ... I'm not sure."

"Why not?" My voice starts to rise.

"I didn't say no," Mom replies, "I was thinking."

"She could even stay over," I suggest. "They could find a cot for her. Remember," I say before Mom can object, "how important your state of mind is when you're sick. In fact, I was just reading about that while I was waiting at the dentist's last month."

Mom puts up her hands. "You're right, Miranda. Company would probably be good for you. But not overnight. They'd never permit it."

"But, Mom!"

"No! But how about this? I'll get Daddy to pick her up before dinner and you guys can order your favorites."

I can see that there is no point in arguing, and at least having her here will be something to look forward to.

As soon as I get back to the room I call Emma with the good news.

The rest of the day I spend in bed listening to a book. It is a really neat story about a girl who suddenly develops psychic powers.

Dad drops Emma off and then goes to pick up my favorite Mexican food from my favorite restaurant, which also happens to be Emma's favorite as well. After he leaves the food with us, he and Mom leave to get their own dinner. Emma and I eat at a small table that Jean has set up for us.

My eyes have improved enough during the day that they seem *almost* back to normal.

"So? Can't get them to let me stay overnight?" Emma says, more a statement than a question.

"A definite no," I say between bites. "But you're here now. Come on. Let's wander around. Maybe we can see something."

Emma stuffs the last bit of taco into her mouth and then follows me.

We go out into the hallway and I show her all the things

73

Mom showed me earlier. We meet Jean in the hall but she is on her way to my room to change the bedding. Emma and I hurry down to the far end of the corridor.

"This is where it should be," I say.

"But where is the original room you were in?" Emma wonders. "The one with the yellow flowers on the wallpaper?"

"You're right. We should find that first. Let's check all the rooms."

We peek our heads into the rooms, one by one. Not all of them, though. One or two are locked. Outside of that, everything seems to be exactly as it is supposed to be. Discouraged, we wander back to my room.

"Maybe the disease *is* affecting my memory," I sigh. "I mean, you weren't there every weekend, Emma. We don't know for sure it isn't a simple but stupid explanation."

Emma shrugs. "I guess. I'm just so used to being suspicious of everything adults tell me. Mom and Dad always fudge the truth 'for my own good.' Still," she adds, "there *are* a couple of locked doors, so we aren't sure the room doesn't exist."

Dad walks in ready to take Emma home. I'm given my sleeping pill and I drop off, hoping I won't have any more nasty dreams. I guess I don't, because the day nurse, Mona, is there when I wake up. My sight is totally clear. She suggests I wash up and says she'll go get my breakfast. I look at my phone. 6:15 a.m.

I have a quick shower but Mona still isn't back so I peek out into the hallway. All is quiet. A door opens at the end of the hall and Dr. Mullen bustles out. I realize that the room he is leaving is one of the ones that was locked last night. I wonder if *that's* where they are keeping the girl—if she actually exists outside of my dream world. I take a second look around. Dr.

74

Mullen has gone into a room across the hall and shut the door. I scamper down the hall.

The room Dr. Mullen just left is an office, and it looks like burglars have just finished with it. Papers are strewn everywhere; boxes filled with papers are piled one on top of another; file cabinets bulging with papers are too full to shut. I look nervously at the door across the hall. It's still closed. I sidle into the office and over to his desk. I don't have any idea why. I mean, he wouldn't have the girl hidden in one of his filing cabinets or anything. I just can't help feeling that everything isn't quite adding up. I glance at the desk. A jumble of papers, logs, and in the middle a large diary open to a series of entries. The date on the open page catches my eyes. November 1, thirteen years ago.

Subject #2, suspected premature aging. 3 years, two months, 5 days. Time of Death: 10:15

I look closer. Lots of incomprehensible medical words. I take a deep breath, check the door, flip the pages. A year later there are more entries.

Subject #5, kidney failure. 9 months, 3 days. Time of Death: 1:05.

Who are these "subjects"? Why are they dying? Are they patients? I turn the pages quickly. More and more data. None of it makes sense to me and I'm too nervous to stay in the room any longer. Quickly, heart racing, I try to find the place where the diary had been left open. I can't. I have to get out of the room. How could I ever explain my presence here? Talk about bad manners! I hurry to the door, then start walking backwards down the hall.

Dr. Mullen comes out of the other room. I stop. "Oh, hello, Miranda," he says brightly. "What are you up to?"

75

"Nothing," I say, "I'm just bored."

"Well, dear, you'll soon be out of here." And he hurries back into his office. I turn and run down the hall back to my room. Shortly after, Mona comes in with breakfast. As I dig into my hotcakes I wonder what it is I've just seen. Probably nothing more than a diary of experiments on lab rats. Perhaps I have to accept Mom's explanation: tumors are pressing on my brain, making me imagine, dream, even making me paranoid.

I decide to stop worrying about all this nonsense and do what the doctor says—just concentrate on getting better.

Another serving of hotcakes would be a step in that direction. I peek out my door to see if Mona is around and see her stepping into a room a couple of doors down.

"Mona," I call, hurrying after her because I've forgotten my slippers and the floor is cold. "Mona!"

She turns just as I get to the door. Swiftly she moves out of the room and shuts the door behind her, holding onto some clean sheets, but not before I get a clear, if brief, view of blue wallpaper, dotted with yellow flowers. My breath catches in my throat.

"Yes?" she asks.

"I, I, just wanted more hotcakes," I manage to get out.

"Good for you. I'll bring them in a few minutes."

I stand there staring at her.

"Back to bed," she says. "Look at you. No slippers."

"Oh, right," I mutter, "bed. Back to bed."

I turn and race back to my room, and to the phone. I have to talk to Emma!

I wake her up, of course, and she is so groggy and I am talking so fast that it takes a few minutes before she can make sense of what I'm saying.

76

"What are you going to do?" she asks.

"I don't know." I put my slippers on. "I think I'll go on a reconnaissance mission. See what else I can find."

"Take me with you," Emma suggests. "We'll FaceTime."

"Good idea." I hang up, then FaceTime Emma back. I peek out the door. "The coast is clear," I inform her.

"Then go check out that wall again—where you thought the room was. If you were right about one thing, maybe you were right about the other."

I hurry down the hallway and look closely at the wall, which I'd thought was a door. "It's just a wall, Emma."

"Are there any buttons?" Emma asks.

I run my hands up and down the corners and suddenly I feel something. It's the exact color of the wall but it's slightly raised and round. I push it. The wall swings open easily.

"Emma," I hiss, "I'm in!"

Chapter 10

Emma answers me. "I can tell you for a fact that you aren't dreaming. Or else I am, too!"

"I can't see much though. It's dark in here. It was brighter the other night."

"Look for a light switch."

I fumble around until I find a dimmer switch and then I turn it up. Immediately I see the child in her bed. She sits up. She stares at me, rubs her eyes, stares again.

"Who are you?" I say, walking over to the bed.

"Miranda!" It is Emma. "What's happening?"

"She looks exactly like me," I whisper to Emma, "exactly. I tap my phone's back camera icon. "Can you see?"

"Can I ever," Emma says, her voice low.

I move closer to the girl.

"What's your name?"

She just stares at me.

"What do people call you?"

"Oh! Ten. I am called Ten. I have been here ten years. Last year I was called Nine."

"Your name is your age? And it changes every year?"

"I am called Ten," she repeats. "That will be my last name. I will never be called Eleven."

"Why? I don't understand. Who are you? Are you my sister? My name is Miranda Martin. Can you see how much

78

you look like me?"

"I am exactly like you," she says, her voice matter of fact.

"But who are you?"

"I am made for you. My destiny is you. Soon I will fulfill my destiny. Thank you. I have been waiting."

"Are you hearing this?" I ask Emma.

"Yes I sure am, but it doesn't make any sense. I mean she *does* look exactly like you did at ten."

"They lied to me!" I declare. "Again!" I pause for a moment just staring at "Ten."

"I'm going to find out what's going on."

I stride over to the door, pull it open and yell at the top of my lungs. "Hey! Anybody around?"

Then I talk to Emma. "Emma hang up and call my parents. Tell them where I am. Tell them you won't say anything to your parents yet, but that they'd better get over here. Tell them they have some explaining to do."

"Okay," she agrees, "I'll do it." And she hangs up.

Just then Mona runs into the room.

"Oh no! Come on, Miranda, let's get you back to your room."

"So Dr. Mullen can stick me with a needle again and pretend this is all a dream? I don't think so. I know it isn't a dream. I've just been talking on my phone," I hold it up and show it to her, "to my friend Emma. So you see, I'm going to wait here for Dr. Mullen and for my parents and I'm going to get an explanation."

Mona puts her hand over her mouth and goes running out of the room.

"Hah!" I say to the child. "That showed her."

She looks at me puzzled. "You speak loudly. Why is that?"

79

"I'm upset!"

"Upset? Upset?" She shakes her head.

"You know, like when you were crying last night. Why were you crying?"

"Oh, I am not worthy. I cannot tell you why I allowed tears."

"Tell me."

"No, then you will not want my gifts. You will think me unworthy."

"I won't. Tell me."

She pauses and looks at me. "I was ... I cannot explain it ... apprehensive concerning my nonexistence."

"What?" Who taught her to talk? She doesn't sound like any ten-year-old I've ever met.

"To not exist," she repeats. "What does it mean? Will it be like sleeping? That's what Lynda says."

I sit on her bed. "Is Lynda your mother?" I ask. "Is Allan your father?"

"I never thought," she muses. "We have never discussed it. They created me. They are my creators. And Dr. Mullen, of course."

"So they are your parents," I say. "Look, that means you're my sister! You can tell me what's wrong with you. Are you sick like me? Why are you here? Why have we never met?"

Dr. Mullen runs into the room, panting, trying to catch his breath.

"Miranda, please stop talking to her. You'll only upset her."

"And what about me?" I say. "Don't you think I'm upset?"

"Of course you are. Please. Be reasonable. Come back to your room. Your mother and father are on their way. They'll explain everything."

80

"More lies, you mean."

"There's no point in that any more, is there?" he says, pulling me gently away from the child. "Come along."

Reluctantly, I go with him. The girl looks after me with such an odd expression ... what did she mean by gifts?

I allow Dr. Mullen to lead me back to my room. I sit on my bed, hugging my knees to my chest. "Are you going to tell me?" I ask.

"Let's wait for your parents."

We wait in silence. I am so confused, so angry, so shocked, I really can't even think straight. It's not long before Mom and Dad hurry in, both of them looking haggard. When they see my expression, which must be pretty dark, they stop dead in front of the bed.

"Well?" I say through gritted teeth. "Will you *finally* tell me the truth?"

Dad sits down on the bed. Mom stands on the other side. Dad tries to take my hand. I pull it away.

"Miranda," he says, "you must try to remain calm. We'll have to talk about this in a reasonable way."

I scramble past him out of the bed. I can't stand to be near to him. "Reasonable? I have a sister and you've never told me?"

"We couldn't."

"Why not? Why is she here? What's going on?"

"She's not well," Dad says. "She's ill. She's mentally ill. So if she said anything to you, anything odd ..."

"*Everything* she said was weird," I exclaim, exasperated. "But you don't lock up mentally ill people."

"You do," Dad says, "if they are a danger to themselves and to others."

81

"What do you mean?"

"She, well, she tries to hurt herself. And others."

"She's too little!" I object. "And she was never at home, so how did you find that out?" I pause. "And I *think* I would have remembered Mom being *pregnant*. Or have I just 'forgotten' that too, like I forgot about that picture?"

Dad and Mom look at each other, seemingly at a loss for words.

"Miranda, may I speak to your parents privately for a moment?" Dr. Mullen asks.

"Sure." I shrug. "I don't care."

The three of them leave the room. I call Emma back.

"Well?" she says.

"They're still lying," I say, feeling queasy. "They're so bad at it I can see right through them. But *why* are they lying, Emma? I'm really scared. The one thing I thought I could depend on was them and how straight we always were with each other." I pause. "That child is really strange. She said all kinds of things. She calls my parents her creator."

"Creator? Like God?"

"Well, I suppose that's what our parents are. But," I add, remembering, "she included Dr. Mullen too."

"Oh my gosh," Emma exclaims. "What else did she say?"

I'm starting to get a horrible feeling in my stomach. I almost don't want to think about what she said.

"You heard what she said about her destiny. Her destiny was me. I mean, what could that mean?"

The three adults come back into the room.

"Is that Emma?" Mom asks, her voice sharp.

"Yes."

"Has she told anyone?"

82

"Not *yet*."

"Good. Tell her not to. Better yet, let me speak to her." Mom grabs the phone from me. "Emma, listen to me. If you say *anything* to anyone you will be directly responsible for your friend's death."

"Mother!" I gasp.

"Do you understand me? Good." She hangs up.

Then Mom starts to talk in a rush, her voice hard, her eyes hard, as if that's the only way she can get the words out.

"All right, Miranda, we are going to tell you something now which is bound to upset you. But I think it's better to be upset than to be dead. So, here it is." She takes a short breath. "That girl is an exact duplicate of you. She was created from DNA taken from you at birth. She's your insurance policy. So many children die in car crashes or of some horrible illness, all because they can't get a replacement organ or some bone marrow or something. We, your father and I, were determined that you would not suffer that fate. We were not going to see you die. So we made a duplicate. She was created here, with the sole purpose of donating to you anything you might need."

My knees suddenly feel wobbly and I get so shaky I begin to topple over. Dr. Mullen puts me in a chair.

"Like a liver," I say, my voice barely a whisper.

"Yes," she says, her voice defiant. "Like a liver."

"So you are going to sacrifice her to save me?"

"It must be done. She's not a real person, Miranda. She's a copy. She's been raised in a laboratory."

"But she talks. She feels. She's afraid!"

"Nonsense. This is the moment she's been waiting for."

I can't speak. I am so shocked, I can't think. A duplicate. A ... a ... and then the word comes to me and I say it out loud.

83

"A clone." I start to laugh. "It's a joke, right? It's just a big joke." They look at me in silence. I stop laughing.

"You're not my parents," I scream. "You're some horrible monsters. This isn't happening. It's not real! It's all a dream. A dream. I want to wake up. I want to wake up!" I'm laughing and crying and screaming. I think I'm losing my mind.

I turn to Dr. Mullen. "Give me something so I can sleep," I demand. "I just can't stand to be awake any longer."

Dad looks like he is about to cry. Mom just looks angry. I go back to bed and lie down. I want blackness. Oblivion. I can't handle another second awake.

Chapter 11

When I wake up I am groggy but alone. I look at my phone: it's 2:15 in the afternoon. I must have slept all morning. Then I realize that I couldn't have checked my phone unless my eyesight was clear. I lie back on the pillows, exhausted. Everything is wrong. Everything is upside down. Everything I thought was true was a lie. My parents, who I thought were so reasonable, who I never argued with because there was no need, who stressed honesty over all else—they were honest in every little detail but lied about the biggest thing: my life. Suddenly Prospero from *The Tempest* pops into my mind. He used magic to make his daughter happy. It's what Mom and Dad have done. But their magic means someone must be killed. They'll be *murderers*!

That notebook of Dr. Mullen's. Those notations of deaths. Were they rats? Or has he been experimenting on people? I slip out of bed and go to the closet. My clothes are hanging neatly on hangers. Quickly I change, pull my hair back with an elastic, splash water on my face in the bathroom to get rid of the remaining drugged feeling from the pill.

I open the door to my room a crack. My parents are standing with Dr. Mullen just outside his office. He is talking fast and leads them into his office. Jean is walking into Ten's room. I may not have another chance. I open the door and run down the hall. I push open the outer door and race down the

85

driveway. I have to find Emma. I decide to go to her home.

Then I stop dead. My habit of forgetting my phone may have just doomed my plans. How could I have left the clinic without it? I look around. I have no money, no way to get to Emma's. I spot a gas station down at the end of the road. I run down the street, burst into the shop and ask the kid behind the counter to call me a cab. He does, and within minutes it arrives. It takes about ten minutes to get to Emma's house. I stare out the window, trying not to think. Trying not to panic.

Emma lives in a bungalow at the bottom of a short street in Palm Desert. When I get to her house I tell the driver to wait, I'll have to get his money. Just as I get out of the cab, Emma appears on her bike. She rides up to me, sees the look on my face, and gives me a big hug. I explain about the cab and the money. She runs into the house and returns with cash, then hurries me into the house, telling me that her parents won't be home for hours as they are out running errands and her two older brothers, Josh and Ben, are at Josh's baseball game. We have the house to ourselves.

We sit at the kitchen table. Emma gets us each an iced tea. My hands shake as I raise my glass.

I take a deep breath. "You won't believe it."

"I already feel like I'm in some weird Stephen King novel," Emma says. "I mean, mad scientists, a spooky hospital, a sister you never knew you had ... what next?"

"Clones," I say, my voice low, hardly able to utter the word.

"Yeah, right," she repeats. "Clones. That would be the logical next weird thing ..." She stops and stares at me. "You're kidding, right?"

"I wish I were."

Just like me last night, she is speechless. We sit saying

86

nothing for a long time.

"Wow," she says finally.

"Yeah, wow," I echo, my voice still shaky.

"Gee," she says, eyes wide.

"Gee is right," I say.

She shakes her head and lets out a little giggle. "Gee whiz!" she says. "Gee golly whiz!"

"Golly gosh dear," I giggle back.

Soon we can't stop. We're laughing and giggling and all we can say is stupid words like "oh wow," "oh gosh," "oh boy," "gee willikers," "boy oh boy," "jeepers," "wow," "double wow."

We're laughing so hard we both need to stop and drink our tea. Finally our giggles subside and we are left staring at each other again.

"Wow!" says Emma.

This time I don't laugh. Neither does she. But we can't seem to find the words, either. I mean, it is so out of the realm of reality that we can't take it in. Who could?

"You'd better explain it to me," Emma says finally.

I repeat what Mom told me.

"An insurance policy?" Emma asks. "That's what she said?"

"That girl is just like ... I don't know ... spare parts, I guess," I answer.

"To them," Emma comments.

"Right. To them. Not to me. She really is my little sister, Emma. In a way. Well, she's really me, isn't she?" I stop to think about that. "Does that mean that we'd have the exact same personality too?"

"I don't know," Emma says. "Does it?"

"I don't know either. I mean if we are exactly the same personality, then, well, wouldn't we be pretty much the same

87

emotionally? I mean I've seen these programs on twins—Mr. London showed us one in biology. Twins separated at birth who ended up being exactly alike, they even used the same brand of toothpaste."

"But you make it sound like we're just machines, programmed to react in a certain way," Emma objects. "I mean, we're all born a certain way. Does that mean we're going to behave a certain way too? I don't like the sound of that—as if we're just following our programming like a computer."

"What if it is like that?" I ask. "What if, well, what if I could never fight with my parents because I'm just that way? Look at that kid. She'll do anything they tell her. Even die for me."

"Die for you?"

"Yeah, well, you can't live without a liver."

"This isn't good," Emma says, shaking her head.

"I'm not going to let them kill her," I state.

"Then you'll die," Emma protests.

"So I'll die!"

"You don't mean that!"

"What am I supposed to do?"

"You think they'll let you decide? I don't think so. They're going to go ahead with this."

"No. We have to figure out another way," I say.

"What?"

"I don't know."

Again we sit in silence. What? What can I do? I look up at Emma. "I can run away."

"You can't run away," Emma chides me. "You're too sick. Without treatment you won't make it."

"I'm going to die anyway, Emma," I say. "If I run away they

88

won't kill the child and she'll live, at least."

"Where would you go? You're too sick," she repeats.

"I don't know!" I declare, frustrated. "But I can't let them do this."

"If she's your clone," says Emma, "won't she get this disease too, in a few years? It's genetic, right?"

"Maybe," I say. "But, they could treat her with this new gene therapy before she gets really sick like me."

"Maybe I'd better tell my parents," Emma says. "This is too big for me or you to handle alone. We need help."

"I think you're right," I agree. "It would be a relief to tell someone else. And your father's a doctor so he'd know what to do."

"He'd have to report Dr. Mullen," Emma says.

"Good!" I reply.

Emma gets her phone out of her jeans then stops and looks at me.

"It must be illegal, what they're doing."

"Of course it is!" I answer.

"So they'll *all* be arrested. Your parents too."

"I don't care! They *should* be. I'd rather they were arrested for this than for *murder*."

"But you won't be cured then," Emma says. "You'll die."

"Emma," I say, getting up, "if you won't call your father, I will."

"But that's what your mom meant when she warned me I'd be responsible for your death. If I tell … I can't, Miranda."

"Miranda! Miranda!"

It's my dad. The door bursts open and he stands there, face red, sweat pouring off his forehead.

89

Chapter 12

"Miranda!" My dad explodes. "Are you crazy? You're sick! You have to go back to the clinic." He looks at Emma. "What have you told Emma?"

"Nothing!" I say, before Emma can speak. "I just got here." My first lie. It's easy really. Especially when it's to protect someone you love. Is that why it was so easy for them?

Emma understands me immediately. They're crazy, after all. If they know she knows they might ... what? Murder her too?

"What's going on?" she says, playing stupid.

"Emma, it's a mix-up, that's all. I know Miranda told you that she saw her double but, well, she's very sick. Her illness is creating these hallucinogenic experiences that seem *completely* real. I know she thought she was telling you the truth on the phone but she was imagining the whole thing."

Emma nods her head. "I understand," she says softly, appearing to believe him.

I realize it's my turn to play the game. I try to look confused.

"It's not like that!" I protest. "I'm sure it's all real."

"Just come back to the clinic," Dad says. "We'll sort it all out, I promise."

What choice do I have? He leads me out of the house to the car. I see there's a security guard from the clinic with him.

90

They were obviously willing to take me back by force, if necessary.

I look back at Emma as I leave. I don't want to put her in danger. I hope she tells her father. But I have a horrible feeling she won't.

I sit in the back seat of the car refusing to speak to my dad, planning my escape. Next time I won't go to Emma's. I'll go somewhere they can't find me. I won't be responsible for that child's death. When we get back to the clinic my mom is waiting in the front foyer. She puts her hand on my arm. I recoil.

"Don't touch me!" I am so full of anger, no, not anger, rage, that I feel like I could kill her and my dad. "So what is this place, really? The clinic where they carry out all the gruesome experiments you fund? What else is here?" Suddenly I remember the third floor. "Yeah," I mutter, "what else is here?"

I make a dash for the stairs, my parents right behind me. My legs are long, and still strong. They can't catch me. I get to the third floor well ahead of everyone. I can hear Mom calling, "Stop! Stop! Stop, Miranda, stop."

I fling open the first door I find, surprised it isn't locked. But why lock it? Everyone at the clinic knows what's going on. Everyone but me. And I always do what I'm told. Well, not anymore.

A regular office is all I can see. I move to a second door. A lab with a bunch of computers. Then a third room. This one's different. It's like Ten's room but nicer, like a regular apartment. A young woman, maybe twenty, tops, is sitting on a couch watching TV. She is very pregnant. She looks up as I crash in and her face registers shock and then fear.

91

Of course. Why would Ten, as they call her, be the only one? Maybe she was the only one that worked.

Mom and Dad rush in. They see the young girl and me and then they both grab hold of me and pull me out of the room.

"Who was that?" I demand.

"A surrogate," Mom answers. "She's well paid and well taken care of, don't worry."

"Don't worry?" I repeat. "Don't worry?" I take a breath. "This place should be burned down. You are evil," I scream at them as they drag me down the stairs. "Evil."

"We're evil because we want to keep you alive?"

"I don't *want* to be the cause of all this," I scream at them. "It's disgusting. No wonder we never discussed God or religion or anything at our house. You're God, aren't you? Both of you? How many more of me are you going to make? Are you going to grow another one after you've killed that child? And then kill her if something else goes wrong with me? It's *murder*," I yell. "*Murder!*"

By now we are at the bottom of the stairway.

"How could you pretend she didn't exist? That she wasn't *really* your child too?"

"We only thought of her in relation to you—not as a real person," Mom says.

"No," I accuse, "as body parts."

"Which we never thought we'd really have to use," Dad says. "You should have been perfect."

"What do you mean?"

Mom darts a glance at Dad. His color rises a bit but he goes on, "Just that Dr. Mullen checked your DNA before you were born. And everything seemed fine."

"Checked?" I ask, getting suspicious again. "Checked for

92

what?"

"Checked to be sure it was fine," Dad says. "But this clone has to give you her liver. If she doesn't she'll wither away. She's been brought up to believe that is her calling, her reason for living."

"She'll have to find another reason," I say, walking away from them. "Like revenge, maybe."

Dr. Mullen appears out of his office. "Miranda, Miranda, what are you doing? You should be resting. Oh, this was a bad idea having you here at the clinic. A very bad idea."

"Can we talk?" I ask him. "In *private*." And I glare at Mom and Dad.

"Certainly. Step into my office."

We go into his office, leaving Mom and Dad outside.

"They're a little irrational right now," I say.

"Naturally," he smiles, the irony lost on him completely.

"Look, Dr. Mullen," I say, "you need to figure out a way to save me and my clone."

He starts to protest.

"If you're smart enough to create a human clone," I say, "you must be smart enough to figure this out." I pause. "I won't have this operation. I'll run away first. Or if you force me to do it you can't force me to live afterwards. I can always kill myself then." He looks shocked. "I mean it. Think of something."

I turn and walk out. I barely glance at my parents as I head for my room. "No more Ms. Nice Guy," I say to myself. I hurry away from them. I don't want to look at them. I reach my room and sink down onto my bed. Suddenly I remember the picture. I pick up my phone, lying right where I forgot it, and call Emma.

93

"Emma," I say, my voice a croak, "those pictures, those photos that were me but not me, in the overalls."

"Are you all right?"

"If my mom and dad were lying and we can probably assume they were, then ..."

"Then," says Emma, "who is that in the picture? Ten?"

"It can't be. They've told me Ten has never been out of here." I'm quiet for a while. "The photo album," I continue. "I've looked through it a million times. It starts with baby pictures—my mom holding me, right?"

"Right," Emma agrees. She's looked through it many times with me.

"And how does your photo album start?" I ask.

"Well, first there are some really funny looking pictures of Mom when she's pregnant. You know how skinny she is. She looks like a twig that swallowed a moose."

"Yours start with pictures of your mom pregnant. Mine doesn't. What does that mean?"

"Nothing?" Emma asks, hopefully.

"It could be nothing," I admit. "But you want to bet if I ask where those photos are they'll make some excuse?"

"I'm coming over there," Emma says.

"It's better if you pretend you don't know anything," I protest.

"They aren't going to do anything to me," Emma says. "I'll get Mom to drive me so she knows where I am. Okay?"

"Okay," I say, relieved.

If I ever needed a friend, it's now.

Chapter 13

Mom and Dad come into the room. Before they can say anything I ask them, "Why are there no pictures of Mom when she was pregnant with me?"

They don't answer. They just look at each other, alarmed.

"Who is the girl in the overalls, *really*?" I continue. "And those so called Halloween pictures when Mom's hair is short ... don't you think you'd better tell me everything?"

"I can show you pictures of me pregnant," Mom says. "I'll go home and get them."

"Pregnant with who?" I ask.

"Whom," Mom corrects me automatically.

"*Whom*?"

She is silent. I sit down on the bed. It's all starting to make sense. If this can be called making sense. A girl who isn't me but is me. No pictures of Mom pregnant with me. There can only be one logical explanation for that picture. Even though every bit of me wants to stop, now, I can't. I have to keep asking questions. I have to know the whole truth. So I take a deep breath and plunge ahead.

"I have another question," I say. "Why do you both look so young? You look the same age in the pictures of me when I'm ten as you do with your *first child. The one you had before me.*"

Mom and Dad look desperately at each other before

looking back at me. The silence stretches out as they seem incapable of replying. I wait. Finally Mom shakes her head and reluctantly tries to answer.

"We've both had some plastic surgery done," Mom says quietly, "so we'd look younger. So no one would question our being too old to have you."

I realize I've been holding my breath. My stomach turns over with Mom's answer, and I feel lightheaded. My conclusion was right. "What happened to that child?" I ask.

"She died," Mom says, her eyes filling with tears. "She died of a brain tumor."

"Just before she died," Dad says, "Dr. Mullen took her DNA."

"Allan!" Mom exclaims.

"She has to be told the truth," Dad says. "All of it."

"No!"

But Dad ignores her. "Dr. Mullen recreated Jessica, our first child. She's the one in the overalls, standing in front of the castle. He used her DNA to make you, Miranda. You were carried by a surrogate because by then your mother was too old to carry you without risking complications."

Suddenly I can't seem to quite catch my breath. The room spins around me, I feel like I'm falling, falling. I stare at Mom. At Dad.

"I'm not even a real person," I say softly. "I'm just some scientific experiment."

"That's not true!" Dad says. Mom has started to cry. "You're as real as Emma. Just because you were started off differently ... you're as human as any of us."

"But Dr. Mullen *made* me." I'm trembling. "I remember when you said he should have known—he must have made

96

sure I couldn't get cancer like she did."

"He did," Dad confesses. "He edited your genome to make you as strong and as healthy as possible."

"So how did I get sick?"

"We thought we could control everything," Dad says. "We wanted to—but it seems that your body just spontaneously got sick. Or maybe ... the genetic code is so complicated ... some tiny thing went wrong."

"We couldn't face losing another child," Mom wept. "So Dr. Mullen told us that he'd give us this insurance policy. We thought he meant he'd grow replacement organs. We didn't know, at first, he'd been growing other children. And that they'd been dying."

"And when you found out, you didn't stop it, did you? Don't you see how cruel that was? Maybe those infants felt something—loneliness, or fear ..." I shudder.

And then I have another thought. "What else did Dr. Mullen do when he made me? Create someone who is always good? Did he give me my dancing?"

Dad looks so uncomfortable I know I've hit a nerve.

"Well?"

"He may have enhanced your mental and physical abilities," he concedes. Then he gets a wan smile on his face. "After all, if he hadn't made you so smart you'd never have figured all this out."

"You shouldn't have underestimated me, then," I snap.

"No," Dad says, "we shouldn't have."

Mom is still crying. I don't care. I hate her. I hate him. How could they do this? I'm just a freak. Who am I? *What* am I?

"Could you please leave me alone?" I ask.

Dad takes Mom's arm and propels her out of the room.

She's completely out of it, sobbing. "I'm sorry, Miranda," she says as she leaves. "We never wanted you to find out. I'm so sorry. We never wanted you to have any pain. That's why we did all this."

"No," I answer her, "*you* never wanted to have any pain. That's why you did it." I run after them and push the door shut. Then I sit on the edge of the bed, staring into space, too stunned to think, until Emma peeks in.

"Hi," she says.

I look at her dully.

"Miranda?" She comes into the room, sits on the bed. "Your parents were very upset when I started pounding on the outside door. But when they saw my Mom was with me they had to let me in or it would've seemed suspicious. What's happened? Your mother looked pretty bad."

I'm so miserable I can't speak. I lie down on the bed and curl up in a ball.

Emma doesn't say anything. I'm not sure how much time has gone by when she pats my foot and says, "Miranda, tell me what happened. What did they tell you? Who was that child in the photo?"

I lie on my back and stare at the ceiling. "Their first child," I say. "Jessica."

"What happened to her?"

"She died. Of a brain tumor."

"That's awfully sad. Why didn't they tell you?"

"Because I'm her. I was created out of her DNA"

"What?"

"You heard me," I say, sitting up, staring at her. "My mom was never pregnant with me. I was carried by some surrogate who is probably long gone now. I'm a *clone*." Emma just stares

98

at me.

"I'm a freak. A monster. A thing. It's why I'm so smart. It's why I'm always analyzing everything. They *made* me smart. They *made* me athletic." I shake my head. "Go home, Emma. Go find a real friend."

"You're still *you*," she says.

"No, I'm not. You should go to the police or something and tell them everything. They can lock us all up."

"No," Emma objects, "I don't want you locked up. I want you better and back at school."

"Emma, I'm *nothing*. Even if by some miracle I could get better, I'm just a bunch of DNA programmed to behave in a certain way. What's the point of living?"

"But," Emma protests, "we're all like that. I mean we all get certain traits passed on—physical power, or brains, or something. Like Jimmy, he's a bully, right? And so's his dad. But if Jimmy had grown up away from his dad maybe he would have learned how not to be a bully. I mean, maybe it's all there, and we're more likely to be one way than another but we can learn to be different. Maybe that's what being human is."

I stare at her in admiration. "That's a pretty good speech."

"Well," she admits. "I can't take all the credit. There was this great *Star Trek* on Netflix a while ago and it was all about this."

"You and your science fiction," I scoff. I've always thought it was silly. Then I realize what I've said and I burst out laughing. So does Emma.

"Yeah," she agrees, "it's so unbelievable, right?"

"Yeah, right," I sigh.

"There's one more thing," she says.

99

"What?"

"Look, I know you don't believe in any of this but I do. I think we all have souls. And your soul is your own. It doesn't matter how you were made. You'd still have one."

"Would I?"

"Of course."

"I think my parents should let me die so they can have number ten as my successor. Child number three. Why not? She's exactly like me. They can train her to be another me. They won't even miss me."

"Miranda!"

"It's true. That's what they should do. But before I die I'd like to set fire to this whole place."

"Miranda. Stop being stupid," Emma scolds me. "You aren't going to die. That girl can't replace you. What about me? Who'd be my best friend? What about Sue? She's calling me every hour to see how you are. And you said it yourself; the class couldn't get on without the three of us. They might have to start doing some work. Come on. We have to find a different way."

Dr. Mullen pushes the door open and hurries in.

"Hello, girls. Now Emma. I must have your word that you can keep quiet—for the sake of your friend, yes?" He smiles but the threat is there.

Emma nods.

"Excellent. I would expect no less."

He turns to me. "Well, Miranda, I may have a solution."

"What do you mean?"

"I may be able to save both you and Ten."

"How?"

"I could give you *part* of Ten's liver. You each get half. That

100

is, she keeps half, you get half. The liver is an organ that can actually regenerate. If we give you half a healthy one, a perfect match of course, it should grow to full size. And then I will cure you with the gene therapy. Well, it *could* work. It's far riskier for you, but it does give Ten a chance."

"Let's do it, then," I say without any hesitation.

"I'll need your parents' permission," he says.

"Tell them that if they don't give it," I warn, "they may have a healthy daughter but not for long. I'll run away, maybe even kill myself. And I'll turn all of you in."

"Interesting," Dr. Mullen says, making a note to himself. "Aggressive. Decisive. Traits I didn't realize you possessed."

"So the lab rat has some surprises for you?" I say sarcastically.

"Yes," he agrees, "yes, you do."

Emma smiles. "See?" she declares. "You are Miranda. That means you get to be just as confused about who you are as the rest of us."

Dr. Mullen nods his head, writing as he leaves. "*Very* interesting," he mumbles. "Fascinating."

"*He's* the one who's exactly like the mad scientist in a movie," Emma says. "He's the one behaving according to type."

"Maybe he's a mad scientist clone," I suggest.

"Yeah," she agrees, "maybe he is."

Chapter 14

Emma has gone home, Mom and Dad have gone home, and I lie here in bed, wondering about everything. Tomorrow morning I'll have the operation. I'm not scared anymore. I guess I'm too upset to be scared. I mean, you think you're one thing and then you find out that everything you thought was wrong. Still, I suppose Emma has a point. Once we're alive we're all made up of the DNA we are born with. But how do I know now, when I make a choice, whether it's me or my programming?

Or is there a difference?

The door opens and Jean comes in with my sleeping pill, but she isn't alone. The child Ten is with her.

"Hi!" I say, surprised.

"Hello," the child answers.

"She really wanted to see you before the operation," Jean says. "She's upset. I didn't think you'd mind."

"No, of course not," I say.

Jean puts my pill on the night table. She pulls the big chair up toward the bed for the child, who is dressed in a long white cotton nightgown. The child sinks into it, staring at me the entire time.

"I've just thought of a name for you," I say suddenly. "A real name. Ariel."

"What is Ariel?"

"Ariel is a magic fairy. In this play called *The Tempest* he helps save Miranda. It's perfect for you."

"I am female," she points out.

"It doesn't matter. Do you like it?"

"Yes," she nods. "I believe I do." She smiles at me.

"You're very brave to have this operation," I tell her.

"That is the matter I wish to discuss with you," she says, her face becoming grave and serious.

"Yes?"

"I wish you to take my entire liver. It will be far safer for you."

"But not for you!"

"That is irrelevant. I am unimportant. I live only to serve you. This goes against everything I live for."

I stare at her a moment and then I realize how true Emma's words were earlier. I mean Ariel wasn't *born* believing she needed to sacrifice herself for me. But she was born to be led easily, just like me. Dr. Mullen trained her to believe she exists only to save me. But had she grown up with our parents she would have a totally different view of life. Or if she'd grown up with Emma's family, maybe she'd be more of a rebel because, now that I think of it, Emma's family loves her independent spirit, even though it also drives them crazy.

"You are going to have to live for something else now," I say. "I can't accept what you offer, even though it's so generous. You see, you don't know anything else. You can't make a free choice."

"Free choice?" she asks.

"Yes. That's what makes us human," I answer. "And you can't choose freely because you've been taught to think only one way." And then, I realize how true that is, for everyone.

103

"But that's okay," I say excited, "because we all have, in a way. I mean some kids are brought up to hate people of color and some are brought up to hate Jewish people, and some are brought up to hate the government and some are brought up really religious with strict rules."

I jump out of bed. "We're *all* programmed in one way or another. We just have to figure out what our programming is."

She looks at me, puzzled. "It seems to me that would be impossible. If you are programmed you cannot decipher what that programming is. You *are* that programming."

"No!" I exclaim. "You don't have to be."

She looks doubtful.

"We're a mash-up of how we're born and how we're brought up—we have to figure it out, that's all."

"It sounds extremely difficult and complicated," Ariel says. "And I still wish for you to take my liver."

"No." I grin. "I won't. And you'll have to deal with that."

"I feel, I feel ... very hostile toward you," she says in a surprised voice.

"Yeah, well that's because you want to do something and I won't let you," I answer. "Get used to it."

"Why get used to it?"

"You'll be leaving here of course, when this is over."

"I will?"

"Oh, I'll make sure of that. You'll be my new little sister, after all."

"Little sister? You mean a sibling?"

I grin. "Yeah. A sibling."

"This is my home," she says, her eyes full of tears. "I cannot leave it."

"You'll have to," I say. "But you'll like it way better away from here. Have you ever even once been outside?"

"No!"

"It's nothing to be afraid of."

Jean has been standing near the door. She walks up to Ariel and pats her on the shoulder. "Time to go. Tomorrow's your big day ..."

I take her hand.

"You *are* fulfilling your destiny," I say. "If not for your gift I'd die. Now I have a chance. A good chance."

She still looks doubtful but she nods her head. "I suppose that will have to be sufficient. At least I do not have to fear non-being at the moment."

"That's right," I agree, "you don't. And maybe I don't either."

"Take your pill, Miranda," Jean says.

She leaves with Ariel and I reach for my pill.

Chapter 15

I've been in hospital for a month. The operation was a success and the gene therapy has worked too. My tumors seem to have disappeared completely. I feel almost normal. Normal enough to be allowed to go home tomorrow. Normal enough to have to decide what to do about my mom and my dad and Dr. Mullen.

I'm still not convinced they've told me the complete truth. They lied about everything, didn't they? Until I forced the truth out of them. But I can't monitor what they do here. Not really. And someone has to. Because they were ready to kill Ariel.

So now I have to make the hardest decision of my life. I've been sitting here, going over it all, over and over it, reliving everything they said. And the more I think about it all, the more ...

Emma peeks her head into the room. "Hiya!"

"Emma. Don't do that!"

"Don't do what? Boy, you're nervous," she says, as she walks in.

"I ... I ... I'm deciding ..." Should I tell her?

"What?"

"I'm thinking of calling the police."

She sits in the big chair. "What'll you say?"

"I'll tell them what's happened."

"They'll arrest your mother and your father."

"I know."

We are silent for a while.

"Can you *do* that? Can you live with yourself?" she asks.

"I don't *know*." I start to cry. "I don't know. But they would've killed Ariel. Emma, what if there are others?"

"Other clones?"

"There could be, couldn't there? We don't know what else they're hiding. That pregnant woman I saw on the third floor. Aren't the odds pretty good she's carrying one of his experiments? We don't know what Dr. Mullen is capable of. Who'll keep him in check? Can I just pretend nothing happened?"

Emma shakes her head. "I guess not."

"But if I turn them all in, including my own parents ... They love me. They did all this because they love me." I pause. "I still can hardly look at them or speak to them." I look at Emma. "I *have* to call the police. How could I live with myself if they don't stop?"

Then something else hits me. I stare at Emma. "It'll get out, won't it?"

"You mean, that you're a clone?"

"The *first* clone. The *first* human clone. I'll be ..."

"You'll be famous."

"Famous, right. I'll have media trailing me everywhere, my picture'll be on the cover of every tabloid."

"You'll never have a minute's peace," Emma says, the reality sinking in.

"Forever. I'll always be the clone. I'll always be a freak." I feel like my brain is spinning and spinning. I don't know *what* to do. Emma sits beside me and puts her arm around my

107

shoulder.

"Fine," she says, her voice determined. "It's time to put all those brains they gave you to work. *Think*. There must be another way. If you turn them in you'll hate yourself and you'll be miserable. If you don't turn them in you'll never be able to trust them. There must be a different solution."

"You're right. There must be another way." I get up and begin to pace. "They're good parents," I say, "I mean, day to day, at home." I try to think logically. "So the only place they can't be trusted is here, in this clinic. The ordinary clinics are fine, but they can't be in charge of the research clinic," I conclude.

"That makes sense," Emma nods.

"So, I need to get them to agree to turn this clinic over to someone else."

"The hospital my dad works in does research funded by charitable foundations," Emma says. "Your parents could turn this clinic over to a charitable foundation, and someone else would be in charge then—also in charge of Dr. Mullen."

"And they'd *have* to agree," I say, excited, "or I *would* tell. And they'd realize that then they'd be arrested and my life would be ruined."

"What if they don't agree?" Emma asks.

"They're smart too," I sigh. "They will."

"Miranda. Miranda. It is a new day. Please awaken. It is time for our swim."

I open my eyes.

"Buzz off."

"Buzz off? This sounds like another unpleasant saying."

"Go away! I'm sleeping!"

"But we must do our physical therapy in the pool. Ms. Richards will be here momentarily."

I sigh. Having a kid sister isn't everything it's cracked up to be.

"Maybe I'll just skip today," I mutter into the pillow. Emma and I were up last night until 2 a.m. gabbing about Michael Lebowitz's newfound interest in Emma. Michael is extremely cute.

"You must not!" Ariel says. "Only one week more and you may return to school. And I may too. I do *not* want to delay my first day."

And I was worried she'd have trouble adjusting to life outside the clinic. She's thrilled about everything, excited, can't wait ... I suppose that's genetic too. I have to admit, I've always looked forward to new situations, a new class at school, a trip, whatever. So, we are awfully alike. I try not to think about that too much. About my genetic programming. I'm trying just to enjoy being alive, something only a short time ago I never thought could happen.

I'm still trying to figure out how to forgive my parents. I'm very angry with them. They did it out of love, but that's no excuse, is it? I don't think their reasons excuse what they did. It was wrong. I spend a lot of time over at Emma's now. Her parents seem to know the difference between right and wrong.

Maybe, eventually, we'll get back to some kind of normal here. At least they took Ariel in. And at least they agreed to all my demands. They were very upset with me, to say the least. But they are just going to have to take a chance on life and death. So am I. It was tempting to let them continue, in a way. Then I'd always know I had "insurance." But I want to be like

109

everyone else. And I know it's wrong to create people for that reason. Horribly wrong. Dr. Mullen is still doing research on DNA. He has no clue he was doing anything wrong. He just does his scientific experiments and never thinks of where it'll lead. But he's under control now—I hope.

It's a beginning.

"Please awaken!" Ariel says again.

"Wake up," I correct her. "Please wake up."

She throws her arms around me and hugs me. "You are an excellent teacher."

I hug her back.

"And you are an excellent baby sister. I'm awake."

"Good."

"Yeah," I smile. "It's all good."

Part Two

Chapter 16

"Miranda!"

Ariel is standing over me, hands on hips. "Are we not going?"

"What time is it?"

"9:03. Late. Very late. We must train ourselves to rise early. On Monday we return to school."

"You train yourself," I retort grumpily, pulling the covers over my face.

"I *am* trained," she points out. "I am up and ready."

"Then you mean I must train myself," I correct her, turning over, talking into the pillow.

"I suppose."

"Well, I don't need to be trained. I know how to go to school. I've never been late. You're the one who's never done it."

"Yes. I am a novice, as you say," Ariel agrees.

I flip over on my side away from Ariel and run my hand over the slightly raised scar on my abdomen where Dr. Mullen gave me half of Ariel's liver. All the pain from the operation is gone now. In fact, as I lie here, I realize that I pretty much feel completely normal, the way I did before I first got sick.

"I am full of anticipation," Ariel says.

"Are you still there?" I ask.

"Of course."

113

I sigh. Well, I asked for it. And I'm just going to have to get used to it. I propel myself out of bed and head for the bathroom.

"I'll be ready in fifteen minutes," I say. "What's it like out?"

"We are situated on twenty acres, three miles from the city of La Quinta's limits. La Quinta is one of a string of desert cities comprising Palm Springs, Cathedral Canyon and Palm Desert," she replies. "Your parents own a very attractive property, palm trees marking the boundaries. A ranch-style home sits in its center. Landscaped ..."

I am holding in a giggle but I can't contain it for much longer.

"With an assortment of grapefruit, lemon and orange trees, Madagascar palms, aloe trees and *senita cereus* or whisker cactus. An extensive cactus garden surrounds the house, with *opuntia* or prickly pear, *mammillaria magnimamma*—"

"Ariel."

"Yes?"

I can't help but laugh a little. "When someone asks, 'What's it like out?' they want to know about the weather!"

"Then why do they not ask, 'What is the weather like outside?'" Ariel demands, her cheeks turning pink.

"It's an expression," I explain. "You'll have to get used to it."

"Yes," she says. "You are correct. I want to be more like you."

"How much more like me can you be? You're my clone! Try to be more like yourself."

She gives me a puzzled look.

"Oh, it's way too early for this," I say with another sigh.

I go into my bathroom and shut the door. At least here I

114

can have some privacy—well, now that I've made it clear to Ariel, who is sharing my room, that she may not enter while I'm in here. I thought it would be easier for her to adjust if she initially bunked in with me, rather than being in one of the guest rooms. After some prodding, Mother agreed to let Ariel redecorate one of the guest rooms for her own. She's chosen all reds and greens and yellows: bright, vibrant colors. I suppose they're delightful to her after the monotony of the lab. Today's shopping trip is also part of my effort to help her be herself. We go back to school on Monday and I think she should choose her own clothes. Right now she has only the ones Mother bought for her. Besides, after being stuck in this house with her for weeks, this is a great excuse to get out of here for an afternoon.

I go into the kitchen. Lorna has made me a breakfast of fresh grapefruit, a mushroom omelet and toast.

"Would you like to eat it here or outside, Miranda?" she asks.

"Where's Ariel?"

"She is outside, on the patio."

"I'd better join her then."

We have a number of patios. Lorna is pointing to the one outside the kitchen. There is also one off the dining room, which overlooks the pool and tennis court, and another off my parents' bedroom. I like the kitchen patio best. It's surrounded by cacti, and some of them always seem to be in bloom. I join Ariel outside, helping Lorna carry my plates. Ariel's face brightens when she sees me. "Do we leave soon?"

"Yes," I answer. "As soon as I've eaten I'll tell Mother we're ready."

"I have been thinking about Mother," Ariel says.

115

Uh oh. There is no such thing, it seems, as a relaxed morning breakfast when we chat about what we might want to shop for at the mall.

"Emma is meeting us," I say, trying to distract her.

"Excellent. Now about Mother." She pauses. "She really is not my mother," she states. She pauses again. "Or yours. My mother is you, as I am cloned from you. And your mother is the child you were cloned from."

"No," I object, "not really. You are more like my twin, only four years younger, and I am like a twin to the original one, Jessica, their child. So Mother really is my mother, and yours, because she and Father had Jessica. If Mother had cloned herself," I say, "and you were the result, then you would not be her child but her twin. You and I are sisters."

"Of course," she sighs with relief. "You are correct. As always."

"Well, Dr. Mullen engineered extra smarts into you as well as me," I say. "So I'm sure you are just as clever as I am. You just don't know enough yet."

"But today I will learn about The Mall! I cannot wait!"

"Then let me eat," I declare.

She finally shuts up and lets me eat. I eat slowly, which I know she finds maddening, and when I'm done I go in search of Mother.

She is busy on the phone as usual, probably with one of her charities.

"Ready?" I mouth.

She nods and waves. Now that I know how old she really is, she seems to have aged before my eyes. After all, she had me after Jessica died, and Jessica was already ten. Now I'm fourteen, and so instead of being thirty-five like I thought,

116

she's actually in her early fifties. The miracles of plastic surgery. But they can't cover up the worry lines she's developed since I almost died, and since I started hating her. Well, maybe that's too strong a word. But I still haven't forgiven her or Father for what they've done. In fact, I find I can't even call Father "Dad" like I used to, certainly not "Daddy." And Mom is now Mother. I think I would call them Mr. Martin and Mrs. Martin if I could, because that's what they feel like to me—strangers.

Mother gets off the phone and smiles. "You girls all ready for your first day out?"

"We are," I say.

"Take a sweater in case the mall is overly air-conditioned," she says, as she always does before I go to the mall.

"I don't need one," I remind her, like I always do, except now I know why—I'm genetically engineered to have a perfect blood flow and I'm almost never cold. Another little "advantage" Dr. Mullen gave me. Also superior healing abilities, or I'd never have gotten well as fast as I did after the surgery and the treatments.

She nods and doesn't argue with me the way she used to before the truth came out. In fact, our relationship is nothing at all like it was before I learned the truth. We used to be close. Now she behaves as if nothing has happened, as if somehow I'll just forget how they lied to me about my entire life. I take a deep breath. Just looking at her can set me off and get me angry all over again.

It's a twenty-minute drive to the mall in Palm Desert. I convince Mother to put the top down on the convertible and I revel in the hot air blowing in my face. The boulevards are a mass of flowers, the sky is blue and I'm happy to be alive.

Mother screeches up to the front of the mall. "Two hours," she says.

"Three," I demand. "We can't do everything in two."

"Fine," she agrees. She can't seem to argue with me anymore. Sometimes it feels like I'm the mother. And I don't like it. I want to be an innocent kid again. But I guess those days are over.

Emma is already waiting at the main entrance. She's a sight for sore eyes. I'm used to seeing her every day at school and FaceTiming or texting just isn't the same. She's been over to the house a couple of times since the surgery, but it's not like hanging out on our own away from our parents. We give each other a big hug. She hugs Ariel too, who doesn't really understand she's supposed to hug back.

"What do we do first?" I ask.

"I guess we give Ariel the grand tour," Emma says. "Come on."

We begin with a walk up and down the mall, showing Ariel the stores, what people buy in them, all that. Ariel is full of questions.

"But why do people need to purchase beauty products? Can you create beauty like that?"

Emma laughs. "No! And mostly we know that, but we fall for it anyway."

"Fall for it?" Ariel says.

"Yeah," grins Emma. "We know it's not true but we let ourselves be convinced. Just in case, I guess."

"Not logical," Ariel states.

At this point we get to a See's Candies store.

"Shall we?" I say.

"Of course," says Emma.

118

We go in. There's a long line and when it's our turn, I'm ready with my choice, a chocolate truffle. Emma picks a chocolate cream, but Ariel has no idea what to choose. She questions the salesperson about each chocolate, pointing and asking, "What exactly is that one?" Behind us the crowd is getting restless.

"Give her a soft caramel," I finally say to the person serving us, a young girl who is starting to look at Ariel as if she's an alien. I mean, who doesn't know what chocolate is all about?

We take our treats out into the mall and eat them right away. When Ariel bites into hers, she says through a full mouth, "I understand this. This makes more sense than beauty products. I would pay dollars for this."

I can't help but think about how really cruel Dr. Mullen was to her, keeping her trapped like that—and then never giving her chocolate? Maybe he worried that if she knew there were such wonderful things out there she might want to escape.

"Come on," I say. "Time to shop."

We take her into the department store. "There is so much," she declares.

"Yeah, isn't it great?" Emma says. "Oh! Look at that, Miranda." And she rushes over to a rack of summer tops, obviously just in. A rack of bathing suits catches my eye. I'd like a one-piece this season, not a bikini, so my scar won't show.

I am still looking through the bathing suits when Emma comes up to me and says, "Where's Ariel?"

I whirl around. "I don't know. Just figured she was following us. Ariel," I call, peering around the racks of clothes. "Ariel?"

Emma starts calling too, but Ariel is nowhere around.

119

"What do we do?" I say, panicked. "She has no idea about anything! I should have warned her to stay close. She's no smarter than a two year old about the outside world. She could go off with a stranger, or—or anything!"

"A stranger won't know she's not streetwise," Emma reminded me. "She's somewhere. Don't worry."

"We should split up," I suggest.

"Okay. We'll meet in ten minutes," Emma says. "You go look for her. I'll alert security and get her paged. We'll meet at the security desk in the center of the mall."

I hurry off, not knowing where to look first. In the store, out in the mall ... I rush up and down the aisles, asking salespeople if they've seen a girl who looks like me, blonde, blue eyes, but younger, tall for her age, which is ten ... No luck. I hear the announcement. *Will Ariel Martin please report to the security kiosk in the center of the mall.* And then a description of exactly where the security kiosk is. That was smart of Emma.

I have no luck finding her so I hurry out into the mall, over toward security. I see Emma. And then I see Ariel heading over there, too.

"Ariel!" I exclaim, running over to her, not knowing whether to hug her or rebuke her. "Where did you go?"

"Go?"

"You left me and Emma!"

"Is that incorrect?"

"Of course! You could have gotten lost."

"How? We are in an enclosed space."

"But a big space with lots of people. What if you'd been kidnapped?"

"Kidnapped? Abducted by an evil person?"

120

"Yes!"

"Why would anyone want to do such a thing?"

I look at Emma for help.

"There are lots of people in this world, Ariel," she says, "who can be trusted. Almost everyone. But there are a few who can't and we have to be careful. Just in case."

"That is sad," Ariel says.

"Yes," I agree. "But sadder if something bad happens to you. So from now on, you stay with me when we're out. Always. Understand?"

"Yes. I understand."

"Good."

Emma looks at her watch. "We'd better help Ariel," she says, "or we'll leave here with nothing for her to wear on her first day at school."

"I enjoyed hearing my name called throughout this structure," Ariel says as we walk.

I shake my head. What am I going to do with her?

Chapter 17

I wake up every morning now, vowing to have more patience with Ariel. But within minutes I'm so mad at her I could kill her. It's been like this for the whole time we've been back at school.

This morning, for example. I told Lorna I would wear my new grey shirt with my grey pants and my black hooded sweater. Only my grey shirt was nowhere to be found. Well, it was finally found at the bottom of the dirty laundry basket. Why? Ariel wore it last night when she went out for pizza with her new friend Jen. And spilled tomato sauce on it. Tomato sauce! Honestly! I thought it would get better once we went to school and we weren't stuck at home together constantly.

Emma doesn't understand. She says she'd love a little sister. That's only because she has two older brothers who boss her around all the time and she wants someone she can boss around. But I never get to boss Ariel around. I'm either looking after her or letting her walk all over me.

I am thinking all this as I wait for her to get ready.

She flies into the kitchen and stuffs an entire pancake into her mouth in one go as I yell at her.

"You're impossible! We'll be late! Let's go!"

"So we'll be one minute late," she says, although I have no idea how she can talk with her mouth full like that. "So what?"

So what? I feel like I must have smoke coming out of my

122

ears. "So what? So ... we can't be late!"

She washes the pancake down with a giant glass of fresh-squeezed lemon juice—no sugar—then grins. "Ready!"

I shake my head and shudder. I can hardly watch her drink that every morning. Lorna was making her fresh lemonade one day when she grabbed it before the sugar was added and declared it delicious. Now it's her favorite drink.

"Mother, we're ready," I call.

Mother hurries into the kitchen. "Where is your knapsack?" she asks Ariel.

"Here it is," Lorna says. The same thing every morning. Ariel forgets it. Lorna has it ready for her.

"My grey shirt." I glare at her as we go out the door.

The heat hits me, just like stepping into an oven, even though it's only 7:30 in the morning. I stop for a moment and gasp. A spring heat wave. The sky is blue and there are no clouds. The flowers Mother has planted all around the house are waiting patiently for their eight o'clock watering, when the sprinkler will turn on automatically. The lemon tree is heavy with lemons right now, and the huge cacti in the center of the yard are unfazed by the heat, of course. I wish I could be like them. Tall, and stately, and strong. I used to be. Now Ariel has my stomach in a knot and my life turned upside down half the time.

"My grey shirt?" I repeat, as we get into the car, top up, air conditioning on.

"I'm really sorry," Ariel blabs at a mile a minute. "But it was my first time out with Jen and her family and I wanted to make a good impression and you weren't here to ask and I was sure you'd want me to look good, it matched just right with my purple pants. And the purple top I got to go with them was too

123

much, don't you think?"

I open my mouth to answer but she prattles on.

"And then I spilled on myself. I was so embarrassed, I'm really sorry about the shirt, but who knows if they'll ever take me out again!" She looks like she is going to cry.

"Of course they will," I find myself saying. "I mean, if Jen is a good friend she won't let a silly thing like that stop her."

"It's silly?" Ariel asks.

"Yes. Silly."

"Then you aren't mad about it?"

See? She's got me again! How can I be angry when I just told her it wasn't worth getting upset about? It's even more annoying that she's almost impossible to stay mad at. Even though I hate to admit it, because I am so ticked off right now, she's really adorable. She loves me to bits, which is kinda sweet, and she is so enthusiastic about absolutely everything that it's contagious.

Things I take for granted, like fresh air, and candy, and new clothes—they are all marvels to her. Still, I have to start to draw the line with her occasionally, and this is a perfect opportunity. Can't have her stealing my clothes!

"It's different," I explain to her. "Jen won't think it's important because everyone has accidents. On the other hand, you took my shirt without asking. That's not an accident. So I can be mad. Understand?"

"Yes," she says formally, much more like her old self, "I understand."

I'm on a roll, so why stop now?

"You have to grasp," I continue, "that I am your older sister. You need to listen to me. You need to ask my permission before you do things."

124

"Miranda!" Mother interrupts me.

"Well, Mother, this is getting out of control," I complain. "She needs to know I'm the boss."

"You are not the boss, dear. Ariel, your mother and your father are the ones you need to listen to."

"Not Miranda?" she says.

I glare at Mother.

"Well ...," she hesitates. "Not in the same way. Naturally Miranda is full of good advice, and I would consider it in your best interest to listen to her."

"Thank you!" I say.

"But," Mother says, "in a family it is your parents who are the final authority."

I am sure that Mother means that as much for me as for Ariel. She, too, has noticed that I have been deciding what's best and maybe now she thinks it's time for her to be the mother again.

"I think I understand," Ariel says seriously. She pauses and I can almost hear her thinking. "Does anyone, then, ever have to listen to me?"

I laugh. "No! Because you're the youngest."

"She's teasing you, Ariel," Mother says. "Of course we will listen to you. That's part of being a good parent. We all must respect each other."

I decide to let that pass. Respect apparently does not include telling your child the truth if the truth can put you in a bad light. I bite my tongue and say nothing.

"I will try harder to be a good sister," Ariel says. And she looks like she means it.

"Thank you!" I reply, and I suspect I have a smug look on my face because Mother glares at me.

125

"What?" I say innocently.

She shakes her head.

❧

"It's amazing," I say to Emma when we are changing classes. "Ariel and I have the same DNA. And yet she's so different."

"But she was brought up so differently," Emma points out. "And now that she's not in a lab anymore and she's experiencing freedom for the first time ever—well, freedom seems to be the thing she cares about most."

"Freedom to annoy me, you mean," I grumble as we head down the corridor to math class.

"Maybe that's the only way she can make herself different from you," Emma says.

"Differentiate herself," I muse. "That makes sense, I suppose."

"It should cheer you up," Emma points out. "It means you are you, and she is she ... or is that she is her?"

We sit at our desks and instead of concentrating on class my mind begins to wander. What Emma said is true, I guess. Or is it? I don't know—ever since I discovered I'm a clone of Jessica I've wondered who I am. Am I just a preprogrammed package, a copy? Do I have my own personality? Well, Ariel is a clone of me. And she seems to be very different. So maybe Emma is correct and it isn't all predetermined. Or maybe Ariel is just like me, but she is *trying* to be different.

I suppose, since we've only been at school a few weeks since our recovery, she has had lots of adjusting to do. It's amazing that in this short time she has almost completely stopped speaking in that formal, stilted way. I think she's gone a bit overboard, trying to sound like her classmates, but she's very bright and picks up speech patterns quickly. She also instinctively understands how important it is to fit in. And that's what she's been working on. After all, she was brought up in a lab with no other children. She was more like a lab rat than a child—so learning to socialize is her big job now.

It's great that the middle school she attends is in the same complex as our high school. Everyone shares the same library and the same lunchroom, so I see her every day at lunch. She's learning quickly.

I shudder as I replay the scene in the principal's office when Mother and Father told the principal that Ariel was their niece.

"She was raised by my sister," Mother said, looking like butter wouldn't melt in her mouth, "in an isolated research facility with no other children. When my sister died unexpectedly, well, of course we took her in. We would appreciate you viewing her as Miranda's sister, not her cousin, as we are adopting her."

Mrs. Dean was terribly sympathetic. But it was all lies, more lies. And what I hated the most was seeing how good Mother was at lying. I don't see how I can ever trust her again.

As we were leaving the office Mrs. Dean said, "But she could be her sister. She's the image of Miranda!"

Image is right, I was tempted to say. *She looks like that because she's my clone created by a mad scientist at my parents' request so that should I need any replacement organs, she could give them to me and then die!* Wonder how that would have gone over? Love to have seen the expression on Mrs. Dean's face then!

I try to put all these thoughts out of my mind and get down to work, but I can't stop thinking about Ariel. I shouldn't have

127

yelled at her. After all, she gave me half her liver and saved my life. What's one ruined shirt in comparison? I'll apologize as soon as I see her.

"Miranda!"

I look up. Mr. Thomas is glaring at me. "Please pay attention! Exams coming up."

"Yes sir," I say, wondering why I insisted on coming back to school.

Emma winks at me. She'd tried to convince me not to come back. "Are you crazy?" she'd said. "A chance to skip the rest of the year, and they'll give you your grades until now and no exams and you say no? It's that need-to-be-perfect thing, isn't it?"

But I want to get my grades the way everyone else does. I don't want to be any more different than I have to be.

After class we head for the lunchroom. As we sit down I see Ariel on the other side of the room. She is just standing there, staring around in a kind of daze. I wave and try to catch her attention, but she doesn't seem to see me. Then she walks off.

"Hang on," I say to Emma. "I'd better go talk to her. Maybe she's ignoring me because she's still mad about this morning."

I hurry over to her as she is about to sit at a table by herself.

"Hey," I say.

She looks up.

"Oh!" she exclaims. "Miranda!" She says it like she's surprised to see me.

"Weren't we going to meet for lunch?"

"Were we?" she says.

"Well, if you want to be that way, fine," I say, knowing perfectly well she hasn't forgotten. Every day she's made a fuss about eating with me and Emma and my other friends. I forget

128

all about apologizing.

"If you don't want to eat with us, don't," I say and I stalk off back to Emma.

Before she came into my life I didn't even know I had a temper. Now she looks at me the wrong way and I get mad. I glance back over my shoulder to see her sitting there all cool, as if she hasn't just blown me off.

She's obviously mad at me about how hard I was on her earlier. I suppose I'll have to make it up to her. I sigh with frustration as I sit down beside Emma.

"Remind me again how lucky I am to have a sister."

Chapter 18

Today after school Ariel is coming to ballet lessons for the first time, and I'm having my first class since I got sick. I'm starting the spring/summer session late, but at least I'm going to get back into it and I think it should help me regain some strength. Mother is picking Ariel and me up. I say goodbye to Emma and see Ariel already waiting by the school drive. It's the first time since we started school that she's been there before me.

"Hello, Miranda," she says. She smiles. Maybe she isn't mad after all. That would be good. Maybe that little talk had the desired effect and I don't have to apologize.

"Well, hello, Ariel," I say in response.

Silence.

"How was your day?" I ask.

For the last three weeks I haven't had a chance to ask. She's just blurted everything out at a mile a minute.

"My day was fine," Ariel says. "I attended French class but found the work difficult."

"Well, you'll catch up," I assure her. "I mean, you're starting at the end of the year after all, and I don't know why you wanted to start with something as hard as a new language, anyway. You can always drop it; no one will care. You aren't taking exams anyway."

I expect her to contradict me and to insist that she can do

anything—Mother and Father didn't even want her to go to school until next year but she said if I was going, she was going!

Instead of her usual spunky answer she nods her head and says, "Perhaps I should quit, as you suggest."

I look at her, stunned, but have no chance to reply because Mother's convertible squeals up and Mother motions for us to jump in.

"Ready for your first ballet class, Ariel?" she asks.

"Yes," Ariel replies. "I am interested in everything. Everything is new and interesting."

But she doesn't look excited, and yet yesterday it was all she could talk about. She must be really mad at me, really upset. Still, I have no intention of giving Mother the satisfaction of seeing me apologize so I decide to talk to Ariel later.

When we arrive at the dance studio I let Mother take charge of Ariel and I go to my first class. Mr. Lovejoy is teaching this session. He is a retired dancer from the Arizona Dance Theatre, and is the real thing. I've heard he won't take any nonsense. And did I hear right! He puts us through our paces like he's a drill sergeant.

"Taller, taller." He comes up and sticks his finger in my back. "Get that head up! Bum tucked in. Arms extended! Extended!" And this is just in the pliés. By the time the class is over I know I won't even have to wait until the morning to be sore. I'm already sore! And drenched in sweat. But it's great to challenge my muscles and I note that I don't feel weak, a good sign. My scar doesn't hurt either, also a good sign.

"Not entirely awful, boys and girls," he says, clapping his hands. "But from now on we work! Yes?"

I practically stagger out. I can't wait to get home and shower. But I am dying to hear how Ariel liked her class.

As soon as we are in the car I ask her, "So? How was it?"

"Interesting," she answers.

"Just interesting?" I say, disappointed. "But you were so excited. Is anything wrong?"

"Why?" she seems worried. "Is something wrong with what I am doing?"

"No, no," I assure her. "You're just so ... I don't know. This morning you were so keen. You sound different now. Did something happen?"

"I thought you wanted her to be different," Mother interjects. "Make up your mind, Miranda. You gave her a big lecture this morning. She's obviously just trying to please you."

"Is that it?" I ask Ariel.

"Yes, I am trying to please you. Of course. That is my reason."

I sigh. So she is mad. Or overreacting in some mammoth way.

"I'm sorry, Ariel," I say. "I didn't mean to upset you this morning. Just forget what I said. And remember that I am not your reason for living. You have to find your own reason."

"Well, Miranda," Mother says, "you say that, but you don't really mean it. As soon as she acts like herself you say that she's annoying."

"I don't wish to be annoying," Ariel says. "I wish to please."

I am really confused now. Of course this is just what I wanted, but somehow it seems too weird. Why the sudden turnabout? She didn't sound like she had any intention of listening this morning. Could there be some bizarre programming engineered into her that she *has* to listen to me?

She is in the back seat and I am up front with Mother. In a low voice I ask Mother, "Did Dr. Mullen program her in any way I should know about? Why is she reacting this way?"

"I'm sure he didn't, Miranda," Mother says. "Probably she is just trying to find her place with you. Perhaps she feels she went too far and now she's decided to be more compliant."

"You mean she's trying out different personalities?"

"Yes. Something like that. She has no idea yet who she really is."

I feel terrible. I was obviously way too hard on her this morning. On the bright side, if Mother is right, this version of Ariel could be far more accommodating than the last one. Maybe I should encourage her, not discourage her. It could work out that she'll be an excellent little sister, if she can keep this up.

As soon as we get home I take a long hot shower and as the water runs over me I start to feel bad. I mean, how selfish can you get? I can't keep Ariel down just to make my life easier.

Father is already at the table when I drag my aching body to the dining room.

"Hello, Miranda," he smiles. "I hear you have a new ballet teacher."

"More like a sadist," I groan, as I sit down.

"Well," Father says, "you are getting to a very high level now. Many of the others in your class are thinking of a career in dance. Are you sure you want to keep it up?"

"Of course I'm sure!" I say, forgetting about Ariel for the moment as she sits eating quietly. "And who knows, I may want some sort of a career like that myself."

I take a deep breath. It's now or never.

133

"In fact, I want to talk to you about acting classes. Emma and I have found a very good new school and we want to take classes together."

Mother and Father both say "No!" at the same time.

"We've been over this, Miranda," Father says. "This is California. Every child takes acting lessons. Every kid wants to be a movie star. And every kid can be. That's how much talent it takes." He pauses. "You're special. You know you are. You have an exceptional mind. You can be a research scientist, a doctor, someone who could change people's lives."

"As if science is the only thing worthy of me," I scoff.

Ariel is sitting quietly, looking interested.

I turn to her. "And don't think this doesn't involve you! They'll have the same rules for you too, you know."

"But they are the parents," Ariel says. "They decide."

"Aah!" I scream, throwing down my napkin. "Forget everything I said to you this morning. They can't decide everything!"

"They cannot?"

"No!"

"Why?"

"Because ... because ... some things we have to decide for ourselves." I glare at my parents. "I never questioned you before. But things are different now. I have to make my own decisions. And I don't want to be a movie actor, anyway."

"That's a relief," Mother says.

"I want to be on Broadway!" I announce. "And I know I'm a good dancer. But the chorus line is all I'll be able to do if I can't act too. And sing."

"But you can sing," Father says.

"Of course I can. I can do everything! Why give me all these

134

talents if you never wanted me to use them?"

This shuts them up. Because they know it's true. They had Dr. Mullen alter my genes to give me extra abilities—athletic talent and intelligence. The thing is, I don't know about the acting. It's one of the things it seems Dr. Mullen didn't know how to program for. I don't even know if I can do it. That's why I want to try.

"Maybe it'll be something I can call my own—not something I was programmed for." Just then Lorna comes in with the phone.

"Ariel, it's your friend Jen."

"My friend?" Ariel says. "Do I have a friend?"

"Ariel," I scold her, "you've made a friend. Be nice to her."

She looks at me for a moment and then says, "If you say so." Lorna hands her the phone, which she takes. She listens, then holds the phone away from her ear and frowns at me. "She wants to go to a movie together Saturday." She looks confused.

"Say you'll go," I tell her.

"Yes," says Ariel, then hands the phone back to Lorna. A bit abrupt, I think, normally she'd babble on and Mother would have to tell her it's rude to talk at the table. But I need to press my point with my parents.

"So, can I take the acting class?" I ask.

"No," Father reiterates. "I understand what you are saying, Miranda, but you'll thank us one day for saving you from this choice. You are meant for better things."

This is new territory for me. Until I discovered what they'd been up to, I thought I had absolutely perfect parents. I would never have dreamed of going against them, because I wouldn't want to worry them and I assumed that they knew best. Now

135

Father keeps wanting to "talk" but I'm not interested—still, it's at least better than Mother's attempts to pretend nothing has happened. I try to think what to do next. I need lessons from Emma on fighting with parents.

"You're being a snob," I say to Father, unable to come up with anything else. "Why is theatre less worthy than science? Don't the arts make our society what it is? Isn't that important?"

"Of course," Father says, "but let someone else do it. You have other talents."

"You don't know what my talents are and neither do I," I fume. "But," I say under my breath, "I'll find out."

I can see he isn't going to budge so I eat my dinner in silence, then leave the table. I have to phone Emma. This isn't finished. Not by a long shot!

136

Chapter 19

I call Emma as soon as I get to my room. "Emma," I say, keeping my voice low, "they wouldn't go for it."

"I told you your plan would never work," Emma says.

"I had to try the honesty thing first," I insist.

"Okay. You tried. And it didn't work. Of course. So now it's Plan B," Emma continues. "You stop trying to convince them and just do what you want."

"What will our cover story be?" I ask.

"Well," she answers, "Mom and Dad know I'm going. They've even agreed to pay for the classes."

"Lucky I'm so frugal," I say. "After all those years of saving my allowance, I've got enough money to pay for years of acting classes."

"Right, then," Emma says. "The new session starts this week. So let's do it." She pauses to think. "I'm just not sure how you'll get away with it. Your parents know what you're doing every moment of the day."

"Why can't I just say I'm coming over to your house after school?" I ask.

Emma laughs. I can almost see her shaking her head. "Boy, are you green at this. They are bound to phone here and the first thing my mom will say is that we're at drama class. No, you have to do better than that. Let me think."

Ariel walks in.

137

"Gotta go. Talk later." I hang up.

Ariel looks around the room as if she's never been here before. She stares at me.

"What?" I ask.

"What?" she repeats.

"What are you standing there for?"

"What should I be doing?" she says.

"I don't know!" I exclaim. And I wonder to myself just which is more annoying—her not listening to me at all, or this new good-little-sister act. Then I have an idea. "Actually, there is something you can do for me."

"Yes?" she says eagerly.

"You can be my cover tomorrow."

"Cover?"

"Yeah, well, cover story."

"Cover story?"

"Yes. Can you keep a secret?"

"I don't know," she answers.

"Well, can you or can't you?" I say, exasperated.

"You tell me," she says.

"You can," I tell her.

She smiles. "Then yes, if you say I can, I can. A secret," she repeats. "Something that no one can know."

"Exactly!" I say. "Here's the deal. This drama school is located in the mall. I'll tell the parents I'm taking you shopping. You wander around the stores for an hour—if you promise not to talk to strangers—or wait for me in the lobby. We go home. And that's my cover story."

"Cover story?" she asks. "What is the secret?"

"The secret is I'm not going to be shopping, I'll be at an acting class. And you are my cover story."

138

"Will I be useful?" she asks.

Back to that. Born to serve me. "Yes," I sigh, "you'll be useful. Are you sure you are all right?"

"What do you think?" she asks.

I'm not sure if she is really asking me or being sarcastic.

"I'm not sure."

She stares patiently at me.

Well, I can't worry about her weirdness now. I have to get this plan sorted out. "So, will you do it?"

"I will be useful and it will be a good plan." She nods solemnly.

"Excellent," I say.

The next morning as we drive to school my stomach is full of butterflies.

"Mother," I say, "I've promised Ariel to take her shopping after school."

"Oh," Mother says, "but don't you want me to take you both?"

"No," I explain. "We, we need to bond. Can you drop us? And pick us up after?"

"All right," Mother agrees.

Then I have an inspiration. "Maybe we can make it a weekly thing. You know, I'll take her for cake and ice cream at Cold Stone Creamery. What do you think?"

Mother beams at me. "I think it's lovely," she says.

I sit there in stunned silence. I can't believe how easy that was! And she has no idea. No idea at all.

Mother pats my hand. "What a good girl you are, Miranda."

All right, now I feel guilty. But it wouldn't have come to this if they hadn't been so unreasonable. I mean it's not as if I'm asking if I can get a tattoo or stay out all night or anything. I've never touched a drug or had a drink! I *am* a good girl. I just want to take a silly acting class. If I'm ever a parent I vow never to be so stupid.

When we get to school Ariel stops for a minute as if to get her bearings and then heads off.

"So I'll see you after school," I remind her.

"Do we not meet at lunch?"

"Sure. I'll meet you for lunch," I agree. "It's just I thought you'd want to start spending your lunch period with Jen."

"Jen. My friend?" she says.

"Yes. Your friend." I shake my head. "Now get going."

Emma is waiting for me just inside the front door. "Have you come up with a plan?" she asks.

"Yes! And it's working like a charm." I tell her about it.

She looks at me admiringly. "Who knew? You've turned out to be a pro!"

"I don't like it," I say. "But they've left me no choice."

"You feel guilty," Emma says. "Don't. They shouldn't have been so stubborn. I'll tell my mom that I'm going on my own," she adds, "so if our parents ever talk they won't hear about it from my folks." We sit down at our desks. "Are you excited?"

"Am I ever!"

"I'm nervous," Emma says.

I love any new situation. Emma says I know no fear. I can hardly wait for school to be over.

140

Chapter 20

Mother drives us and cheerfully drops us off. The plan seems to be going like clockwork until Ariel and I walk into the mall. Suddenly Ariel grabs my hand, holding on so tight it hurts.

"What's the matter?" I say.

"Afraid," she replies.

I look at her, puzzled. How can she be frightened when she's a clone of me? Almost nothing scares me, certainly not walking into a mall. Anyway, she and I were just here with Emma and she loved it.

"What's scaring you?" I ask, concerned.

"Too many people. Too many things."

"It's a mall, isn't it?" I say, frustrated.

I hope there isn't something unexpected happening to her. Who knows with a clone—maybe the wiring in her brain has gone haywire. I don't like the thought of that. Could it happen to me, too? After all, if I'm the very first human clone and she's the second, well, no one really knows anything about us yet, do they? Maybe her brain has misfired or gotten scrambled or some strange thing. I've been reading all I can find on cloning, and one of the reasons so many scientists are against human cloning is because of all the things that can go wrong, and are going wrong, with cloned animals. When one cloned mouse turned the equivalent of thirty in human years it suddenly became horribly obese. Other clones were born with only one

141

kidney, or blind. I mean, who knows what's in store for me and for Ariel in the future?

Ariel keeps a grip on my hand, an iron grip, and shrinks up against me like a monster is after her. She obviously isn't going to be wandering around on her own like I'd planned. She drags along after me, upstairs, to the space where the new drama school is. I register and pay my money. Then Emma turns up.

"I had trouble ditching my mom," she says. "She wanted to come up and register me but I was afraid she'd see you. Hi, Ariel. Aren't you going shopping?"

"No!" Ariel exclaims.

"She won't let go of me," I complain. I take Emma aside, telling Ariel to wait where she is. "Ariel is acting very strangely," I whisper.

"How?"

"I'm not sure, just less like Ariel. More like she used to be."

"Well, what do you expect?" Emma asks. "She was brought up, from the time she was a little baby, to sacrifice her life for you. You saved her from that. But ten years of having 'You were created to serve Miranda' drummed into her—think about it. When you got angry with her she probably really took it to heart."

"Great," I reply. "So now I won't be able to say a word to her, no matter how annoying she gets."

"Doesn't sound to me like she'll be getting annoying." Emma points out. "She's probably decided that she must be a good little sister at all costs. Even if it means not exploring who she really is."

"But you know I don't want that!" I say. "And what do I do with her now?"

142

"Maybe the teacher will let her stay and watch," Emma suggests. She goes over to Ariel. "Would you like to come in with us? If you're quiet," she adds sternly.

"I will be very quiet," Ariel agrees.

Emma registers. Then the girl who registered us points to a door. We walk in slowly, looking around. It is a large bare room with a few chairs at one end.

"Hello! I'm Tara, your teacher."

Tara has straight brown hair streaked with grey. She's wearing a tie-dyed T-shirt and a long paisley skirt. She's quite happy to let Ariel stay and watch.

There are already four other kids standing around waiting—one of them a drop-dead gorgeous boy with curly black hair and blue eyes.

After we introduce ourselves, Tara starts us off with what she says is a standard acting exercise: mirrors. You get into pairs and you take turns copying each other's moves. Who do I get paired with? Dale, the gorgeous guy! I feel like I'm in a dream the whole time. I get to stare at him and it doesn't look like I'm staring because I'm supposed to.

After that we do a relaxation exercise on the floor. Then we do an exercise where Tara gives each of us a character—mine is a bored computer geek—and then she tells us we are at an office party. It is really funny! The time flies by. When we're finished I go over to Ariel, who has been sitting on a chair not moving a muscle.

"Come on," I say to her. "We have to hurry. We're meeting Mother in the shoe department at Macy's. Now don't forget," I say. "We've been shopping. The drama class is a secret."

"I will not forget," she says. And then I notice a tear trickling down her face.

Emma catches up with us as we're hurrying out the door.

"What's the matter, Ariel?" she says.

"I do not know," Ariel replies.

My heart sinks. Something is wrong with her.

"Why am I crying?" she asks.

"I don't know," I answer, getting more worried. Shouldn't she know? "Are you sad?"

She answers. "I am ... I want to be where I am used to being."

"You want to go home?" I ask.

"Yes!"

"It's okay," I assure her. "Come on. We'll go find Mother."

Emma waves goodbye. "Call me," she says.

"I will."

I take Ariel to our meeting place with Mother, who is there waiting. "So girls, did you have fun?"

"Ariel is a little upset," I say to her. "I think we'd better go home."

"What is it, Ariel?" Mother asks.

"I want to be back where I am used to everything. But I need to comply. I must serve Miranda."

Mother looks bewildered. "Ariel," she says, "you can go back to being the way you were before Miranda scolded you yesterday."

"Scolded?" Ariel says.

"Yes, don't you remember?"

"Miranda never does anything wrong," Ariel says.

Now I have to say something. "Ariel," I say, "I'm really sorry for yelling at you yesterday. I was just annoyed about my shirt. But it was stupid. You can go back to being yourself."

"Myself?"

144

"Like you were."

"Please tell me exactly how to be, and I will be that."

"But I can't tell you that!" I exclaim. "You have to find out who you are. But," I say in my own defense, "it's normal for sisters to fight, so I should be able to yell without you overreacting like this."

"You can yell," she says. "You can do anything. I am made for you."

I turn to Mother in frustration. "Mother, there's something wrong with her! She doesn't even understand what I'm saying!"

"I think you might be right, Miranda," Mother agrees. "Something is off. We'll call Dr. Mullen to be on the safe side. He knows her best."

"Dr. Mullen will be angry," Ariel says, suddenly very alarmed.

"Don't be silly," Mother assures her. "Of course he won't. Come along, dear."

This child is, in fact, a stranger to Mother. She's been home with us for less than two months and only because I forced Mother and Father to take her in. But I have no illusions. It's me they love. They are trying to be good to Ariel, but if she turns out to be defective or sick, they might not want to keep her. I have to wonder if what I said triggered this reaction in her. I feel awful. Really, I love Ariel a lot. I was annoyed with her, but I didn't want her to revert to her former behavior!

We get home and Mother calls Dr. Mullen. Ariel sits in her room as if waiting for her execution.

Dr. Mullen, her creator, still works at the G.R.F. Clinic that Father used to own but turned over to a charitable foundation under the strict supervision of Emma's dad. It continues to do genetic research but no more human cloning. Instead, its research now centers on curing diseases.

He's checked up on Ariel a few times, and me too, since the operation. I'm still so angry I can barely stand to have him near me, but what choice do I have? Let's face it—who understands your makeup better than the guy who made you?

He's over at the house within half an hour. He asks me to leave the room so he can examine Ariel. He comes out looking cheerful. He calls Mother and me over.

"Nothing wrong with her!" he assures us.

"How do you know?" I demand. I don't trust him.

"Because I've examined her and talked to her. She is simply trying to please. Your mother tells me you gave her a little lecture the other day, Miranda."

"Yes," I agree. "A *little* one. But she's never paid any attention to my complaints before!"

"She's a thoughtful child, though, isn't she," he says. "She decided that she was not being a good sister. She's trying hard to be one now."

"Well, tell her to stop," I demand. "She's weird now."

"I can't make her do anything," he says. "I'm sure you wouldn't want me to. Let her find her own way. Be patient. She'll be who she's going to be. I think you'll find this is just part of her learning to be in the real world," he says to Mother.

I go into our room and find her sitting on her bed. When she sees me she gets a big bright smile that looks as phony as anything and says, "Hello! Let's have some fun!"

"What did Dr. Mullen say to you?" I ask, suspicious of this put-on cheerfulness.

"He said that I must tell you that he is my doctor and all our talks are private."

So he's told her not to tell me anything. Why?

"But you can talk to me," I coax. "I'm Miranda."

She looks confused, so I relent. I'd better not add to her confusion. It might make her worse. "Never mind," I say. "You just do what Dr. Mullen tells you."

She smiles. "I will be happy! Let's go have fun!"

"What do you want to do?"

"Have fun!"

I try to think. She's loved swimming ever since she came to live with us. Father, to his credit, spent a lot of time teaching her.

"A swim before dinner?" I suggest.

"Yes! A swim."

We change into our suits, except I have to help her find hers as she seems to have forgotten where it might be, and we go out to the pool. I jump right in. It's cool and feels glorious. Ariel stands by the edge for a minute staring at me as I tread water.

"C'mon, jump!" I yell.

She jumps in after me, and proceeds to sink right to the bottom! When she surfaces she flails about and swallows water and is obviously in distress. I have to put my arms around her and pull her out.

"Are you crazy?" I pant, once we are sitting by the side of the pool. "You have to swim!"

She looks terrified. "Do I know how?"

I wipe the water out of my eyes and stare at her. I don't care what Dr. Mullen says. Something *is* wrong.

Chapter 21

"Miranda, dinner," Mother calls.

I drag Ariel into the house and help her get changed. She's so much like she was when I first met her in that lab, I can't get over it.

We go to the dinner table. Mother and Father are sipping their wine. Lorna has put out our salad already.

"How are you, Ariel?" Father enquires.

"I am fine, thank you," she replies.

I sit down and stab a piece of lettuce. "Well, she's not," I announce. "She's acting as if the last few weeks never happened. She almost drowned right now. She forgot how to swim!"

"I'm sure she didn't forget, Miranda," Mother says. "She simply didn't want to swim."

"That's why she sank to the bottom of the pool?" I ask.

Father smiles at Ariel. "Were you teasing?"

"Teasing?" She brightens. "I am having fun!" she says.

"There," says Father. "She was just pulling your leg, Miranda. You need to relax. Don't see a disaster around every corner."

"You can hardly blame me," I say.

"That's true," he says, trying not to look pained at my words. "But we concealed things for your own good. And now you know. There are no more hidden conspiracies. You need

148

to stop reading so much into everything."

I suppose he's right. I'm suspicious of everything these days.

"Let's have fun!" Ariel says brightly.

"Yes, that's the spirit," Father agrees. "Now eat your dinner."

After dinner I do my homework and then decide to watch something. Ariel has been quietly reading on her bed.

"Want to watch *Pitch Perfect*?" I say. I always watch it when I'm feeling blue or confused—actually, I'll watch it any time.

She nods, and looks pleased. We go into the family room. As soon as the movie starts she begins to mutter quietly under her breath. I realize that she is saying every line. She knows the entire movie by heart.

"I didn't know you liked this movie," I say.

"Oh, yes," she says. "We watch it every day. It's my favorite."

"Who's 'we'?" I ask.

She looks worried suddenly. "Who's we? Who's we?"

"Yes," I say. "Who watches it with you?" But she won't answer. She continues to mouth the words and is so happy that I feel it would be cruel to keep pestering her. I leave her watching and go to my room to phone Emma.

"Hi!" I say.

"Hi! Is it cool? They never suspected?"

"What?"

"The acting class!"

"Oh that! I'd almost forgotten. No, nothing."

"What about Ariel?"

"We've had Dr. Mullen here and everything. He swears

149

she's fine. Except right after he leaves she jumps in the pool and then seems to forget how to swim."

"That's a dangerous thing to forget."

"Mother and Father think she's just having me on, but I think something is seriously wrong. Father gave me this speech at dinner, which sounded good at the time, about how I can't keep being suspicious all the time."

"Hey, you have a right to be!" Emma declares.

"Exactly," I agree. "But I don't know what to do. Listen, can you ask your father if Dr. Mullen is behaving? Nothing strange or bad going on at the clinic? He's not working on mind control now or any bizarre thing we should know about?"

"Sure, I'll ask," Emma says. "But if there is anything going on that shouldn't be, Dr. Mullen wouldn't let my dad see it. Maybe we should go check it out."

"How? Just walk in?"

"No. Let me see if I can work on Dad. I'll think of something."

"Great. Thanks."

"Hey," Emma says, "what about Dale?

"Is he gorgeous, or what?" I sigh.

"Or what!" she agrees. "But listen to this! Michael Lebowitz called to ask me if I want to go to a movie on Saturday."

"No!"

"Yes!"

"Why didn't you tell me right away?"

"I was saving it. I couldn't believe it. 'Course, Mom doesn't want me to go. 'You're too young to be going out alone.' Blah, blah, blah."

"Too bad Dale and I can't come with you," I giggle.

"Yeah, well, Michael's older brother is going to drive us and take us home. I think Mom may come around. I'm still working on her."

Just then Ariel comes in. "Go away," I say, waving her out of the room. She scurries out.

Emma and I are still chattering away when Mother comes into the room dragging Ariel.

"I found her walking down the driveway. What did you say to her?"

"Emma, hang on," I say, then turn to my mother. "I told her to go away. I'm talking to Emma."

"She obviously took you literally," Mother says. "Careful what you say."

I shake my head. "Did you hear that?" I say to Emma.

"Yeah."

"See what I mean?"

"Something's not right, I agree with you," Emma says. "I'll see what I can get out of my dad."

"Okay. Talk later."

Mother is turning to leave when suddenly Ariel clutches her head. She lets out a small squeal.

"What is it?" Mother asks.

I run over to Ariel and kneel down by her.

"My eyes," she says. "My eyes are behaving strangely. I do not see clearly."

I must turn white as a sheet because I feel like all the blood has drained from my head and dropped to my feet. I am so lightheaded I can't stand. I sink to the floor.

"Miranda," Mother says alarmed. "Are you all right? Come. Lie down."

She drags me over to my bed and puts some pillows under my knees. I'm sure I was about to faint. I turn my head and

151

see her walk Ariel over to her bed. She speaks in that really calm voice she gets when she's trying not to panic.

"What is the matter with your eyes?"

That's how it started with me, of course.

But Dr. Mullen gave Ariel every single test in the book and told me she was just about as perfect as you could get. She didn't have the disease, which meant that mine must have been a spontaneous mutation. Although, I *had* secretly wondered if Dr. Mullen was telling the whole truth.

On the other hand, maybe Ariel *was* just more perfect than me. Maybe he'd just done a better job on her. Made a few little changes. Improvements.

But now if she has it too ... Mother is laughing. She is laughing hysterically.

"What's so funny?" I say, trying to sit up.

Mother holds out a small piece of lint on her fingertip.

"Ariel had something in her eye," she says, still laughing.

"Really?"

"Really."

"Can you see now, Ariel?" I ask.

"Yes. I can see very well."

I flop back on the bed. That would have been too much.

"Shall we have fun?" she says.

I shake my head. "Bedtime," I say. But I am still not convinced there isn't something very wrong with her.

Chapter 22

Ariel is sound asleep.

I can't sleep. There is too much is racing around in my head. It's so hard to accept how much things have changed in such a short time. Like, a few weeks ago, I would have thought myself incapable of lying to my parents. I am still surprised that I did it yesterday and that it felt so easy. But I suppose I have a lot of resentment built up. Fine, I admit it, I'm mad. Really mad.

I believed they were so noble, so honest, so good. And yet they were willing to sacrifice Ariel, *murder* her, let's not sugarcoat it, to save my life. And I still don't think they feel anything for her, except thankful that she saved me. Well, maybe they are *beginning* to like her. But this personality change, for instance. If it was me, they'd be all over it. Dragging me to a psychiatrist, no doubt, within seconds. But because it's her they are just willing to take Dr. Mullen's word for everything.

And who's to say they aren't in on it with Dr. Mullen like they were last time? Maybe they've all agreed to lie to me. But why? And what exactly could they be lying about?

Something suddenly occurs to me. I sit bolt upright in bed and I can feel myself break out into a sweat. I know my imagination is probably running away with me but I can't shake this idea. I grab my phone and sneak out of my room.

Mother and Father are asleep and the house is dark.

I pad silently through the house until I reach the family room. I sink into the couch and call Emma.

"Emma?"

"Miranda?" She's groggy.

"Sorry to wake you, but this can't wait."

"What?"

"I know this is paranoid," I say. "But the swimming thing. People don't just suddenly forget how to swim, do they? I mean, you could change your attitude, maybe even your personality, although I find that hard to swallow, but you can't just forget how to swim. I'm sure she wasn't teasing me like my parents are saying. She kind of went along with that, but she didn't really seem to believe it."

"Yes. Go on."

"Well, then you add up all the other stuff. How she's talking different all of a sudden, how she doesn't seem to have any idea who she is anymore. I simply can't believe it's all because I told her off about a stupid shirt. Come on." I pause.

"You don't think ...," Emma whispers. Then she stops.

"Emma," I whisper back, "what if it isn't *her*?"

"Oh my gosh."

"I'm a clone. She's a clone. What if this Ariel isn't the real Ariel? What if she's been substituted?"

"But why?" Emma exclaims. "Isn't it more likely, if there's an evil plot, that they've done something to her mind? Or even worse," she adds. "Maybe her mind is malfunctioning and there's some sort of problem with the whole cloning process?"

Just what I, too, have been worried about. And a malfunction would be worse. For Ariel. To lose your personality all of a sudden. It's true that Dr. Mullen had lots

154

of failures before he succeeded with us. Maybe he didn't really succeed with her at all. Maybe she is malfunctioning. Does that mean it could happen to me? Maybe I'll be next. Maybe I'll suddenly forget to be who I am. After all, I've gotten sick once already—that certainly wasn't planned by Dr. Mullen!

"Whatever it is, I'd better find out," I say, "for her and for me. One thing I'm sure of, something isn't right. After Dr. Mullen was here it was almost like he'd given her instructions to lighten up and have fun like the old Ariel, but this one has no idea how to do it. She just keeps repeating 'Let's have fun. Let's have fun.'"

"I asked my dad about the lab," Emma says.

"And?"

"Nothing. He says it's under strict supervision and Dr. Mullen is behaving. But your dad owns lots of clinics, doesn't he, all across the country?"

"There's another clinic here in town," I say. "You know, not the research one, the one where I go. My pediatrician works there."

"Maybe Dr. Mullen has other secret ones," Emma suggests. "After all, you didn't know about his clinic and that was one of your dad's."

"But how do I find out? Dr. Mullen won't want me to know. And are my parents in on it or not? It's terrible not being able to trust your parents," I add.

"Yeah, it's not right," Emma agrees. "It should be the other way around."

I laugh.

"Miranda?" It is Ariel, standing by the door.

"Hey, she's here."

"Talk to her," says Emma. "See if you can't get some more

155

out of her."

"Right. See you tomorrow. Sorry about waking you up."

"I'm used to it," she says. "Maybe I should be a doctor. I'm already used to not sleeping through the night."

"Not my favorite profession right now," I say to her. "Stick to singing. Bye."

"Bye."

Ariel is still standing by the door.

"What is it?" I ask.

"You were gone when I awoke. I must be sure that you are safe."

I roll my eyes, even though she can't see me. "Come in."

"It is dark."

"You can see in the dark," I say. "I can."

"I cannot."

"Since when?"

"I do not know how to answer that."

"What happened yesterday?" I demand.

"What do you mean?"

"You're different. What happened?"

"I am just trying to be Ariel."

"Why are you *trying* to be Ariel? Aren't you Ariel?"

"Yes," she says, but she sounds uncertain. "I am Ariel."

"Do you feel any different than you did a few days ago?" I press her.

"No."

"Did Dr. Mullen do anything to you?"

"No."

"Did he tell you how to behave?"

She doesn't answer.

"He did, didn't he?" I think I'm on to something. "What?

156

What did he tell you?"

"Many things."

"What?"

"I cannot say. He says all our conversations are private. Secrets, like you and I have. I can keep a secret!"

This is too frustrating. Obviously Dr. Mullen is involved in something. But what? What?

She says, "Am I not a good Ariel? Are you unhappy?"

"You're different," I answer. "And yes, that makes me unhappy because I don't understand it."

"But I should not make you unhappy."

Aha! This might be her Achilles heel. She may have promised Dr. Mullen something, but the old Ariel was brought up to serve me. Indoctrinated. Even if this is a different Ariel, she may have been brought up the same way. Maybe if I play up what she owes me she'll have to tell me the truth.

"It makes me unhappy," I say, "not to know why you suddenly seem so different."

Long pause.

"I do not know what to do," she answers. "Dr. Mullen made me promise, but you are Miranda ..."

"Come on," I say. "Let's go to the kitchen and get a snack. Remember how you love to eat chocolate sundaes late at night? Remember how that makes you feel better?"

I get up and take her hand. We walk through to the kitchen where I turn on the light.

"Why are you different?" I say. "You must tell me. You must."

She is staring at me wide-eyed, obviously distressed. As I stare back at her it strikes me again how identical we are—but wait. I look closer.

157

"What's that?" I ask.

"What?"

"You have something on your forehead."

She puts her hand up and covers the spot. "It is ... it is ... a freckle," she says.

"You have a freckle?"

"I am not perfect. I am useless. I am not good for anything."

Suddenly she cries out and puts both hands to her head. "My head. It hurts. It hurts terribly."

"Go lie down in bed," I tell her. "I'll get Mother."

I rush to my parents' room and knock on the door. My stomach is all knotted up. Now what? Ariel really sounded like she was in pain.

"Mother? Father?"

"Come in."

Mother sits up in bed.

"What is it?"

"It's Ariel. She has a terrible headache. I'm worried."

"I'm sure it's nothing, Miranda," Mother says. "She's been checked. She's fine. Give her a Tylenol and both of you get some sleep."

"But ..."

"Miranda. It's the middle of the night. Not now. Go to bed. We'll check her in the morning. You are over-reacting to everything. Headaches are normal. Everybody gets them."

"But ..."

"Now!"

I turn and leave the room. Just another example of how little they care. If it had been me they would have been hysterical. Well, I care about her. I won't let her down.

Chapter 23

I lie in bed, trying to wake up. I gave Ariel a Tylenol and then sat up with her as she whimpered in pain for what felt like hours. She fell asleep, clutching my hand. I had to extricate my hand from hers without waking her and eventually was able to crawl into my own bed where I lay, staring into the darkness, until it began to get light. I must have finally dropped off.

How do I find out if Ariel isn't Ariel? That freckle. I've never seen it before although I know they can appear suddenly if you've been in the sun. And we're always in the sun. But if she isn't Ariel, where is the real one? It is just starting to sink in what this could mean. Has she been kidnapped? If so, by whom? She was almost murdered once. Is her life in danger? Is she somewhere alone and terrified?

I notice that Ariel, or the child who says she is Ariel, is up already, standing by the window. She is quite still, gazing out. I have an idea. A simple one.

"Ariel," I say.

No answer. No response. The real Ariel would have at least turned. This one doesn't even recognize her name.

"Ariel," I say again.

"Oh!" This time she turns. "Yes?"

"How are you?" I ask.

"My headache is better, but not gone."

159

"I'm going to try to get Mother to take you to the doctor," I say. "And if she won't, I will."

"You will?"

"Yes."

"Why?"

"Because I'm your big sister. I need to take care of you."

"No," she corrects me, "I am made for you."

"I thought we'd gotten past that," I chide her.

"Past that?"

"Over it. Over and done with. You aren't made for anyone but yourself."

"My self. What is that?"

Good question, I think. One I've thought a lot about ever since I found out I was a clone.

"Well, that's hard to say." Now I am almost positive I am not talking to Ariel. "It's who you are. Inside."

"I am made only for you."

I am totally positive Ariel had gotten over this stage. But if this one is telling the truth and is spouting all this garbage, she must be another of Dr. Mullen's Miranda clones. And yet he swore there were no more.

"Part of finding out who you are," I say, "is to look at the choices you make. You have to think for yourself. You don't just do what everyone tells you."

"I do what you tell me," she says confidently. "And you do what your parents tell you."

"I used to do everything they told me," I agree, "until I discovered they'd been lying to me. It's all right to do what other people tell you if you think about it and agree with it. But not if you are just doing it because you've been trained to."

She shakes her head, confused.

"You have to tell me who you really are," I say. "And where the real Ariel is." She looks alarmed.

"Why?"

Now's the time to get tough. "You must. You need to listen to me, and I want to know."

"You just told me I do not have to listen."

Me and my big mouth. I'm trying to figure out how to get around this one when Lorna bustles in.

"Hurry up, you two. You'll be late. Miranda, what do you want to wear? It's going to be a scorcher today."

"Shorts," I say. "And a short-sleeved shirt. And a sweater for school." Even when I wear shorts they are cuffed and ironed. Ariel prefers much less formal clothes.

"Ariel?"

She doesn't answer.

"Ariel? What do you want to wear?"

"I like the bright purple," she answers. That, at least, is like the old Ariel.

I take a quick shower, dress, then go find Mother. She's in the kitchen drinking coffee. I have to talk to her but I don't even know if I can trust her. And how do I bring up the whole "we might have an extra clone" thing? I decide to start simple.

"Mother," I say, "you must take Ariel to the doctor. She's sick."

"Ariel has just been seen by a very capable doctor," Mother says. "Please stop this, Miranda. You are obsessing."

Obsessing, am I? I'll give her obsessing.

"Yeah, well," I blurt out, "I think it's much worse than her just being sick." I take a breath. "I think she might not even be Ariel."

"Meaning?" Mother says.

161

"Meaning I think she might be another clone. And I'm very worried about where the real Ariel is and what's happened to her."

Mother rolls her eyes.

"Stop that!" I say. "You have to listen to me. I'm not being paranoid."

"You are," she says. "You are worried the whole thing is happening over again, except to Ariel this time. I promise you that everything is fine. Why would we need a second clone? It's ridiculous. I think that maybe you need to talk to someone."

"Like a shrink?"

"Yes."

"And I tell this shrink I'm a clone and he puts me away in the loony bin."

"I guess that's a problem," she admits.

"No kidding. Anyway, I don't need a shrink. I need you to listen to me."

"Obviously, if Ariel really gets sick, we'll have Dr. Mullen look at her again. But not until then. He was just here and he says she is fine."

"Not Dr. Mullen! He can't be trusted. And he's not a pediatrician, anyway."

"But he knows you both, and your case," she counters.

Ariel comes in. She sits primly at the table and eats one piece of toast. Her fresh squeezed lemon juice sits by her plate. I push it over to her.

"Take a big drink," I say. "It's your favorite."

She takes a gulp, swallows, then makes the funniest face. "That is *horrible!*"

"But only yesterday you loved it," I say, looking

162

meaningfully at Mother.

Mother refuses to acknowledge that there is anything wrong. She ignores the entire thing. "Come along, girls. Time to go."

When we get to school Ariel goes off and I find Emma.

"So?" she says.

"I'm sure it isn't her. She practically admitted it. She doesn't answer to her name, she hates lemon juice ..."

"What can we do?" Emma asks as we hurry to class.

"We have to get into the clinic," I say. "Dr. Mullen must be up to something. But what? It has to be him, don't you think?"

"If there's something bad going on we can assume that he's behind it, yeah," Emma agrees. "The question is, what we can do about it?"

Classes drag by. I spend my time trying to think up a new name for the one who isn't Ariel. If she'll let me do it, I'll be absolutely positive. Ariel loved her name. I should call her Poser. But that wouldn't be nice, would it? If she is posing, she's doing it because Dr. Mullen is making her. Maybe she should be called Dupe.

What about something simple, like the name of a flower? A name of her own would help her think of herself as an individual who can think for herself. If I could get her to do that, maybe I could find out what happened to the real Ariel. I think hard. I know! Not a flower. Adam. The first man. Eve. First woman. She should be Eve. For being brand new.

I hurry to find her at lunch.

"Do you know the story of Genesis?" I ask her.

She shakes her head.

"Well," I say as we sit down, "there is this book called the Bible. It tells stories. Stories of how the world began."

163

"Oh!" she says. "I do know. Myths of creation. I have studied them. Genesis is Adam and Eve, correct?"

"Yes," I say. "And since you are starting a new life, I think you should have a new name. Eve."

She looks at me bewildered. "You do not want me to be Ariel?"

"No," I say firmly, "because even though you won't admit it to me, I know you aren't Ariel. So it's wrong to use her name."

She begins to object, but I continue. "And you should have your own name, shouldn't you? I gave Ariel her name. And now I'll give you your name. Eve. You'll be my other new little sister."

She looks at me then, her eyes full of hope. "You will still like me? You won't want to dispose of me if I am not Ariel?"

That's it! That's what Dr. Mullen threatened her with. I take her hand.

"Of course not! You'll be Eve. You'll be my sister, too. But you have to help me find Ariel."

She clutches the table. "Miranda!"

Just then Emma and Sue join us.

"What is it?" I say, alarmed.

"My head. It hurts."

I grab my phone and call Mother.

"Yes, dear?"

"Mother, Ariel's got another horrible headache. If you don't come and take her to the doctor now, I'll do it myself. And not Dr. Mullen. My doctor."

"Miranda!"

"I'll tell the principal you aren't available and I'll get a cab over there with her."

"I'll be right there," she says grimly.

164

"Good." I hang up. "Come on, Eve, let's go wait at the front. Emma, can you tell the office we're going?"

When Mother comes we get into the car and I buckle Eve up. And then I say, "Mother, meet Eve."

"What do you mean?"

"I mean this is not Ariel. This is Eve."

"Miranda," she says, "that is quite enough. I will take Ariel to the doctor, but stop all this nonsense."

I don't reply. I try to think how I'm going to find the real Ariel. Where could she be? And why was this switch made?

Chapter 24

I am terrified by what the doctor might find. Is this a repeat of my disease? And if so, why? How? Mine was a spontaneous mutation, I thought, not something in my DNA. I am sitting in the front seat and the radio is on so I figure Eve can't really hear too much.

In a low voice, I say, "Mother, I want you to tell me the truth. Did Dr. Mullen ever figure out why I got my disease?"

She pauses for a minute before she answers. I think she is trying to decide whether or not to be honest.

"Mother!"

"It was a genetic mutation," she answers. "Spontaneous. He checked Ariel thoroughly and she does not have it. In fact, her genetic structure seems to be quite perfect. At any rate, her symptoms are different. She has a headache, not blurry vision."

"But Ariel doesn't have it," I point out to her. "This is Eve. She's sick. We don't know where Ariel is."

Mother doesn't answer, but I can see her gritting her teeth.

"Dr. Corne hasn't ever seen Eve, has he?"

"Stop calling her that!"

"Has he?" I persist.

"No, he has not seen Ariel. You know that."

"Good. At least I'll know he isn't in on it." I turn to the back seat. "Eve. How are you?"

166

"My head hurts," she complains.

We drive into the parking lot and I help Eve out. It is so hot it's hard to walk, even from the car to the front door of the clinic. Eve stumbles. I practically carry her inside. The air conditioning feels wonderful.

As usual the waiting room is filled with screaming babies and fighting children. Mother makes sure we are taken through right away. The perks of owning the place! I insist on going in with Eve and Mother. I don't trust Mother to go in alone. Who knows? Maybe Dr. Corne is in on all this too— although I really doubt it.

"Hello, Miranda," he says in his usual serious way. "I'm so pleased to hear about your full recovery. And Ariel here turned up just at the right time for you, didn't she?" He turns to Eve and extends his hand. "Hello. I'm Dr. Corne."

She doesn't respond.

Dr. Corne calls for his nurse and then sends both me and Mother out of the room. We sit and wait in the examining room. He comes out after what seems like ages.

"I'd like your permission to do an MRI of her brain, and perhaps an angiogram. I have some concerns."

Mother consents. She calls Father. Eventually he shows up. We wait. Finally Dr. Corne calls us in to his office. He motions for us to sit down.

"Ariel is resting in one of the examining rooms," he says. "I'm afraid you need to be prepared for some very bad news." I hold my breath. "She has a brain tumor."

"You mean tumors, like I did?" I ask.

"No, Miranda. One brain tumor. Almost certainly cancer already in an advanced stage. I doubt we'll be able to operate. Have you noticed any other symptoms besides the headaches?

167

Clumsiness? Nausea? Even a personality change?"

"Yes," we all say at once.

"Definitely a personality change," I say.

"That is a common symptom, and often the most distressing one, as it feels like you've lost a person close to you." He turns to Father. "You were able to help Miranda in your research clinic. I understand you've given it over to a charitable foundation. But maybe they could still help. There are trials going on for this type of cancer, but they are hard to get into. If you can pull some strings, use your contacts ..."

I can't believe it. I am so stunned I can hardly breathe. So it really is Ariel and she's got a brain tumor, just like Jessica— Mother and Father's first child. Jessica died from hers and it sounds like Ariel will too.

They keep talking about treatment and what to do, but I don't really hear it. I can't take all this in! I was so convinced that this wasn't Ariel and now it seems that it is, but that she's going to die!

I get up and run from the room to find Ariel. The nurse shows me into her examining room. She is getting dressed and I notice her scar. I'm so stupid! Why didn't I just think to check to see if she had a scar. Only Ariel would have one—so she couldn't be a different clone. I've been sunk in paranoia and I've been no help to Ariel at all. She's ill and all I've done is make it worse. I go over and hug her.

"We'll find a cure," I say. "We will."

She says nothing. I help her get dressed and then Mother and Father come to fetch us. I sit in the back seat of the car with Ariel as Mother drives, and hold her hand.

"Mother," I say, "you were right. While Ariel was dressing I saw her scar—only Ariel could have that scar."

"I should have thought of that myself," Mother says.

"I am very sick," Ariel says.

"Yes," I agree.

"I have to go to a hospital," she says.

"You do," Mother says from the front, "but we don't know which one yet, dear. Father has to call Dr. Mullen."

"Dr. Mullen said she was fine!" I object.

"Still," Mother says, "he knows all the latest experimental treatments, where they are happening. He's our best bet."

"Dr. Mullen knows everything," Ariel says.

I hate this. She's just like she was before. She's lost everything that made her herself.

We get home and put Ariel to bed. I go to the kitchen. I had turned my phone off while we were at the clinic. I turn it back on and notice there are two missed calls.

The first message is from Emma.

"Hey. I'm home. Call me."

The second one is Ariel.

"Miranda? Help me. Help me."

Then a click and the phone going dead.

I play it again.

"Miranda, help me. Help me."

She sounds desperate. Frightened. I stand frozen, staring at the phone. I have just accepted that Ariel is here. But then how could she be calling me and asking for help, when I was with her most of the day? I check the time on the message. 10:05 a.m. We were in school then. I am hopelessly confused.

I save the message and run to our room. Ariel, or Eve, or whoever the heck she is, is lying in bed.

"Ariel," I say, "did you call me today?"

"I called your name."

169

"No, I mean did you phone me?"

"Phone? No," she says. "I was with you all day. Why would I telephone you?"

"Are you positive?"

"Yes. Why would I? You were at school with me. Should I want to talk to you, would I not come and find you, since we have to keep our phones turned off in class?"

She hasn't lost her ability to reason.

I go back into the kitchen and look at the numbers on the caller display. *The number is there but no name.* But it does say, "Palm Desert, California."

I let out a scream of frustration, then call Emma.

"Emma!"

"Hi!"

"Can you come over? No wait. Better if I come there. I'll see if Mother'll drive me."

"Sure," Emma says. "What's up?"

"Tell you later," I say as Mother walks into the kitchen. I replay the message for her.

"Miranda, Ariel has a brain tumor! She's forgotten already that she called you. You weren't with her every minute of today, were you?"

"No," I admit. "But she says she never would have even thought of calling me."

"Stop this nonsense, Miranda," she says. Then she looks at me sympathetically, for a moment letting down the guard she seems to have put up.

"We have a very sick child and you have to adjust to the fact that she may not get better. But Father and I will always be here for you. You know that, don't you?" In a flash I understand why she's been so cold. She's terrified. She's afraid

170

she's lost me forever. She's afraid I'll never be able to love her again. The scary thing is—she might be right.

"But you're going to try to help her, aren't you?" I ask.

"Of course we are. Dr. Mullen is in the middle of something and can't get away immediately ..." I start to object. Mother raises her hand to stop me. "But he will come over after dinner."

"Can you drive me to Emma's?"

She thinks for a minute. "Perhaps that would be a good idea. Dr. Mullen can examine Ariel and I'll pick you up around nine. What about your dinner?"

"I'll eat there," I say.

So off we go to Emma's. Living outside La Quinta is annoying. I can't go anywhere without being driven. Probably part of their plan. Easier to control me that way. But something is out of control here, and I have to find out what it is—and fast.

The scar proves it is Ariel. But the phone call says it isn't.

Chapter 25

Emma's street ends in a cul de sac and there is a hiking path that begins there, affectionately known by the locals as Doggy Poop Trail—for obvious reasons. Emma has a dog, a golden retriever, and I arrive just as she's getting ready to take him out. It's almost six o'clock and it's still broiling hot. We decide to take Merv for a short walk up the trail.

"Miranda," Emma's mom calls out, "will you stay for dinner?"

"Sure," I say, "thanks." And to Emma I add, "I was counting on that."

Emma laughs. "My mom and Shabbat dinner? Only one possible outcome."

Emma and I set off. The trail winds up the hills behind the street and we quickly get a lovely view of the city. The trail is packed with other hikers, most of them with dogs. Fortunately Merv is quite well trained and doesn't lunge at the other dogs, which is a good thing since half of them seem to be pit bulls. I guess I'm not the only paranoid person around.

Emma and I discuss all the latest news. It's hard to know whether Ariel is sick or if it isn't Ariel at all. The thing is, if it isn't Ariel, the real Ariel is out there somewhere and I need to help her. But how do I find out? We seem to have reached a dead end.

"I wish we could drive," I sigh.

"Why?"

"Dr. Mullen is on his way over to our house right now. If we could drive to his clinic and get in while he's away, maybe we could find out what's going on."

Emma looks at me in amazement. "Talk about personality change."

"Meaning?"

"Meaning you know very well that two months ago you never would have thought of that."

"That's true," I admit. "Do you think Ariel has a tumor?" I wonder. "I suppose that could explain everything, and she really is Ariel after all."

"It does explain everything," Emma says. "And the scar is pretty definite evidence. But I'm with you. I still feel like something isn't right. Plus, why did she get sick? I thought Dr. Mullen said she was perfect." As we turn to start down the trail she says, "Maybe one of my brothers would drive us over there."

"You think?"

"We can ask. Say you're supposed to pick up a special prescription or something. They won't know the difference."

It never ceases to amaze me how quickly Emma can come up with a good cover story.

On the way down we pass all kinds of people who are jogging up the trail. I find walking in this heat quite enough. I hope I never turn into that kind of a crazy adult.

Both Josh and Ben are home for dinner because Emma's mom insists everyone be there for Friday night Sabbath dinners. She lights the candles, then says the blessings over the wine and bread. I know all the Sabbath blessings by heart, I've been over for dinner so many times.

173

We have a great meal of roasted chicken and I find I am starving. I've hardly eaten the last few days, I've been so worried.

Emma works on Josh after dinner, because at sixteen he's the youngest, closest to us in age. Ben who is eighteen is already on his way back to his friends on campus. Reluctantly Josh agrees to drive us and wait while we go into the clinic. We figure it's safer that way—we won't just disappear like maybe Ariel did.

"Make it quick," Josh says, as he pulls up in front of the clinic. "I have plans tonight."

"I will," I say. "Emma, want to come?"

Emma says, "Sure."

Ms. Yellow Teeth, otherwise known as Jean the nurse, answers the bell when we ring.

"Miranda. What can I do for you?"

"Dr. Mullen called me at Emma's," I lie, "and said we should meet him here. He said to wait in the office."

She opens the door for us. "Come in."

We follow her into the foyer. "Best wait here," she says. "He's been out for a while. I'm sure he won't be long."

We sit down. As soon as she goes off to do whatever it is she does—I briefly wonder why a nurse would be working at a clinic that no longer has any patients—I motion to Emma. We get up and I lead the way to Dr. Mullen's office. I try the door handle. Not locked! We step in.

Dr. Mullen is seated at his desk, smiling. Emma and I jump a mile.

His grin broadens. "I've been expecting you."

I can't answer. Emma grimaces.

"Have a seat, girls."

174

"My brother is waiting outside," Emma warns. Neither of us moves from the door.

"Yes, well then, I'll be brief," Dr. Mullen says. "I understand, Miranda, that you are trying to convince your parents that Ten is not really Ten."

"I think it's a possibility," I say, my heart still beating so hard I can barely hear my own voice. "And her name is Ariel now."

"I want you to stop talking to your parents this way."

"Why?" I ask.

"Because they might eventually believe you. And that could cause a lot of trouble for me."

I don't like the sound of this. Emma and I are standing close to each other as if that will protect us. From what, though?

"Just spit it out," Emma demands.

He smiles again. "Yes, good plan. The direct approach. Here's the thing. Ten has been removed. The child in your home now is not Ten. She is a defective clone I made immediately before I made Number Ten. I call her Eleven at the moment because she is actually older than Ten, and I name them each year by their age. Tests on her revealed that she was imperfect but I decided to keep her as a backup should I ever need her, and now I find I do."

I grab Emma's hand.

"But where's Ariel?" I exclaim.

"Ariel is somewhere safe," he says.

"But why? Why have you done it?"

"You don't need the details of why or where. All you need to know is that if you tell your parents, I will kill Ariel. I assure you that I am quite capable," he says lightly, "of doing so. I can

175

always harvest her DNA before I do away with her. So you and Emma should just forget this little talk and try to help the other child. She'll need it."

"How do we know Ariel is safe?" Emma demands.

"You don't," he says. "But I am telling you that she is, and that she will remain so. Unless you force me to kill her to cover up her abduction." He stands up. "Are we clear?"

"You can't!" I say.

"I believe I can," he says.

"Wait ... what about the scar? It *must* be Ariel."

"I made a small incision in Number Eleven and stitched her up again in order to convince your parents that she is the same girl. They cannot discover that I am still doing human experiments. And now you must go."

He ushers us out of his office, down the corridor and out the front door. We stand there so shocked we can't move. Josh honks. That startles us. We clamber back into the car.

"You girls look like you've seen a ghost," Josh says. "Everything okay?"

"Can I sleep over?" I ask Emma in a small voice.

"You'd better," she says.

"What's up?" Josh asks again.

"Nothing!" We both answer at once.

Josh drives us back to Emma's house. I call my parents. My dad answers.

"What did Dr. Mullen say?" I ask.

"He was very sorry to hear about the test results. He says he doesn't know of any treatments, that we have to prepare for the worst."

"There must be something," I say.

"I don't think so, Miranda. Are you ready to come home?"

176

"No. I'm sleeping over here tonight."

"I think Ariel needs you," he says.

"I know. But I need to be here."

"All right," Father says. "We'll come get you tomorrow. Call."

I hang up. Emma and I go to her room and sit on the bed. I stare at her.

"What are we going to do?" I say.

"Something," she says, voice determined. "We are not going to let him get away with it."

"But what?" I repeat. "And poor Eve. To him she's just some experiment gone wrong. I mean, to go so far as to cut her open just to give her a scar. Even a small one! He's horrible!"

"He is," Emma agrees. "And we have to stop him."

"Why would he tell us all that?" I wonder aloud. "The scar just about had us convinced. He didn't have to tell us, did he?"

"Yeah," Emma agrees. "Maybe none of it's true! Maybe he's trying to confuse us."

"But he'd figure that we would consider that," I counter. "So maybe he told us the truth, figuring we'd never believe him."

"Reverse psychology," Emma muses.

"We'll have to follow him," I say. "If it's true, he'll lead us to Ariel. We just have to figure out how to do it."

177

Chapter 26

Saturday morning, and we have it all worked out. I'm borrowing Ben's bicycle so Emma and I can bike together to the clinic. It's nine o'clock when we set off. It takes us about half an hour to get to the clinic. We both have baseball caps under our helmets, which we pull down as a disguise as well as protection from the sun. We also borrowed baseball jerseys from Josh so we look like kids on our way to a game. Since it's already blistering hot, we arrive out of breath and sweating.

The clinic is set back from the street with its own driveway. There's only one way out, so Emma and I plant ourselves behind a large truck parked just at the end of the driveway. We spot Dr. Mullen around 10:15 as he drives past us into the clinic driveway. Both Emma and I figure that Ariel isn't at the clinic. It's being closely watched now and has a different administrator in charge. Dr. Mullen must have Ariel stashed somewhere else. But where?

Around eleven he goes out. It isn't easy to follow him on the bikes but we just manage to keep his van in view. And he doesn't go far. He stops at a small strip mall and hurries into a Starbucks. We peer in the window and see that he is sitting with an older man and they are deep in conversation. The older man then hands a briefcase over to Dr. Mullen, who takes it and leaves. We sneak around the corner in the nick of time so he doesn't catch sight of us.

He doesn't go back to the clinic, though. He gets onto Highway 111 and heads south.

Now it's impossible to keep up on our bikes, but thanks to bad traffic and lights, we manage to keep him in view for a while. Eventually we lose him altogether, and we pull up at a big intersection to decide what to do.

"Look, look," Emma says. She points left. Down the street is a large industrial park and what appears to be Dr. Mullen's van parked outside the building closest to us.

There are rows and rows of office buildings, all painted a pale pink. Set behind those are a group of larger buildings that appear to be warehouses of one sort or another. We turn down the street and move closer. The van looks like it is Dr. Mullen's, but we can't be sure. Why didn't I think to memorize his plate number? And I'm supposed to be so smart.

"What do you think?" I pant.

"No one would suspect," Emma says, "if that's where he's hiding her. But why here?"

"He's devious," I say. "No one would think to look here. The question is, how do we get in without being seen? How do we find out?"

"We wait until he leaves," she says. "And then we get in."

That seems the only logical answer so that's what we do. Since we don't have to watch the place we decide to go get lunch. We are overheated and need to cool off. We find a nice little place nearby that makes huge sandwiches. We both call home and say we're fine, but that we won't be back until dinner. With a grimace Emma calls Michael and tells him she will have to postpone the movie.

"How did he take it?" I ask.

She shrugs.

"I'm sorry!" I say.

"Don't be. Ariel needs us. We're all she has."

By the time we return, Dr. Mullen's van is gone. We drive our bikes around the side of the building and leave them there. Then we try the front door. It's locked. We walk around to the back where there's another door but it, too, is locked.

We are just about to give up and are heading around to the front when the front door opens. We flatten ourselves against the side wall. A large man walks out. We watch as he wedges a small rock between the door and the jamb to keep the door from locking behind him. He lights a cigarette and walks down the path.

I know we have to act fast. I motion to Emma. We sprint to the door and into the building. There is a long corridor ahead of us. We have to get out of the way or he'll see us as soon as he returns. There are doors off the corridor. I open the first one. An office. Empty of people. Full of computers. The next door is the same.

"Hurry," Emma hisses.

We open the third door. A man in a white lab coat is standing beside all sorts of equipment: test tubes, vats, computers. He whirls around and sees us. We back out. Right into the cigarette man who grabs us each by our jerseys and lifts us into the air.

"You two lost?" he growls.

"Yes," Emma says.

"Well, get out of here," he snarls, "and don't come back!" He starts to drag us down the corridor.

But the man in the white lab coat calls, "Hold up a minute. Don't let them go!"

He takes a good look at me. He comes closer and knocks

180

the hat off my head.

"Look who it is," he says.

"Hey, she looks just like the other one!" the cigarette man says.

"You must be Miranda," the other man smiles.

He is a short, skinny fellow, completely bald, but young, maybe twenty-five at the most.

"Get off me," I yell. I try to fight, but I'm being held in the air and all I can do is flail around.

"Bring them," the short guy says.

Emma and I both protest and shout, but who's going to hear us? The short guy points to a door. The big guy throws us into a room. We hear the door lock.

We both run at the door and bang on it and turn the knob, all the stupid things you see people do in bad movies but we do it anyway. It's useless, of course. I look around. No windows. A few long tables with lab equipment and some chairs.

"This isn't good," I say to Emma.

"That's for sure," she agrees. "If he was willing to kill Ariel, who's to say he won't just kill us too?"

"And no one has ... wait a minute. I've got my phone." I laugh.

"And I've got mine!" Emma exclaims.

Emma pulls hers out but she gets no service.

I try mine. It works! Eve answers.

"Eve!" I exclaim. "It's me! Miranda."

"Hello Miranda."

"I need help. I'm in trouble. I'm stuck in Dr. Mullen's lab, in the industrial park off ..."

"Trouble?" she interrupts.

181

"Yes!"

"Dr. Mullen is here with me. He would like to know what trouble."

"No! Don't tell him! He's the trouble. You have to ..."

Suddenly I hear his voice.

"Hello?"

"Put Eve back on," I say. "Or my parents."

"Your parents are speaking to a specialist I brought over. I am examining Number Eleven. It occurred to me there is more to discover about her condition." His lab rat, I think.

"Oh, just a moment, my phone is ringing." He hands the phone back to Eve.

"Hello?" she says.

"Eve," I say, "we're trapped. You have to help me ..."

Then Dr. Mullen's voice again.

"I thought I warned you to leave all this alone, Miranda. I just got a call from my colleagues. Apparently you are my guest."

"Yes," I exclaim. "And you'd better let us go!"

Just then the door opens and the big lug comes back in. He grabs my phone and Emma's, walks out and slams the door.

"Great!" I exclaim. "Just great!"

"What?" says Emma.

"It's Dr. Mullen. I got through to Eve but Dr. Mullen was there and now we're really in trouble."

We stare at each other.

"I'm sorry, Emma," I say. "I never should have let you get involved. I just didn't think. I didn't realize how dangerous it could get."

Emma throws her arms around me and gives me a hug.

"It's okay," she says. "We had to try to save Ariel. I guess we should have gone to my dad, though. We're playing in the big leagues here. Way over our heads."

I sink down on one of the chairs. She's right. Or is she?

"Maybe," I say. "But I should be smarter than all of them. Dr. Mullen made me that way, after all. I just have to think. I just have to think."

Chapter 27

I look around. They've stuck us in some kind of lab. Emma and I check out what's around us. There are little bottles and vials and test tubes all over the long table, but I have no idea what most of them are. We do find some hydrochloric acid, which I know hurts like anything if you get it on you.

"When the big guy comes in next," Emma says, "we throw this at him and run."

"It'll burn him," I object.

"Oh, but it's all right for them to kidnap us. We should just sit here and take it, I suppose?"

Emma makes a good point. I want to be good. But I realize that my wanting to be good could get us hurt. And I have to think about Emma, not just me. I got her into this, after all.

"You're right," I say. "But I hate to do it."

"This is like war," Emma says. "We have to save ourselves."

"But this isn't a war and anyway, we aren't positive that they want to harm us." I pause to think. "Dr. Mullen believes that the end justifies the means. But does it ever?"

"Yes," says Emma. "Sometimes it does!"

"You shouldn't do to others what you wouldn't want done to yourself," I say.

"Do you think Dr. Mullen would let that stop him?" she counters.

I know he wouldn't. So we position ourselves on either side

184

of the door, each one holding an open bottle of acid, and wait. And wait. And wait. I look at my watch. Three o'clock.

"Dr. Mullen's obviously making other clones," I say. "Why is he doing it? What's he up to? It's horrible to think about how I was created."

"And yet," Emma smiles, "you still aren't perfect."

She can make me laugh even when we're trapped in a mad scientist's lab waiting for who knows what to happen.

"Yeah, how's that possible?" I say.

"It's not just possible," says Emma, "it's necessary. Now if you were perfect—the thing you are always striving for, by the way—you wouldn't be human."

"What's the matter with Dr. Mullen?" I ask. "Can't he see what he's doing is wrong?"

"He thinks he knows what's best for everyone," Emma says.

"Yeah," I agree, "dictators think that too. Never mind dictators, look at my parents. They were willing to kill Ariel to save me."

"Dad always tells me that I have to do what is right," Emma says, "and not worry about the consequences."

I look at the acid in her hands and in mine. "Well, we aren't exactly following that advice are we? If we were, we wouldn't hurt this guy despite the consequences for us."

Emma stares at me for a minute before she answers. "But he wouldn't want us to get hurt either, I know that," she says. "Still, you have a pretty good point."

"I told Eve that her choices make her who she is," I say. "But, Emma, I can't get away from this—people make choices for the weirdest reasons. Half my choices are made because I've been bred to be good and the other half because I've been brought up to be good. So I'm conditioned to choose a certain

185

way. I mean, how free am I?"

"Maybe we're all programmed like robots or, machines, you mean," Emma says. "If not by our genes then by our parents ..."

"And friends," I interrupt, "and magazines and movies and ..."

Our discussion is interrupted by the lock turning and the door opening. Don't do to others what you wouldn't want done to yourself. Still, we have to make sure he won't hurt us either. Well, I wouldn't want that stuff thrown in my face, so I aim for his hands. Emma hits him on the back of the neck. He yells, dances around, and drops the key. I grab it and Emma and I are out the door before he can grab us. Not that I think he could with his hands hurting like that.

We slam the door and lock him in. Then we look around.

"We have to find Ariel," I whisper. "And get out of here."

We are more careful this time. Instead of opening each door wide, we open each one a crack and sneak a peek in.

The first door opens onto a room with a woman sitting at a computer. She doesn't notice me. The next door leads to a room full of equipment. Behind the third door is a large partition. I can't tell what's on the other side without going in. We slip in and shut the door behind us.

I peek around the partition. The room is separated by large screens into three sections. Sitting directly in front of me on a cot is Ariel!

"Ariel!"

"Miranda!"

She leaps off the cot and throws herself into my arms.

"You found me! You're so smart! You are so good! How did you do it? Hi, Emma." She hugs Emma too. "Are we leaving?

Can we go home?"

"Yes," I say. "Let's get out of here before Dr. Mullen gets back."

"Dr. Mullen is here," Ariel says. "He was just in to visit me."

"Oh, no," I groan. "Then he'll find the big lug any second."

"The back door," Emma suggests. "There's a back exit, remember?"

"Yes," I say. "Let's make a run for it."

I take Ariel's hand and we creep toward the door. I hear it open. It's probably Dr. Mullen. I point at the partition. Emma nods. We both push it and it crashes over. I recognize Dr. Mullen's voice as he yells. The only trouble is that the partition is now against the door and although he's under it, we can't get out.

"Get this off me," he shouts.

"Not unless you let us go," I shout back.

"Can't do that. Help!" he starts to call at the top of his lungs.

I whisper to Emma. "I'm the strongest. You and Ariel lift it up. I'll shove him out of our way. Then we run!"

She nods and motions for Ariel to help her lift the partition. They do, and it falls backwards. Dr. Mullen is trying to get up but I don't give him a chance. I push him down and we all shoot past him out into the hallway.

There are a couple of people in the hall, but they are coming out of the offices toward the front of the building. The corridor toward the back door is clear, although there are one or two heads peering out of offices.

"Run!" I hiss.

We run. A young woman rushes out of a door and tries to stop us. I fight her off, giving her a good kick in the knees. Her legs buckle. We reach the end of the corridor and the door.

187

The door is locked. But there is no deadbolt we can open from the inside. It must be locked from the outside. We're trapped. Quickly I look around. There are corridors going off from the back door on either side. One is clear of people.

"Come on," I say. I push them both to the right. "Check all the doors."

"This room is filled with stuff," Ariel calls to us. It is filled with boxes almost up to the ceiling.

"At least we can hide in here," I say.

We dash in, shut the door behind us, and crouch at the back behind the boxes.

"Are you all right?" I say to Ariel, trying to catch my breath.

"He hasn't hurt me."

"What happened?" I ask.

Emma interrupts. "You can talk about all this later, but right now shouldn't we be thinking about getting out of here? In case you've forgotten," she says to me, "Dr. Mullen *did* threaten something very nasty if we got involved. And he's sure to be checking all the offices as we speak."

She's right. We have to get out. But how on earth? We're locked inside a building full of his people. There are no windows. No phones. And no one has any idea where we are.

"But there must be a way," I mutter aloud. "We just haven't thought of it yet."

188

Chapter 28

"Let's look in the boxes," I suggest. "Maybe there's something we can use to escape."

The boxes are piled almost to the ceiling, and it's a problem just to get one open. Ariel is small and dexterous so we send her up like a mountain climber. She gains a foothold on each box and slowly makes her way to the top where she perches. Unfortunately, since she is sitting on the box, she can't open it.

"Can you reach the one next to you?" I call up. "Maybe you can open that one."

She looks around for a moment, and then calls down. "Miranda. There is something more interesting up here than the boxes."

"What?"

"An air vent in the ceiling."

"Really? Can you open it?"

"Let me see." She stands up slowly, reaches for the vent above her, and pulls. It comes away. She pulls herself up so her head is in the opening, then drops back onto the boxes.

"There is a long passage here," she says. "It has porous tiles all around."

"Big enough for a person?"

"Big enough for us," she says.

"Can you see where it goes?"

189

"No."

I look at Emma.

"Let's try it," she says. "The minute we go back into the hallway they'll catch us. And they're bound to check here soon and find us."

"Right. You go first. I'll catch you if you fall."

Emma slowly climbs up the boxes. Although she and I love to hike together I know she doesn't like steep drops.

"Just don't look down," I encourage her.

She gets up with little trouble and helps boost Ariel into the overhead passage. I reach the top and boost Emma up. Then I pull myself up with Emma's help. The tiles lining the tunnel look like the kind we have in our music room at school—used to soundproof the room. With the extra crawl space lined with tiles, this office building would be completely soundproofed to the outside world. Why? I shudder as I think of the only logical explanation: Dr. Mullen's experiments. Were there clones born here? Did they die here? Did they suffer? The sound of screaming babies would never leave these walls.

Ariel leads the way as we slither through the crawl space. Every little while there is another vent and we are able to look down and see what is happening. We reach a room where two people are working away at computers. No one is talking and there seems to be no concern about the three of us. In the next room, we can see the top of some huge vats. Another room, and we see a few people in lab coats working with test tubes. Another room seems to be an apartment like the one that surrogate was living in at the other clinic.

"We need to get back over the front corridor," I say, "so that we can get out the front door. They can't have locked that from the outside."

"Look," Ariel says, "I think that's where I was being kept."

I tell Ariel to move ahead a little and I peer down. It does look like the same room, screens and all.

"Let's go down here," I say. "We'll be close to the front door."

"But how?" says Emma, looking down. "No boxes."

"But there is a cot, right under the vent," I point out.

"Yeah," says Emma, "far under. Far enough that we might not hit it, or hit it on the side, and break every bone in our bodies!"

"Let me go first," Ariel offers. "I can jump down easily, and then put some of the mattresses on top of each other for you two."

"Are you sure?" I ask.

"Yes," she answers. "I'm the smallest; it'll be easiest for me."

"All right," I agree.

I pull the grate off and push it aside. Ariel squeezes past us. Emma takes one arm, I take another, and we lower her down as far as we can.

"Now?" I say.

"Now," she replies.

Emma and I let go on the count of three. Ariel drops onto the cot. She scrambles up and grins at us. Then she runs to the other cots, pulls the mattresses off them and piles them onto the cot below us.

"All done," she calls.

"It still looks very far away," Emma groans.

"I agree."

Emma shakes her head. "Let me go first and get it over with."

191

"No," I say, "let me. I've got a better chance than you of not getting hurt."

"Your superior physical abilities," Emma says.

"Not to mention all my dance training," I point out. "And then Ariel and I can catch you if necessary."

"All right," Emma says.

I grab the edges of the opening, hang for a minute, take a deep breath, then drop. I land hard on the mattresses and roll off, but get up basically unhurt.

"Come on, Emma," I call.

Ariel and I watch as she lowers herself, grabs on to the edge and quickly lets go. She falls slightly off the mattresses but I am there to catch her and push her back onto them.

"Whew!" she sighs as she scrambles off with my help.

"All right?" I ask.

"Yeah, okay."

I lead the way to the door, open it a crack and peek out. The big lug is walking down the corridor. I close the door.

"Not yet," I say. "We'd better wait. The big lug is out there."

"Big lug?" Ariel asks.

"Big guy? Very big?"

"I haven't seen him," Ariel says.

I turn to her. "Tell me what happened? How did they take you?"

"After you left me Dr. Mullen called my cell and told me that you had suddenly become sick. He said you were asking for me, and that Mother agreed he could come and pick me up. But when I got in the car we came here and he put me in this room. He made me change my clothes and then he went away. When he came back he took me to a room that has lots of medical equipment. He took blood, did lots of tests and

192

then brought me back here and left me with nothing to read and no TV and nothing to do but worry and worry!"

"He substituted you," I tell her.

"What do you mean?"

"There's another clone. I've named her Eve. She's pretending to be you. No wonder he had you switch clothes. He put her in the ones you were wearing so I wouldn't suspect anything."

"So no one would know I was missing." Ariel nods.

"I knew."

"How?"

"Because you are you. And she wasn't behaving like you."

This seems to interest Ariel. "How is she different?"

"Tell me why you are here," I say. "Do you know?"

"Not exactly," Ariel replies. "Except that after Dr. Mullen did all those tests he said I was perfect. More perfect than you. More perfect than Eleven."

"That's Eve," I say.

"Probably," says Ariel. "I don't know if there are others. But I overheard him saying something about needing a prototype."

"So he really *is* going to make others," I say.

"But why?" Emma asks.

"Who knows," I grimace. "He's nuts. No doubt in his own mind he's got some great reason."

I open the door a crack and peek out. "It's clear. Are you ready?"

"Let's go, then," Emma agrees.

I open the door and lead the way, running full speed. We reach the front door at the end of the corridor with no problem. I go to unlock it when suddenly a voice carries down the hallway.

"Leaving so soon?"

I don't turn around. I am trying to turn the deadbolt and I do, but before I can even yank the door open, the big lug is there. He pushes me away from the door, and stands in front of it. Another very big man comes up beside him. I whirl around. Dr. Mullen is walking toward us.

"Let us go!" I yell, although I know no one outside will hear me no matter how loud I shout.

"Calm down, my dear," he says. He reaches us and says, "Follow me."

The big guy gives us a shove. I look at Emma and Ariel. My heart sinks. I see no alternative though so I nod to the others. Well, what other choice is there?

We follow him into an office near the room from which we just escaped. He sits behind a desk, which looks similar to his desk at the clinic, covered in books and papers. There are three chairs already placed in front of the desk. Three? Was he expecting us? We sit.

"Ah, Miranda, I see you have noticed that I have three chairs waiting here." He picks up his notebook and scribbles in it. "Most interesting. You have been very useful to me today, thank you so much."

"What do you mean?" I ask.

"Do you really think I am stupid?" he asks.

"Yes," Emma smiles. I can see she doesn't want him to feel he's scaring us.

"Ah yes, Emma. You did spoil the experiment a little. I would have preferred to watch Ariel and Miranda on their own. Still, I think I have an excellent idea of their reactions now, and I know what needs to be done."

194

"Could you speak in English, please?" I say, getting more and more angry, less and less afraid.

"But I am," he protests. "Don't you understand? Think."

I think. He says he is not as stupid as we think. And three chairs waiting. I gasp.

"You knew we were following you? You knew we were here before I called home?"

"Good for you, Miranda," he says. "That is correct. This has all been an experiment. And you've been my little guinea pigs. I gave you the bait in my office, thinking you would have to try to find Ariel. But I wanted to be sure you would behave in the way I expected. And you did, right down to your escapade with the acid and your trek through the vents. Excellent."

Chapter 29

I just sit and stare at him. He knew everything?

"Look up," he says.

We do. I don't see anything but a ceiling.

"See that little clock on the wall?"

"Yes," I say.

"A camera," he beams. "Clever, what?"

"You've been watching us?" I say, incredulous.

"Oh, yes. Most certainly. From the start. Even before you came to my office. I thought it possible that when I took Ariel, you would notice. It would have been easier if you had not, of course. But once you did I wanted to observe how much you would notice, how far you would go."

"Why?" Emma asks.

"Because," he smiles, "Ariel is a perfect prototype. *Physically*. But *emotionally*, well, that is harder to quantify. You showed some surprising characteristics when you discovered you were a clone, Miranda. Surprising. I need to know what other surprises you clones might have inside you. Stored away. Hidden. Yes, personality seems to be far less predictable."

"So let me get this straight," Emma says. "You knew we were following you. You let us in. You let us throw acid on that poor guy. You've followed our every move."

"Just a minute," I say. "That guy—his hands weren't

196

bandaged."

"I didn't want you to hurt anyone," Dr. Mullen answers. "That was just foul-smelling water. But I was very interested in the fact that you were willing to do it. Very interested in that." He flips through his notebook and nods and clicks his tongue.

That makes me feel really sick.

"Why are you doing all this?" I demand. "It has to be more than just scientific curiosity. After all, you could always ask us to come in for tests, couldn't you? I'm sure you could have convinced my parents it was necessary for some reason."

"Clever, clever," he smiles. I wish I could wipe that smile off his face.

"You said prototype," I press on. "I think I should know if there are going to be more of me!"

"Here is the problem," he says. "You know in the movies when they say, 'If I tell you, I'll have to kill you?'"

All three of us squirm a little.

"Isn't it best if you don't know?" he asks.

"So does that mean you are going to let us go?" I ask.

"Oh, yes," he says. "Eventually. But I do think you need to calm down. If I let you go now you might run off to the police. I'm going to put you in a room for a little while so that you can cool off and think. After all, if you go to the police everyone will know you are a clone."

"But what about Ariel?"

"She stays here."

"That won't do," I say.

"It will have to."

"Why? Tell me," I insist. "Whether I know or not, you'll still have Ariel. I'll still be tempted to go to the police. Maybe if I

197

know why, I'll be less likely to go. My imagination might come up with something worse than what is actually happening."

He looks at me for a full minute, thinking. "You are attached to Ariel, then?"

"No, I just came to rescue her for no reason."

"And do you not care about the one you call Eve? She is very ill."

"Of course I'm concerned about Eve."

"But not as much as Ariel."

"Well, no."

"Why not?"

"Because I know Ariel better," I say, "obviously."

"Not obvious," he states. "It seems you have developed a rebellious streak, something I certainly did not calculate as a possibility. It also seems that friends can play a more important part in shaping a person's character than I had assumed." He stares at Emma. She glares back at him.

"After all," he continues, looking back at me, "you should accept what has been presented to you. Why assume Eve is not Ariel? Especially when presented with evidence of a tumor?"

"Because," I say, frustrated, getting up from the chair. "I could tell it wasn't Ariel. And," I add, "I don't trust you!"

"That at least is logical," he comments. "Fine," he agrees. "I will let you in on my little scheme. I intend to produce babies. Perfect babies. You are aware no doubt that there is a huge demand for babies. I will supply that demand."

"For millions of bucks, no doubt," Emma scoffs.

"It is an expensive business," Dr. Mullen states. "I am only covering my costs. I do this as a scientific project first and foremost. As a humanitarian. But I need to do more work on

198

the genes that control our emotions, our personalities."

"Babies who aren't any trouble?" I ask.

"That is correct."

"But," Ariel finally speaks up, "I have been trouble. So I am not perfect. Therefore you should let me go, too."

He beams at her. "Excellent reasoning, Ten," he says.

"Ariel," she corrects him.

"Ariel," he says. "But you are the most physically perfect specimen I have ever created. You will serve as the basis for all my new clones. Up until now, I have been using Miranda's DNA, but as you can see from Eve, it is not going as planned."

This gives me pause. What's wrong with my DNA? Is it defective in some way?

Dr. Mullen continues speaking to Ariel. "From now on I will use only your DNA."

"You will experiment on me?"

"Don't worry," he says gently. "I would never hurt you. And in a way, you can think of yourself as mother to all the new clones that come out of our work."

"Not very original," I say, trying to needle him. "Every movie you see on TV has a mad scientist cloning babies for sale."

"That is because it's the logical next step, isn't it?" he says. "Mass culture is often very accurate about where the world is heading." He rises from his chair. "Now, girls, it's time for you to go to your room. I believe you know the way. I'll send in dinner."

"Our families will start to worry soon," I warn him.

"Oh, no," he corrects me. "Eve—who sounds just like you, Miranda—has left a message for Emma's parents saying Emma is at your house. And she's told your parents, Miranda,

199

that you called to say you were staying at Emma's. I think we have a little time for you to think about what to do. Think carefully."

"We can't talk privately if we are being watched," I object.

"Ah, the camera. I'll turn it off."

"Why should we believe you?" I scoff.

"Come with me. I'll show you."

We follow him. He leads us to one of the first rooms we looked in, full of computers. He shows us the screen, which displays the room with the cots. They are still piled high.

"You will have to clean up your mess," he comments. I don't bother to answer. He's worried about a mess? He flips a switch and the picture goes off.

"As soon as we're gone you'll put it back on," I point out.

"There is a tiny green light on the second hand," he says. "If it is on," and he points to a matching clock on the wall behind him, "you are being watched." He throws another switch. I see the light go off. "When it is off, the camera is off, too.

"Ariel," he orders. "Show your friends to your room."

Ariel leads the way. We get to the room and I check the clock. Green light off.

"I suppose we can talk," I say. "But I suggest we talk quietly. He may have microphones hidden, who knows?"

"Who knows anything?" Emma sighs. "He says we're free to go. What if he only wants to see what decision we'll make? What if this is still part of the experiment? What if we are never getting out of here?"

200

Chapter 30

"Selling perfect babies," I mutter as we sit on the cot. "And all little Ariels. Imagine."

"We have to decide what to do," Emma says.

"We can't just leave Ariel and pretend nothing has happened," I say. "That's out of the question."

"You must," Ariel states.

"Why?" I ask.

"Because if you don't, it's possible we'll all die," she points out. "He's giving you a chance to live. You have to take it. It's only logical."

"I don't care if it's logical. I hate it and I'm not doing it! I can't leave you behind and pretend Eve is the real you."

"I think we should try to escape again," Emma suggests, getting up and pacing. "I can't stand the thought of him getting away with all of this."

"But at least no one will die," Ariel says. "He doesn't want to hurt us. He's a scientist. He values us."

"Only as experiments," I remind her. Then I remember that he practically brought up Ariel. The only father she's ever known. That's a creepy thought.

"What if we don't agree?" I asked. "What do you think he'll do?"

"The logical thing," she answers, "is to kill all of us. That will leave no one to tell on him. He can take my DNA and

201

create new clones after we're gone. Actually it's quite kind of him not to kill us. It would be easier and more logical to do so."

She's talking like we have no choice. But there is always a choice—of some sort. I suddenly remember something I read when I was stuck at the clinic after the liver transplant. I looked up everything I could about genetics and free will. An article I read said that research shows that genes make up fifty percent of our choices, the environment ten percent. And the other forty? That's our free will. I doubted that when I read it because I felt like I was just this puppet Dr. Mullen had created. But now, well, I have to believe it. And I have to believe we can do something unexpected or make a choice he won't see coming.

The door opens and a young woman comes in, followed by the big lug. She is carrying a tray piled high with hamburgers, fries and Cokes. When that familiar greasy smell wafts over the room, I realize that I'm starving. It does flash through my mind that if Dr. Mullen wants to drug us and then kill us, the food would be a way to go. I notice Emma looking at it suspiciously, too.

As if reading our thoughts Ariel says, "He has never tried to trick me with the food. It's probably safe." She grabs a burger and starts to eat. After a minute Emma and I join her.

After we've eaten we know we have to make a decision. I don't know what to do—I'm not willing to go along with Dr. Mullen. I have to think of something else.

Just then the door opens and, well, I would say Ariel walks in. But it couldn't be Ariel, because she is sitting on her cot. Could it be another clone?

The girl closes the door behind her. Ariel is staring at her.

They are exact doubles. Then I recognize the outfit she is wearing.

"Eve?"

"Hello, Miranda."

"Eve! How on earth did you get here?"

"I used to live here," she says calmly. "And when you said you were in trouble, in a lab, I figured you must be here."

"How did you get here, though?"

"I hid in Dr. Mullen's van," she says, her tone very matter of fact.

"You did *what*?" I can't believe my ears.

"After he had been stopped for a few minutes, I got out. I waited until Bob went outside to smoke. Then I walked in. I did not hurry. People are used to seeing me here."

"But they think you are me," Ariel says. "I'm the one they think lives here now."

"I want to help you to escape," Eve says.

"Eve, that's wonderful," I say, "but we can't put you in danger."

"What danger?" says Eve. "I do not mind being here. I miss it. It is my home."

"Is this the place you were homesick for?" I ask.

"Yes."

"But wouldn't you rather be with us, in a real home?"

"I do not know," Eve answers. "I am not used to your home. I have to pretend. And I am not very good at it. I do not know how to be Ariel." She pauses. "I watched carefully at the drama class to see if I could learn how to pretend but I was not able to fool you."

Suddenly, I have an idea. "Oh! Oh! Oh!" I exclaim.

Emma looks at me hopefully. "You've had a brainwave!"

203

"Yes. Yes. What if Eve does stay? Only she pretends to be Ariel? And Ariel pretends to be Eve? Wanna bet Dr. Mullen saw Eve come in on the cameras? He probably knows she's here." I look at Ariel. "Do you think you could pull it off?"

"Pretend to be Eve?" she says. "I don't know. I've never met Eve, remember."

She's right. I draw them together. "Eve, meet Ariel. Ariel, meet Eve."

Ariel smiles at Eve. Eve looks solemnly at Ariel.

"But Eve," I say, "if you agree with my plan, you'd have to stay here."

"I am dying," she says simply. "I wish to do that where things are ... familiar."

"But you would have to pretend to be Ariel," I caution, "and you weren't too good at it before."

"I can tell her what to do," Ariel offers.

I look at Emma and draw her aside. "What do you think? Would it be awful to leave her here?"

"Not if she wants to be here. We can try to come back for her later," Emma suggests. "And let's face it, it might be our only chance."

I think. I have to take care of Emma too, and Ariel. I can't be responsible for Dr. Mullen killing anyone.

"All right," I say, turning back to them. "Let's do it. First you have to change clothes." I look up at the camera to be sure it is still off. It seems to be, so the girls quickly switch clothes. Ariel has her hair pulled back in a ponytail, Eve is wearing hers straight. Ariel gives Eve her scrunchy and Eve pulls her hair back.

"Now," I say, "I'm going to ask Ariel a question. Eve, you listen. Ariel, how do you feel about this decision?"

204

"Okay, I'm not crazy about it because I really liked being with Miranda and going to school and all that, but it's logical so we have to do it." Ariel answers. Eve mimics her, just like in the mirror exercise.

I turn to Eve. "Eve, why did you hide in my van?"

"I am made for Miranda. She said she was in trouble. I must help her."

Ariel copies her.

Soon Ariel realizes that she just needs to remember the way she spoke before she began living with me. It's easier for her. Eve has the more difficult task.

"Remember," I say to Eve, "how we had to pretend to be characters in that acting class?"

"Yes," she replies.

"Well, just pretend the same way. And don't worry. Ariel is upset now, so she's not happy the way she was at home. Use contractions, like 'can't' instead of 'cannot.' And sometimes try to be a little cranky or not nice."

"I am nice!" Ariel objects.

"But you've learned to think for yourself," I say. "And that's an important part of Ariel."

"He will discover I am Eve soon," Eve says. "When I get sick again."

The door opens.

"Ah, Number Eleven, I saw you come in." Dr. Mullen says as he walks into the room.

I knew it. He must watch everything. But he is talking to Ariel, not Eve. So far it's working.

He speaks sternly. "You should not have come back. I told you what you had to do."

"But I cannot pretend well," Ariel says, pretending to be

205

Eve. "I could not fool Miranda."

"You do not need to fool Miranda," he points out. "You only need to fool her parents. And they are convinced you are Ten." He turns to us. "Well, what is the decision then?"

I step forward. "I think you are horrible," I say. "Really horrible. But we can't think of any way out of here unless you let us out. And I can't be responsible for you hurting Emma. Or Ariel. So we've decided to leave Ariel behind. She says she'll do it. She doesn't want us to be hurt."

"Of course she doesn't," he says. "Of course not. She was brought up to serve you. To give up her life for you. But she doesn't have to die now. She'll be a valuable prototype. And we'll all be happy."

"What about Eve?" I say. "Can't you do anything for her?"

"I'm afraid not," he replies. "Well, time to get you girls home. Let's put those bikes in my van and I'll drop you at Emma's house. Ten, you come with me."

Before I can stop her, Ariel turns. Reflex action, I suppose. But then Eve, who is supposed to go with him, says, "He said Ten! Not Eleven. Honestly!" She turns to me, talking very fast, just like Ariel. "Goodbye, sis. It was great while it lasted. I had lots of fun. I'll, I'll always remember you ..."

She throws her arms around me. I can feel her tears on my cheeks. They are real tears, not fake. And I suddenly wonder if she was pretending when she was talking to me—convincing me she'd rather be here than at home with me so that she could save us.

She pulls away, and then hugs Emma too. "Bye, Emma." She looks at Ariel. "Goodbye, Eve."

"I'll be back for you girls in a minute," Dr. Mullen says.

They leave. We stand there. Fearful of talking, afraid we've been discovered. Time goes by slowly; every second seems like hours.

But Dr. Mullen returns about ten minutes later without Eve. He leads us down the hall and out the front door. It is dark. The sky is clear and full of stars. The air smells so sweet. I take a deep breath and realize how close I came to never taking another one. We get into the van. I'm still not sure I can trust the good doctor, but within fifteen minutes we are at Emma's house unloading the bikes.

"Remember," Dr. Mullen says. "Tell no one. If you do I cannot guarantee Ariel's safety. Or any of yours." He drives off, leaving us standing outside the house.

Chapter 31

The three of us hurry into the house. Emma's parents run over to us, frantic.

Emma's mom says, "Where have you girls been? Miranda's mother called because she couldn't find Ariel and was worried, thought maybe she'd come here. And I told her you girls were at her house, although I wondered what had happened to your big date, and she said no, you were here, and we've all been worried sick!"

She pauses to catch her breath. Emma's dad is standing just behind her. He's got a temper, and I can see he isn't pleased. Actually they both have tempers. But at least you know where you stand with them. Unlike my parents, who are always calm, except it turns out they are lying to you half the time.

Emma is obviously at a loss for words. What do we do? I decide we need to tell someone. They already know about me and about Dr. Mullen.

"We need to tell them, Emma," I say.

"What? About Eve?" she replies.

"This might be her only chance," I reply.

Ariel is quiet for once.

"Tell us what?" asks Emma's dad, suddenly more concerned than angry.

"Come on," her mom says, "and sit down. Anyone want

208

something to drink?"

She gives us juice. While waiting for the kettle to boil so she can make tea, she calls my parents, assures them we're all right, and suggests we stay the night as it's awfully late to drive all that way.

When we're all settled in at the kitchen table, I tell them what's happened. I try to shorten it, but it's at least an hour before I'm finished and they've asked all their questions. Emma doesn't have a lot to complain about on the parent front. They are both calm and neither of them look at me as if I am some kind of freak. It doesn't seem to occur to them.

"Dr. Mullen has to be stopped," Dr. Green says. His voice is grim and his expression is even grimmer.

"But how? If we call the police, everyone will know about Miranda and Ariel," Emma objects. "Their lives wouldn't be worth living—TV cameras around them every single second. It would be horrible."

"Let me think." Dr. Green says. "Wait a minute." He looks at Mrs. Green. "The security guards at the clinic? I handpicked them. They're tough and loyal to me."

Mrs. Green nods. Dr. Green motions for us to leave the room while he makes his calls.

The three of us flop down in the living room. I obviously crash right out because the next thing I know Mrs. Green is waking me up. Ariel and Emma are just waking up too.

"Girls," she says, "it's almost midnight. Dr. Green is going with the guards over to the lab. We need to know where it is."

Emma opens her mouth when I interrupt. "I'm not sure, are you, Emma? I'd have to go," I say. "I could show them."

"If you describe the streets they will be able to find it," Mrs. Green says firmly. "There's no need for you girls to go."

209

"But we want to, Mom!" Emma objects. "Eve is there, and that horrible Dr. Mullen is so creepy. I want to make sure they've got him. Besides, Eve doesn't know Dad. She'll be scared."

Mrs. Green goes out and then comes back in a few minutes.

"You can go over there in your dad's car," she says, although she doesn't look thrilled about it.

We scramble up and get ready, first telling the guards—who are waiting in the kitchen and who are even bigger than Bob and his pal—where the lab is. Emma grabs us all jackets. It feels cool out now, even though it was so hot earlier.

We pile into Dr. Green's car, Emma in front, Ariel and me in the back. I go from being tired to being wired with nervous energy.

As we drive through the night, it is completely quiet in the car. It reminds me of that first night trip I took with my mother to the clinic—was it only a few months ago now? I was afraid I was about to die. But maybe death isn't the worst thing in the world. Back then I didn't know what I really had to be afraid of. Then I found out that I was a clone. I found out that my parents, whom I loved, were willing to do anything to cheat death. And it forced me to think about who I am. I look at Ariel sitting beside me. She is staring out the window. I wonder if she is thinking the same thing. Who are we really?

Ariel takes my hand. "I'm scared," she whispers.

"Why?"

"If Eve and I can be switched so easily, what does it matter if I'm here or if she's here?"

So she has been thinking similar thoughts. Doesn't that prove what she just said? We are so much alike, engineered to be the same, that we even think the same. Maybe there is no

210

point.

Dr. Green speaks. "I couldn't help but overhear, Ariel. May I suggest something?"

"Yes," she says.

"You have a soul," he says. "That's unique to you. At least I believe that. Even if you don't believe in a soul, the truth is that you and Eve and Miranda are all different in ways that science can't quite explain. You'll make different choices in your lives. Maybe when you look at those choices you won't like some of them. So you'll change. Life is complicated.

"Ariel," he adds, "it isn't easy growing up. Even if you aren't a clone! Right, Emma?"

"Yeah," Emma says. "That's for sure."

"Let me tell you a little secret," he continues. "Life isn't that easy when you're an adult either." He pauses. "I had two twins as patients a number of years ago. One developed cancer, the other didn't. And yet they were identical in every way, they were brought up the same way, they ate the same way, and they both did the same activities. So far, we can't explain why one developed cancer and the other didn't. Life isn't a straight path. If it was—well, we'd all know where we were going."

"That would be nice," Emma says, "with road maps and directions!"

"If only ..." I sigh.

All conversation is cut short as we turn into the drive that leads to the lab. My heart is in my throat. What if Dr. Mullen found out about Eve after we left? What would he do to her? Did we make the right choice? It seemed we did at the time, but maybe I was just looking for an easy way to save my skin.

The cars pull up to the front door. We watch as the two guards go to the front door. Much to my surprise, they enter

211

the building right away. I wait. Will Dr. Mullen try to escape? What will happen?

Finally I see the men come out. No one is with them. I can't stand it. I get out of the car.

"Miranda!" Dr. Green warns me, but then he gets out too. One of the guards comes toward us.

"What's happening?" Dr. Green says.

"I don't know," the guard answers. "There's nobody there. The whole place is empty."

I am so stunned I can't speak for a moment.

"It can't be!" I exclaim.

And then I'm running. Emma and Ariel are right behind me. We burst through the unlocked door. I open the first door, to the room that had all the computers in it. Empty! We race from room to room finding the same thing in each one— nothing! The cots are still in the room we were held in, but all the equipment, computers, people, are gone. The three of us stop finally, out of breath.

"He must have known we'd go to your father," I say to Emma. "I don't know how your father can say Ariel and I are individuals," I add, disgusted. "Dr. Mullen knew exactly what we'd do! And he should. He made us!"

I sink down on the floor, head in my hands. "Poor Eve. He'll find out soon. And he'll be really mad."

Emma sits beside me. "He knew you'd tell, not because he made you but because he knows you are a good person and that you'd be more worried about Eve than about your own safety."

"But do you think we'll be safe?" Ariel asks. "Maybe he'll be mad at us. Maybe he's watching us this very minute." She looks up at the camera on the wall.

212

I get a chill down my spine. "He could be," I say.

"Ugh," Emma grimaces.

We hurry outside.

"What if Ariel is right?" I say, once outside. "He'll know now for sure about Eve."

"He's probably too busy getting out of town to be keeping tabs on us," Emma says.

"Come on, girls," Dr. Green calls. "Time to go. There's nothing left for us to do here."

I put one arm around Emma and the other around Ariel and we walk back to the car together. It's all over for now.

Chapter 32

I am sitting in bed thinking about Eve, because it is exactly a month since she and Dr. Mullen disappeared. I stare out the window. The sun is shining, as usual, and Ariel is sound asleep, the morning breeze making the drapes billow just over her bed. My phone rings and I jump.

"Hello?"

"Miranda?"

It's Eve!

"Eve!"

"Yes, yes, it is me!"

"I was just thinking about you!"

"I know. Because it is a month ago exactly that Dr. Mullen took me. I had been planning to call you today. But I only have a minute. It was complicated to arrange this." She hurries on. "I know you must be worried about me. But when Dr. Mullen found out it was really me and not Ariel, he vowed to cure me so he could use me to showcase his creations. I don't know whether he can cure me or not, but he seems to think it is possible. He will not be able to use my DNA, as he would have done with Ariel, but I will serve as a model for his clients. I cannot make him angry, though. He is my one chance." She pauses. "I miss you."

"I miss you too," I say fervently. "But I am so glad you are alive."

214

"Dr. Mullen saved enough of Ariel's DNA so he can carry on with his experiments. And he is showing me off to many strangers."

"But how is your health?"

"Will I live, do you mean?"

"Yes, yes."

"I do not know, but I am on a new drug and I will soon have surgery and he says we will know in a month or two."

"Will you call? I want to help get you back."

"I will try. Now I have to go."

"Wait, wait!" I try to think. "Where are you?"

"If I tell you, I know you will put yourself in danger."

I hear something. It sounds like a foghorn. "Are you by the ocean?"

"Miranda, I have to go."

"Come home," I say.

"I'll try."

The line goes dead.

Ariel is sitting up in bed. "Eve's alive!"

I nod.

Ariel comes over and sits on my bed. By rights she should be in her own room, but she says she gets lonely in there and half the time she sleeps in here with me. "What did she say?"

"She sounded all right," I say. "She thinks Dr. Mullen might be able to cure her. He's trying. And he saved your DNA and is using it."

"To make his perfect babies," Ariel says.

"Apparently."

We sit for a moment. I'm just glad Eve is alive. I thought she might be dead. I've cried many nights. I've worried about my decision. I've wondered if I didn't take the easy way out—

the end justifying the means. I've wondered if Dr. Mullen has somehow programmed that into me. Maybe my so-called goodness was only my wanting to be good because it produced the desired result: peace with my parents and teachers.

What does it mean to act with goodness, for the right reasons, without thinking about the result? But we never know what the result of our actions will be. I was sure Dr. Mullen would let Eve die. Instead the opposite has happened. I suppose the only thing I know for sure is what Dr. Green said—life is complicated.

"What are you thinking?" Ariel says.

"A bunch of stuff," I reply.

I don't like to talk to her about all of this because I don't want her to feel any of it is her fault. It isn't! She has enough to get used to. We're on holiday now, school is over, so we're home more and Mother and Father have to deal with her more. In a way it's almost funny because she's not at all the goody-goody I used to be. Yesterday she went out with Jen and came home two hours late and was hardly sorry or worried or anything! I wouldn't have dreamed of doing anything like that.

Of course, Mother and Father are still recovering from the news that I was right about Eve and Dr. Mullen. I'm pretty sure they didn't have anything to do with his nefarious plans. Pretty sure, but not one hundred percent positive. I mean, if they could lie that way once—the way they did to me, letting me believe I was a normal kid—they could certainly lie again.

Father keeps taking me out to dinner so we can talk "one on one," and I listen. He assures me that I can trust them. I'm just keeping my options open.

"I'm glad Dr. Mullen is taking care of her," Ariel sighs. "I

216

only wish she was free. Not his—"

"His lab rat," I finish for her.

"Isn't there a way we can find her?" Ariel asks.

"Let's think about it," I reply. "And talk to Emma."

"We'll see Emma at acting school today," Ariel reminds me.

"I know," I say.

Ariel is taking a class for younger kids at the same time as my class. Mother drives us. When I told them about Eve I also told them about our class. I don't want to live surrounded by lies anymore. They gave in, but it was funny when they tried to tell me I shouldn't lie to them. Funny in a weird way, not a laugh-out-loud way.

"Want to go for a swim?" Ariel asks. She looks at me hopefully. I have to smile back. Since I've got her back I don't get angry with her as easily. I'm just glad she's here safe and sound. Since I've lost Mother and Father as family I can trust, at least I have her. We've become pretty close.

I get up and look for my swimsuit.

"What are you thinking now?" Ariel says.

"I'm wondering what else Dr. Mullen is up to," I reply.

She looks at me. "I wonder, too."

Part Three

Chapter 33

"Will Miranda Martin please come to the office?"

I look up in surprise. Me? I'm never called to the office. I'm never in trouble. I'm Little Miss Perfect. In more ways than one.

"Miranda?" Mr. Edgers prompts me. "Are you going?"

I look at Emma. She shrugs, like, Don't look at me, I have no clue.

Slowly I gather my books, grab my knapsack and head for the door. I can't imagine what they might want me for. Unless someone's hurt—like Ariel. That gets me moving, and I reach the office in a minute. The secretary nods when she sees me and motions me toward Mrs. Dean's office. That can't be good. I peek in the door.

Mrs. Dean notices me and beckons me into the room, pointing to a seat.

"Is Ariel okay?" I ask, unable to wait for her to speak. I am clutching my knapsack as if it'll keep her from saying something I don't want to hear.

"Ariel is fine," she replies.

"My parents?"

"As far as I know, they're fine."

I am at a loss.

Mrs. Dean clears her throat. "Miranda," she says.

"Yes?"

221

"I really never thought I would need to have a conversation like this with you." She waits.

"Like what?" I ask.

"Come with me," she says and suddenly gets up. This is getting stranger and stranger. "Just leave your gear here."

I put my books and knapsack on the floor and follow her down the hallway—silent except for the sound of her high heels clicking on the floor. We get to the end of the hall at the back of the school and she opens the door to the outside. I am now completely mystified. She walks a short way down the path then turns back toward the building. Sprayed on the yellow stucco are large red letters: *Desert High Sucks!*

"Not very original," I comment.

"No," she agrees.

"I don't know who did it," I offer, "if that's what this is about."

"That's not what this is about, Miranda. We know who did it."

I stare at her. Why on earth involve me?

"See the camera there?" She points up to a spot on the building where a small camera is located.

"So whoever did it is stupid, as well as unoriginal," I say.

"Miranda, please stop this."

"Stop what?"

She puts her hands on her hips. "We know it was you. We have it recorded."

"*What*?"

"You heard me, Miranda."

"That's impossible! I didn't do it! Why would I?"

"I don't know why," she says, staring evenly at me. "You had to realize you'd be caught. You certainly aren't stupid."

222

"But I didn't!" I repeat. "How could you think for one minute I would ever do such a thing?" I pause, at a loss for words. "It's so, so ... *childish!*"

"We can certainly agree on that," Mrs. Dean says. She pauses for a moment and then says, "Miranda, if you have a problem you can tell me. Often these incidents are a simple cry for help. I know it must be hard for you—having your cousin, well, now your sister, come to live with your family."

"Well, that's true," I agree. "Ariel can be pretty annoying. But I'm okay. I even kinda am sorta fond of her now."

Mrs. Dean raises her eyebrows.

"Well, just because I don't express myself well while talking about her doesn't mean I don't like her. I do."

"You can't deny the evidence."

"May I see it, please?" I ask.

"Of course."

We take the same silent trip back to the office. I stand as Mrs. Dean loads the file on her computer, then plays it. The girl looks like me, all right. Almost exactly. She is spraying the wall, quickly, efficiently, seemingly with no nervousness at all. My heart sinks. "When was this taken?"

"This morning, around six o'clock."

"I was home, in bed."

"Can anyone vouch for you?"

"No, they were asleep."

"Miranda, it couldn't be anyone but you." She pauses. "Or Ariel."

Ariel has sprouted up over the summer. When she first came to live with us it was obvious she was younger than me. And it's still obvious because she hasn't developed any, shall we say, curves. She looks like she's eleven. But the girl in the video is wearing a loose sweatshirt and an Angels baseball cap on her head, hair tucked into it. Ariel had her hair cut over the summer, and she wears it in a really cute bob, unlike mine, which is long and straight. But the hat makes it impossible to tell anything that way. Still, to me, whoever that is looks like Ariel in age, like me in appearance. So what could that mean?

My mind starts racing, searching for an answer. Those clothes? I don't recognize them. It couldn't be Ariel. I'd know if she were up to something—wouldn't I? But if not me, or Ariel ... Eve? But Eve is with Dr. Mullen ...

I realize I need to say something to Mrs. D.

"Mrs. Dean, I'll pay for you to get the wall cleaned."

"Thank you, Miranda. Of course, your parents will be called."

"Of course."

"And I want you to see the school counselor. I've made an appointment for one o'clock today. Don't miss it."

"I won't."

She waits.

"You aren't ill again, are you?" she asks.

I immediately think back to the illness that almost killed me—and would have, without Ariel's sacrifice. But what if there is something else wrong with me now—like something wrong with my brain?

I gulp and answer, "Not as far as I know."

Could I have done it without realizing? Surely not! I woke up as usual in my bed only a few hours ago. Unless ... now my head starts to spin. Unless I did it and managed to then get myself back home. Or maybe it was Ariel ... I realize that Mrs. D. is staring at me and that, again, I need to say *something*.

"I'll do everything you say," I answer weakly.

224

"Fine. Go back to your class."

The lunch bell rings just as I reach class. I almost bump into Emma rushing out the door, no doubt coming to find me.

"So?" she asks.

"You won't believe it. Come with me. We need to talk."

We throw our books into our lockers, grab the brown bags we both brought today and head outside. When it's 115 degrees in September, mostly everyone stays inside, so we have the table at the back of the school to ourselves. We can see the graffiti from where we sit.

"Not too original," Emma comments.

"Exactly what I told Mrs. Dean."

"Mrs. Dean showed it to you?"

"That's not all she showed me. She has a video of me doing it."

"*What?*"

"Exactly my reaction." I grimace. "Sometimes I wonder if it's you who's my clone, not Ariel."

"But Miranda, what does that mean?"

"A variety of not especially attractive answers come to mind," I reply.

"Let's list them," Emma says, ever practical, as she takes a swig of water from her bottle. Only a minute out in the sun and we can both feel all the moisture evaporating from our bodies.

"Fine," I say with a sigh. "Option one. It was me and I was under some kind of spell."

"Or you are sick and don't know what you're doing," Emma says quietly, not looking at me.

"But I have no other symptoms—no headaches, no blurry vision, nothing. I feel totally normal."

225

"Well, that's something," Emma says. "So I doubt it's that. Let's move on. Option two?"

Neither of us want to dwell long on option one.

"Option two. It was Ariel and she is either sick or gone crazy."

"Don't like that one," Emma grimaces.

"Option three," I continue. "It's Eve."

We both fall silent for a moment, thinking about Eve.

"That's pretty unlikely," Emma says finally, "since Dr. Mullen has taken her away, and the chances of her escaping from him are close to nil. And why would she want to? He might be the only hope to cure her brain tumor! I mean, when she called you last she said Dr. Mullen had done something to help her and that she was getting better, right?"

"Which brings us to option four," I say. "There's a fourth clone."

"But surely we would have found out about a fourth clone by now," Emma objects.

"Why?" I counter. "Dr. Mullen could have hidden one somewhere and as she was growing up, kept her a secret. Now she's either escaped from him or is doing his bidding."

"And his bidding is what?" asks Emma. "To spray-paint graffiti on school walls?"

"It does sound kind of stupid," I say. "But I did get in trouble. And maybe that's the motive."

"But why would anyone want to get you in trouble?" Emma demands.

This stymies both of us so we resort to the next logical thing to do. Eat. Maybe it'll stimulate our brains.

Emma and I gave up on school cafeteria lunches ages ago and now always bring our own. Lorna has made me roast

226

turkey with cranberry sauce on whole grain bread. This is one of my all-time favorite sandwiches, but today I can hardly taste it. I gulp my water.

"Maybe Dr. Mullen is still mad at me for rescuing Ariel."

"He could be," Emma says. "Although he did already take Ariel's DNA. Well, I should say he did already *steal* her DNA," she corrects herself, "but maybe he wants an unlimited supply of DNA, i.e. Ariel *herself*, for his perfect babies scheme. So he gets you in trouble, damages your reputation. But I still don't see how the two are connected."

"Do you think he's plotting something," I ask.

"Maybe," Emma nods.

"You think I'm in for more trouble?"

Emma looks at me. "What do you think?"

"I think I'm in for more trouble," I sigh.

"Come on," says Emma, "let's get inside."

"We need to find Ariel," I say.

"Plus, there's no use having our brains fried, just when we need them," Emma says with a grin.

I try to smile back. But it isn't easy. Something inside me just wants to stay out here in the heat and the unrelenting sun, because it's quiet and peaceful and I have a very, very bad feeling. Whoever has done this doesn't have my best interests at heart, that's for sure.

Slowly I follow Emma into the cool hall. The door slams behind us with a huge bang and involuntarily I jump.

Chapter 34

We have two counselors at Desert High, Mrs. Sanchez and Mr. Bell. The general agreement at school is that the former is cool, the latter is a goof. Naturally I get stuck with Mr. Bell. We call him Mr. Saved by the Bell. He always has this crazy smile plastered on his face.

"Oh, you're getting bad grades? Laugh it up! Kids are picking on you? Let a smile be your guide!"

I suppress a sigh. What on earth am I going to tell him? Let's see: *Mr. Bell, I'm a clone of my dead sister Jessica, created by the mad scientist Dr. Mullen. My so-called sister, Ariel, is a clone of me. I discovered her at Dr. Mullen's lab when he was treating me for a rare illness. It turns out that my parents had her created as an insurance policy, in case I ever needed spare parts, but I wouldn't let them murder her for that. Instead she gave me half her liver, which cured me just fine, thank you, and then she came to live with us. She's four years younger than I am so she doesn't look exactly like me, but she will. And oh, yes, there's a third clone, Eve, who has a deadly brain tumor, who at first pretended to be Ariel and fooled me, and swapped herself for Ariel when Dr. Mullen wanted Ariel back, and tricked him, too, and also made him pretty mad. And now there's a fourth clone, we think, and it doesn't look good for me right now.*

Yeah, they'd lock me up in a second.

"Miranda?" Mr. Bell is looking at me curiously. "Miranda, you're talking to yourself."

"Did I say something out loud?" I ask, horrified.

"Something about things not looking too good for you."

"Oh," I say, relieved. "Well, that's true. They don't."

"I understand you refuse to admit you've done this, even though we have an actual recording?

"Maybe I'm sleepwalking?" I suggest, grasping at straws. "I've heard that crazy things can happen when you sleepwalk."

Mr. Bell brightens. "That's true! Why, that's a perfectly logical explanation."

I can't believe he's falling for it. But his brows knit together.

"Still, what we need to figure out, Miranda, is why your subconscious would make such a statement. You have a 4.0 average. You dance brilliantly. Everything you do, you do well. Perhaps you are putting too much pressure on yourself to be perfect."

"But I have to be perfect," I say.

"Why?" he asks.

"I'm just made that way, I guess."

"Miranda, I must disagree," Mr. Bell counters. "We can choose who we are."

"Do you really believe that?"

"Of course I do! Otherwise I'd be out of business, wouldn't I?"

"Do you choose to be Mr. Smiley Face all the time?" I blurt out.

The grin fades from his face for a moment and then returns stronger than ever.

"Touché," he declares. "But yes, I do. Okay, I'll admit I'm naturally cheerful. But I could easily make myself miserable,

229

I'm sure."

"No, you couldn't," I object. "See, I upset you for a second, but your default position is to be happy. Mine is to be perfect!"

"Let's say for a moment that's true," he concedes. "I have read studies that suggest we all have a certain set point. People who win lotteries go back to being the way they were about a year after they win. People who have bad luck—become paralyzed, for instance—also go back to their set point, happy or depressed, a year or so after the terrible event. Your set point is, perhaps, to be perfect. But what if a part of you doesn't want to be perfect anymore."

Wrong, I think. A part of whoever that clone is doesn't want me to be perfect anymore.

"Or," he suggests, "are your parents pressuring you to do well?"

"No," I sigh, "they think I'm perfect no matter what I do."

"That's both good and bad," he says. "You might feel you always have to live up to that."

I need to wrap this up. After all, I can't really level with him.

"Maybe you're right," I agree. "So what do I do?"

"Just cut yourself some slack," he advises.

"That's it?"

"That's it."

"So, can I go?"

"Sure. But you'll need to check in with me twice a week for the next month or so. Agreed?"

"Agreed," I say.

Well, that wasn't so bad. I start to walk back to class.

The PA system crackles: *"Will Miranda Martin please come to the office?"*

I stop dead. My heart sinks. Now what?

230

I turn slowly and head over to the office. Classes are changing; the halls are full. Everyone is looking at me. A few kids shout at me. "In trouble again? Oooh, Miranda, bad girl!"

Bad girl? Wow, never thought I'd hear that said about me. I get to the office. Two police officers are in the outer office talking to Mrs. Dean.

"Please," she says to them. "In my office."

She shows them the way. I follow, heart in my throat.

"Miranda Martin?" The police officer is a young woman. Her partner is an older man.

"Yes?"

"We have evidence that you have been shoplifting at SuperMart."

I stare at her. "I've never shopped at SuperMart in my life."

"I didn't say shop," she says sternly. "I said *shoplifting*."

"It wasn't me," I say, but I know it's in vain. They'll have it recorded.

"We have the evidence. We showed a still from the security camera to your principal, who identified you. It wasn't too bright of you to wear a Desert High sweatshirt, which led us right here to the school."

"When did this supposedly happen?" I ask.

"Yesterday afternoon at five o'clock."

"I was at home with my sister," I say.

"How old is your sister?"

"She's just turned eleven."

"Were there any adults present?"

"No."

"Well," she says, "we'd better speak to your sister."

Mrs. Dean calls the middle school office and asks them to send Ariel over. We all stand around awkwardly while we wait

231

for her to arrive. When she comes in looking happy, curious, and so innocent, I get a rush of feeling for her and want to dash over and give her a big hug. I don't, though.

"Ariel," Mrs. Dean says, "what did you do yesterday?"

"I was at school," she answers with certainty. "And after that I hung out with Miranda," she adds rather proudly.

She loves to hang out with me, but I'm usually busy with Emma or my other friends and I encourage her to hang with her own friends. Still, her favorite thing is for the two of us to swim in the pool or go shopping. Yesterday, even though it was way too hot, I agreed to a swim.

"Where were your parents?" Mrs. Dean asks.

"I am unsure," she answers, "but they were not at home."

The policewoman hesitates for a moment. Ariel certainly seems to be telling the truth, and I'm sure the policewoman is experienced at picking up on whether people are lying or not. "Thank you, Ariel. You can go back to class."

Ariel leaves, and the policewoman turns to me. "This is a very serious offence. Do you understand?"

"Yes, I do. But really, I didn't do it! You can see that Ariel and I were together."

"You might have told her what to say," the woman says.

"Well, I didn't! Can I at least see the video?"

"The store intends to press charges. You can see the video at some point."

"I would really like to see it," I insist.

The two officers look at each other. "We can show you the still photo," the woman says.

It's grainy and not a great shot. The hair is under a cap and the sweatshirt covers the body, but it looks to me like a younger version of me. If Ariel hadn't been with me, I'd have said it was, in fact, her. I wonder why in both cases the adults are jumping to the conclusion it is me and not Ariel. I guess the Desert High sweatshirt is enough to make them think that it's someone from the high school. Not that I'd ever consider pointing them in Ariel's direction! Still ...

"May I call my parents?"

"Yes, all right."

I use the phone and call. Mother, thank goodness, is home.

"Mother, please stay calm." I quickly explain what has happened.

"It wasn't you, Miranda?"

"No, Mother."

"Of course it wasn't. You would never do such a thing. But what about Ariel? She could have done it!" Of course it's my mother who immediately jumps to that conclusion!

"We were together," I say, trying to stay calm and not blow up at her.

"I'll be right there."

I hang up. "My mother is on her way."

We wait for about twenty minutes, me sitting on a chair in the outer office. Mother and Father arrive and Mrs. Dean shows them into her office. After a few minutes the police come out, walk past without a glance and keep going. Mrs. Dean calls me back into the office.

Father speaks first. "Miranda, I've assured Mrs. Dean that this is some kind of hoax. We've seen the photo and although we admit it looks like you, it could easily be someone made up to look like you. Mr. Gonzales, our lawyer, will be dealing with the store and I doubt they will press charges after he gets them to see reason."

Mrs. Dean looks at me with some relief. "Well, I'm sure

233

you'll get this all straightened out," she says lamely. "Do you want to go home with your parents now?"

"Maybe that would be best," my father says, not letting me answer. "Ariel will have to come, too."

"I'll just get my books," I say.

Instead of going straight to my locker, I head to chem lab and peek through the window until Emma sees me. In a minute she's out in the hall whispering with me.

"What was it?"

"Only the police! Caught me on video—shoplifting at SuperMart!"

"You? At SuperMart? That's a laugh!"

"Emma, my parents are here. They're taking me and Ariel home."

"Don't worry, Miranda," she says. "We'll figure this out."

She goes back to class and I head back to the office after grabbing my knapsack and books. Ariel is already in the outer office with her stuff.

Once we're all in the car Mother starts. "Mrs. Dean told us about the graffiti as well. Now Miranda, can you assure us that wasn't you?"

"Yes," I say, exasperated. "It was not me."

"Ariel," mother says sternly. "Perhaps it was you?"

"Me?" Ariel repeats. "I fail to understand. Why would I paint graffiti and steal? I would never shame Miranda in such a way."

I notice that when she gets upset she reverts back to the formal way of speaking she learned in the lab from Dr. Mullen.

"Where are we going?" I ask, noticing Father hasn't taken the exit that leads to our ranch.

"To the clinic, of course, to see your doctor," Mother

234

replies. "They're expecting us."

I almost object, but then when I think about it for a moment I realize that I'm actually a bit relieved. At least Emma and I can rule out my being crazy because of some sort of tumor or something ... *if* all the tests come back clean.

I roll my eyes. Could my life be any more complicated?

I go through all the tests—bloodwork, an MRI and a physical exam by Dr. Corne. But this time all my results are normal. Mother looks years younger after Dr. Corne tells us the good news. And I must admit it's a weight off my mind. Ariel is also put through all the tests. Dr. Corne seems pleased—he almost smiles—to see that Ariel has recovered so well. Father tells him some tall tale about this new drug one of his clinics is developing. And Dr. Corne has no idea it was Eve who was so ill anyway. It's kind of mind blowing to see how easily Father can pull the wool over Dr. Corne's eyes. Dr. Corne believes Father is a good person who tells the truth and so he believes everything he says. Creepy.

On the way home Father again turns to the problem at hand.

"What worries me is that whoever is behind this seems intent on harming you," Father says, as he drives.

"I know!" I agree. "That's what Emma and I think. But why?"

"Why indeed?"

"Maybe we shouldn't go away this weekend," Mother says to Father.

"I don't like leaving either," he agrees. "But we need this deal." He thinks for a minute. "We'll cut it short, be sure to be back by Monday. Do you think you'll be all right?" he asks me.

"If I don't end up in jail, you mean?"

235

Although normally I'd be glad to be rid of them, I'm a little nervous now about their leaving. I mean, who knows what else someone will try to pin on me?

"If this deal doesn't go through, we'll be ruined financially," Father says. "The buyout from our clinics was just enough for us to be able to acquire this company. It's a great deal and you'll be set for life. This is important too, Miranda."

"I think I'm smart enough to make my own living," I answer sullenly.

"You are. But," he answers slowly, as if reluctant to say it, "we don't know what kind of medical costs you and Ariel might incur."

"No," I snap, "we don't."

Who knows what the cloning might cause. Premature aging? Cancers? Madness? I sigh.

"We'll get back as soon as the deal is signed," Mother assures me. "In the meantime stay close to home. All right? Mr. Gonzales will be on call all weekend in case you need him. He won't let anyone put you in jail, no need to worry about that. In fact by the time he's finished with SuperMart they'll be wishing they never bothered with that video."

For once I'm glad to have one of their ruthless cohorts on my side.

But I have a bad feeling. If Dr. Mullen is behind this, why stop at shoplifting? He must have other nasty surprises up his sleeve. Just how far will he go? But the bigger question is, why? *Why* is this happening?

236

Chapter 35

It's Saturday morning. The phone wakes me up. It is Emma. She is screaming into the receiver. Something about N. *N*?

"Emma, stop!" I exclaim. "What? I can't understand you."

"CNN!" she shouts.

"What about it?"

"CNN. Turn it on!"

I grab the remote from the floor where I tossed it last night and turn on the TV just as Ariel walks into the room. She points to the screen and shouts, "Dr. Mullen!"

"Shshsh!" I grab her arm and pull her onto the bed.

Dr. Mullen is speaking. "Yes, I repeat, I have created the first human clone."

I stop breathing. Ariel lets out something between a gasp and a cry.

I whisper into the phone. "Has he said my name yet?"

"No, no," Emma screams back. "Not yet. Quiet."

I clutch the phone and listen. And stare. Underneath Dr. Mullen is a headline that announces in bold letters: **CLINIC IN BELIZE**.

"Belize?"

"Belize is a country situated in Central America," Ariel states.

Then a thought strikes me. I'm probably still dreaming. That's it! This is, of course, the nightmare I've feared ever

237

since I found out that I was the first human clone. Discovery. CNN and all the rest camped out at my doorstep. School an impossibility. My friends looking at me like I'm some sort of— well, like what I am. Not quite human. Unable to protect Ariel from the media, unable to lead a normal life. I close my eyes and will myself to wake up.

"Did you hear that?"

I had tuned out. Why listen? It's all a dream anyhow.

"No," I say.

Emma is screaming into the phone again. "It's not you!"

"What?" I say.

"Listen! Look!"

A picture fills the screen. A beautiful face. A perfect face. Black hair. Large blue eyes. A baby.

"Adam," Dr. Mullen is saying. "We call him Adam. He is the clone of a young man who died all too young. His parents saved some tissue. And this, this is the result."

The camera pulls back. A nurse walks onto the stage holding a small bundle and then presents it to the camera. The crowd of reporters gasps.

"Emma," I say into the phone. "This is a dream, right?"

I know how silly a question that is, but it's okay to be silly in dreams. I would like to wake up though.

"Miranda," Emma says, finally not screaming, "this is no dream. You are awake. I swear."

"You'd swear in a dream."

"Get Ariel to pinch you."

"What will that prove?" I say. "She could pinch me in a dream."

The call waiting beeps. I look. It's Mother.

"That's my mother," I say.

238

"Is she part of the dream too?"

"Hang on."

"Miranda?" says Mother.

"Yes."

"Are you watching TV, by any chance?"

"Yes."

"Now stay calm."

"I'm calm. I'm dreaming."

"No, dear, you aren't. Unless it's the same dream the rest of the world is having."

The phone drops from my hand.

"Miranda?" I hear her voice from far away.

Ariel picks up the receiver. "Mother?"

I can't hear what they are saying. I stare at the TV.

Dr. Mullen is speaking. "Adam is healthy and completely normal in every way."

"Mother and Father are catching the first flight home," Ariel announces. "And Emma is on her way over. It appears," she adds, "that this weekend will be slightly more interesting than we expected."

I continue to stare at the screen.

"We'd better hear the rest," I say. "He could name us next."

The news conference seems to drag on forever. Ariel and I sit and watch, waiting, waiting, for Dr. Mullen to tell the world about us. But then it's over. Well, the story isn't over. CNN is now interviewing every scientist and senator they can find. But nothing about us. Nothing.

"I don't understand," I say to Ariel. "I'm the first human clone. Why is Dr. Mullen saying it's this boy?"

"Adam," Ariel says.

"Adam," I repeat. "Poor kid. Still, I don't get it."

239

"Perhaps," Ariel suggests, "Adam's parents want the world to know. Or it was part of the deal they made with Dr. Mullen."

"And we didn't want the world to know," I reply. "Plus he can't tell the world about us—he was going to murder you for your liver, and who knows how many other clones may have died. This way, he's done nothing illegal."

"Yes, that is accurate," she agrees.

Lorna comes in.

"I thought I heard you calling."

I've never figured out how much Lorna knows. She's not stupid. She must know a lot. But every time I've asked her she just shrugs and says, "Your parents do what's best, Miranda."

"There's quite a news story on CNN," I say. "The first human clone. And Dr. Mullen is announcing it."

She goes pale. "They give a name?"

"Yes," I answer. "Come on, Lorna. Tell me. You know all about this, don't you?"

"I know some things," Lorna answers reluctantly. "What name did they give?"

"Adam," Ariel interjects.

"Adam? But that's a boy."

"It appears that Dr. Mullen has cloned a boy," I confirm.

"Well, well," Lorna nods. "What do you two want for breakfast?"

"Breakfast?" I exclaim in disbelief. "Who could eat?"

"*I* could," Ariel says. "Could I have a red-pepper omelet please, Lorna? And pancakes?"

I stare at Ariel. "You're joking, right?"

"No," Ariel replies. "I'm hungry!"

"Emma is on her way over, Lorna," I say. "Could you make enough pancakes for her, too?"

240

Lorna nods. "Emma can always eat," she says with approval. "You should be more like that."

I go to the bathroom, scrub my face and brush my teeth, then put on brown capris and a short-sleeved brown-and-green striped shirt. Talk about being programmed—despite the catastrophe I still am picky about how I dress! When I emerge I see that Ariel has also gotten dressed. She's in jeans and her new sandals and an orange Polo T-shirt and she's watching TV again.

"Dr. Fisher. Do you think this is the real thing?" the CNN anchor asks.

"We have no way to know unless they allow us to verify the entire process independently."

"I understand," says the anchor, "that a very large sum of money has already been offered to the parents for their story. And that the publishers have hired their own medical team."

"Yes, I've heard that as well," the doctor answers. "I'd love to be part of that team."

The doorbell rings.

"Emma!" I exclaim. "Thank goodness."

Chapter 36

"Is that pancakes I smell?" Emma asks as she waves goodbye to Josh, who has just dropped her off.

"Yes," I say, punching her on the shoulder.

"Just because the world as we know it is coming to an end doesn't mean a person can't be hungry," Emma protests.

I follow her and Ariel to the kitchen and watch as they tuck into their breakfasts. I eat half a grapefruit, picked fresh from our tree, and a piece of toast with marmalade. I steal a corner of Ariel's omelet.

"Hey!" she protests.

"So now what?" I ask the two of them, ignoring Ariel's dirty look.

"I'm not sure," Emma says, waiting until Lorna is out of the room. "So far it looks like this won't affect you and Ariel. Maybe Dr. Mullen is going to leave you out of this altogether."

"If you think we're getting out of this free and clear," I say grimly, "you've got another think coming. No good can come of this. Something is bound to go wrong. People are going to find out about us. After all, they'll be snooping into everything Dr. Mullen has ever done. Plus, we can't forget, there may even be a fourth clone. Someone is trying to get me in trouble, and it has to be connected to this announcement somehow. I feel like my head is going to explode."

"What about your dad?" I ask Emma. "Can he tell us what

242

to do?"

"He could if he wasn't hiking with my mom in the desert," Emma says. "But they're supposed to be home tomorrow. I've paged him. If they aren't out of range, maybe they'll come home sooner."

"So both our parents are out of town on the very weekend Dr. Mullen makes this huge announcement."

Emma stares at me.

"You think he planned it that way?"

"What do you think?" I ask.

"He has the resources to spy on us of course," she says slowly. "It *is* a weird coincidence."

Ariel asks, "What do we do while we wait for them to return?"

"Try to keep our heads from exploding," Emma suggests.

I slip out of the kitchen and walk to the pool, sinking into one of the chairs. I don't understand how Emma and Ariel can be treating all this so lightly, digging into breakfast as if this is just another day.

Today is a disaster of the first order. In all likelihood my life will be different from this moment on. It's true that, in a way, my life changed irrevocably as soon as I discovered I was a clone. But at least I could hope for, imagine, a normal life. After all, no one in the outside world knew. Now they are bound to find out, no matter how hard we try to stop them.

Another, more troubling thought occurs to me. Perhaps I *will* have to come forward. If I don't, Dr. Mullen will be viewed as some sort of genius; he'll be revered, instead of shown up for what he is—an evil, horrible man, out for himself and no one else. A murderer. Someone who sees us as property to sell, not human. With enough money, enough support, how many

243

more of us could he create? Yet, if I expose Dr. Mullen, I'll be exposing not only myself but also Ariel and my parents.

My parents could go to jail for conspiracy to murder! Then what would happen to me and Ariel? Some horrible foster home where we would be viewed as freaks? Not to mention the guilt of seeing my parents suffer in prison.

I don't hear Emma and don't realize she's followed me until she sits on the wicker chair next to me.

"How are you?" she asks.

"Brain exploding as we speak."

"I know, me too. This has so many implications for everyone, doesn't it? Like my dad, who knew all about it but didn't turn in your parents. Even he could get in trouble, maybe lose his medical license."

"I hadn't thought of that," I say. "It just gets worse and worse."

"True," Emma agrees, "but I don't think we should upset Ariel any more than we need to. She doesn't realize what this could mean."

"Yeah, you're right."

"So what should we do?" she asks.

I put my head in my hands. I have a strong urge to burst into tears. We can hear the phone ring and soon Ariel is out on the patio, phone still in hand. She puts it down on the table.

"Your parents are at the airport in Frankfurt. They won't be home till tomorrow morning, though."

"Just as well," I mutter. "They'll only make things worse, no doubt."

Ariel grimaces. "Miranda, you are very hard on them. They have been trying to make it up to you. They love you." She pauses. "You are fortunate."

The phone rings again. It's a number I don't recognize right away. I answer.

"Miranda," a small voice says.

"Yes."

"It's Eve."

"Eve!" I shout at Emma and Ariel. "It's Eve!"

"Is she all right?" Emma asks.

"Are you all right?" I repeat.

"So far."

"What does that mean?" I ask.

"Dr. Mullen seems to have forgotten all about me. I don't know where I am. Locked up somewhere. He hasn't been to visit in weeks. Not even to do tests on me or anything."

"Maybe that's a good thing," I suggest.

"Perhaps," Eve replies. "He says I am cured."

"But that's wonderful," I say, giving a thumbs up to Emma and Ariel.

"Yes. Except now the headaches are back. And he's lost interest in me. And I don't know what it all means."

"Well, first thing you have to do," I say, shaking my head at Emma and Ariel, "is find out where you are. We need to get you out of there. Who's minding you?"

"A couple of nurses."

"What are they like?"

"Bored."

"Bored," I muse. "Well, then you should be able to take advantage of any lapses they have. Or outsmart them. You're calling here. How did you manage that?"

"I lifted the phone from the living room."

I check the phone display again. Dr. Mullen must be getting sloppy because he hasn't blocked the number. I can see it's a

245

760 area code.

"You're here! Right here in the desert. You just need to get out of there and we'll find you."

"Must go."

And then, *click*, the line goes dead.

"You heard?" I ask Emma and Ariel.

"She's here?" says Emma.

"And I thought Dr. Mullen would take her far away so the authorities wouldn't find him—or her," I say.

"Perhaps he did. He might have flown her back here without her knowing. Or made sure she was so drugged she couldn't remember. Is she all right?"

I tell them what she told me.

"Maybe he needed to get her out of the way before he made the announcement about Adam," Emma suggests.

"Possibly," I agree. "A defective clone isn't good for business, is it?"

"In that case, I think we need to find Eve," Emma says with some urgency.

"You're right. I wouldn't put anything past Dr. Mullen. Maybe he's left her to die." Then something occurs to me. "You don't think he would be keeping her at his old clinic, do you?"

"No, my dad cleaned it up, fired everyone who used to work for Dr. Mullen."

Of course. I'm not thinking straight. I knew that.

"I can find the address for this phone number online," I say. I grab my phone. And discover that the house is surprisingly close by!

"Why would he stick her anywhere so obvious?" Emma asks. "It's too easy."

I pause to think about that. The worst scenario comes to

246

mind.

"Maybe it doesn't matter where. He figures she'll be dead soon, and then she won't be a problem."

Ariel and Emma stare at me. I can see that makes sense to them—too much sense, unfortunately.

"We need to find her," I continue. "If she's dying we don't want it to be with strangers."

"But how?" Ariel asks.

"Yes, how?" Emma echoes.

"It is so annoying being stuck out here," I say, stating the obvious. Although even if we lived in one of the cities, I'm too young to drive a car. Like everywhere in California, you pretty much need one—or a parent to drive you. "Bikes?" I suggest.

The other two nod. No choice. I'm strong enough to double up with Eve if we're lucky enough to find her. Ariel has a brand new bike. I also have a new one, and there are two pretty decent older ones my parents use. Emma takes my mom's.

I check Google Maps first, and then we set off—after Ariel has made sure we are slathered with sunscreen. She's become some sort of health fanatic because she worries that both of us are susceptible to all kinds of diseases, especially cancer. Who knows what our genetic makeup might spring on us next?

It takes us about forty-five minutes to get close to the address, which turns out to be near the Polo Grounds. It's in a subdivision of large homes, a gated community with a guard. This poses a problem. How to get in?

247

Chapter 37

We huddle together on the grass, away from the gate so the guard doesn't see us and become suspicious. We are exhausted. I drink half my water and make Ariel do the same. It's *only* 105 degrees today, which feels almost cool compared to the 115 it's been for the last week.

"Do you think we could come up with a story the guard would believe?" Emma asks.

"I doubt it," I reply. "They won't let you in unless you have a person to call." I look at the wall around the complex. "It isn't too high," I remark. "We could probably climb over if we used our bikes to stand on. Let's ride around and see if we can find a spot where no one will see us."

We get onto our bikes and drive down the nearest side street. When we reach the end, we see that the complex is part of a large golf course, with condos built around the links.

"We may be able to get in through the golf course," Emma suggests.

She's right, of course. I've always wondered why people bother with the gates and guards when you can just get in a back way. We keep riding until we finally see an opening, a fairway that flows into a wash. We get off our bikes and walk them over the wash, hurry across the fairway—I really don't want to die being hit on the head with a golf ball—and find ourselves at the back of a cul de sac.

248

This neighborhood is made up of large, detached homes. Million dollar homes, no doubt. I check the map on my phone.

"We're on ...," I look around, "Hummingbird Drive. And the address is here," I point, "on Blackbird Way. So we go," I pause to get my bearings, "that way."

It takes us another ten minutes before we reach the right street. We ride by the house once, checking it out, and stop a few numbers down. The house is a long, low bungalow, probably at least three or four bedrooms, with a two-car garage. There's no obvious activity. We leave our bikes and casually walk around the house checking all the windows, but no luck. They are all dark and shuttered.

"Now what do we do?" Ariel asks.

"We could just go knock on the door," I suggest. "If one of the nurses answers, we could push our way in. Maybe Eve will hear us and she'll manage to get out."

Emma shrugs. "I can't think of anything better," she says. "Let's do it."

We grab our bikes and walk them over to the house, leaving them near the street, on the well-manicured grass that someone has managed to keep green despite the past month of scorching sun. We walk up to the door. I pause for a second to work up some courage, then bang on the door. We listen intently. Nothing. No sound at all. I bang again. Nothing.

I turn the handle with the intention of rattling it and yelling, except the handle turns easily and the door opens.

"Whoa!" I exclaim.

"That's weird," Emma says.

"Too weird," I agree. "Should we go in?"

"Of course we should," Ariel declares, as she pushes past me. "Maybe she's sick. I wouldn't put it past Dr. Mullen to

249

leave her here to die all alone."

"Neither would I. But let's hurry. I don't like this. It's too ..."

"It's too B movie," Emma finishes my sentence.

We step into the foyer. It's dark and cool, a relief from the terrible heat. The foyer opens onto a living room/dining room. The house is furnished in typical southwestern-desert style. There is a couch and an armchair in the living room and a TV that is on, tuned to CNN, with the sound off. It looks like more on the cloning story, but I try to ignore it and concentrate on my surroundings. Drapes cover the front windows and longer ones in the dining room probably cover sliding doors to the backyard.

"Hello?" I call out. "Hello?"

No answer. The house has that quiet feel, no one around.

"Let's split up," I say. "Emma, you and I will check the bedrooms. Ariel, look in the kitchen and out back. If we can't find Eve, maybe there will be evidence that she's been here."

Ariel heads off and so do we. This feels wrong. Plus there is a strange smell in the air. I hurry and check one of the bedrooms. It has twin beds. I look in the closet. There are clothes that would fit a girl Eve's age. So maybe she is here somewhere, or was. I look in the bathroom. Three toothbrushes. There is a door off the living room, probably a den. I open it and draw in a quick breath. It looks like a complete operating theatre with two beds, machines, wires, lights in the ceiling—and a funny odor. I walk into the room. Emma comes in after me.

"The two rear bedrooms are completely empty," she says, "but wow, look at this!"

Just then a strange tingling sensation begins in my fingers.

250

My knees feel all wobbly and my head starts to spin. I hear Emma's voice behind me.

"Miranda, I don't feel very ..."

She doesn't finish her sentence. I turn toward her. She crumples to the floor. My head is spinning and it feels like there's a hurricane in my ears, the roar of rushing wind. Ariel comes into the room. I see her as I sit down hard on the floor. I grab Ariel's hand as she nears me.

"Get Emma out of here," I say, my voice a whisper.

Ariel drags Emma out and soon is back for me. She helps me up and I stagger out into the fresh air. I collapse on the grass beside Emma, gulping air.

"Miranda," Ariel is saying, "can you hear me?"

My head starts to clear, the noise in my ears subsides, and I crawl over to Emma. Her eyes are open. She stares at me for a moment, then speaks. "What the heck just happened?"

"I'd say we were set up. There was some kind of gas in there and if Ariel hadn't gone outside we all would have dropped like flies. Ariel, can you get us our water?"

Ariel runs to our bikes and brings back the water. I help Emma sit up. We take deep drags from our bottles.

"If someone is out to do us harm, I suggest we get out of here as quickly as possible," Emma says.

I agree. "Can you get up?" I ask her.

Slowly she stands, as do I. I feel like I've been hit on the head with a hammer. We walk shakily over to our bikes and start off slowly. We ride out through the front gates and then head toward Palm Desert. I'm in the lead. After about ten minutes, I notice a small strip mall on my left, down a side street. I spot an ice cream place. We turn in, park our bikes, go inside, order some smoothies and sit down in a booth.

251

"What's going on?" Emma pulls her hands through her thick hair. It's gone all frizzy from the heat and the ride and her eyes are looking wild.

I shake my head and take a sip of my drink.

"Do you think it was some kind of poisonous gas?" I ask.

"Must have been," she says.

"Was the place booby-trapped?" Ariel asks.

"Maybe set to go off when we opened that door," Emma replies. She stops. "If you hadn't looked outside," she says to Ariel, "we would all be dead."

Ariel nods. "Yes. That is obvious."

"Not so obvious," I say. "We don't know what that gas was. Perhaps it was to knock us out, not kill us."

"Why?" Ariel asks.

"Could Dr. Mullen be after you again, I wonder?" I say, looking at Ariel. "Maybe he can't cure Eve so he still wants you back. You're the perfect clone, after all."

"So he knocks us all out and takes Ariel," Emma says. "Based on that theory, what happens to you and me?"

"Maybe we don't wake up," I say. "Maybe we know too much."

"Or if we survive somehow, no one believes us because you have already been caught doing crazy things."

And my parents wouldn't fight to get Ariel back, I think to myself, not wanting to say it out loud in front of Ariel.

"But why would Dr. Mullen need me?" Ariel objects. "He has Adam now."

"Adam is just a baby," I point out. "What if he grows up with health problems like Eve? Or like I had? He'd want a backup, some proof that he could create a perfect clone. You are still that proof. Not to mention the disgusting baby-selling

252

plan—nice blonde baby girls ..."

I feel cold all over, despite my overheated body. Is this what we have in store for us? Will Dr. Mullen never leave us alone?

"Let's say Dr. Mullen figured out we'd go looking for Eve. Does that mean Eve set us up?" Emma asks.

"No!" Ariel exclaims.

"But maybe Eve was being used by Dr. Mullen to get us out to that house," I suggest.

"If all this is true, he is a very bad person," Ariel says softly.

"We know he wouldn't hesitate to kill us," I say. "We found that out when we tried to rescue Eve the last time. What on earth are we going to do?"

"I think we should still try to find Eve," Ariel says. "She may know nothing of this. And she might still be in danger."

"But we're in danger too," Emma reminds her. She looks at me. "Miranda, you have to consider going public."

"Telling the world about the evil Dr. Mullen?" I say.

"Yes!" says Emma. "He *is* evil. I'm sure he's behind this. Who knows what other horrible things he's doing. He could be creating clones and killing off the ones he doesn't like, the ones that aren't perfect enough. We have to stop him."

"No!" Ariel exclaims. "Then everyone will know we are clones. Our lives will be ruined."

"She's right," I say to Emma.

"My father always says you have to do the right thing for the right reason," Emma reminds me, "never mind the consequences. Because we never know what the consequences will be."

"We do," I say. "CNN and the tabloids will take over our lives. We'll never have another normal day."

"And what about Eve?" Ariel interjects. "He could hurt her

253

if he thinks he's about to be exposed. She'd be a hindrance to him and he'd leave her to die."

"That's true, too," I agree.

"If Dr. Mullen is charged, wouldn't our parents be charged also?" Ariel asks, bringing up a subject I prefer not to think about. "I mean, they paid for his work and they were going to have me used for spare parts for Miranda. Couldn't that get them in trouble with the police?"

I sit and try to sort things out. I know that what Emma says is true. But how can I doom Ariel to a life labeled as a lab rat? Because that's what she'll become. If I'm honest, I don't want that for myself either. Is that so wrong? And Ariel has a point about Eve. She may be an innocent dupe in all this. Or she may not be involved at all—left to die by Dr. Mullen. Then there's the question of my parents. I'm mad at them, but mad enough to send them to jail?

Just then my phone rings.

"Hello?" I say after grabbing it out of the knapsack.

"Miranda?"

"Eve?"

"I've escaped! I'm ... I'm at a drugstore ..."

"Where?"

"Hang on," and there is a pause. "At the Westfield Mall on Highway 111 and Washington."

"Stay there. Don't move." I hang up. "Emma, can you call your brother? Think he'd come get us in the van? Eve's escaped, and she's at the mall. And I don't think I have the strength to ride her double all the way back to the house after that little gas episode."

As Emma reaches for her phone, I wonder if we are about to rescue a friend or an enemy.

254

Chapter 38

While we wait for Josh, we discuss how to explain Eve to him. Soon he drives up and helps us stow our bikes in the back of the van.

Emma tells him the story we've come up with.

"Josh," she says, "this is a secret. Not from Mom and Dad. As soon as they get home we'll tell them—just from your friends."

"Why?" he asks. Emma and I know lots of Josh's friends from school. Some of them are even hot.

"Well it's all about this custody battle. See, Ariel has a twin. And when she came here ..."

"I thought she was an orphan—your cousin," he says to me. "That you call a sister because your parents adopted her.

"She is my cousin," I answer. "But her father isn't dead. He took the other twin. And he raised her."

"Weird."

"Yeah," I continue, "and here's the thing. Apparently my mom hates her dad and they don't speak. So Eve, that's the twin, found out about Ariel a month ago, and she's run away and come here. But it has to be a secret!"

"I don't like this," Josh says. "Her dad will be worried sick. The police will get involved."

"No. Because she told him she's going to stay with a friend here, and she's calling him every day. He thinks it's some kind

255

of school exchange thing."

Josh tilts his head and looks at us all.

"Okay. That's the stupidest thing I've ever heard. What's the real story?"

"She's a clone," Emma sighs.

"Emma!" I exclaim.

Josh laughs.

"Fine, don't tell me. I just hope you guys know what you're doing. Guess it can't be that bad if you're going to tell Mom and Dad. Let's go get this weirdo freak twin clone."

I smile weakly. We head down 111 and sure enough, we spot Eve, standing alone, peering around furtively. She doesn't look sick, which is a relief. She's dressed in a sleeveless white shift, no doubt something the nurses put on her.

She practically leaps into the van as we pull up. I'm at one window, Ariel slides over to the middle, and Eve buckles up beside Ariel.

Emma twists around from the front seat. "Are you all right?"

Eve impulsively throws her arms around Ariel. "I am now," she says. "Let's get out of here."

I reach over and squeeze her hand, so relieved to simply see her alive!

We drive away, none of us able to say much because of Josh. He's blaring his music anyway, so we all just settle in and rest as he drives us back to my house.

"I'll come get you at dinnertime," he says to Emma. "Mom and Dad will be back—we're ordering in."

"Thanks Josh," Emma says. "You can be a fairly decent brother when you try."

He grins. "See you."

As we get into the house, Emma says to me, "I wonder if he likes you."

"Me?"

"Yes, you. Josh never does me favors. Why would he start now?"

Josh is very cute. Curly black hair, tall, a bit gangly and a few too many zits, but all in all not unacceptable. And more importantly, he's a nice guy. Funny. Smart. A little naive. He'd never go out with me if he found out what I was. I grimace.

"I don't think you'd want your brother hooked up with a freak."

"You aren't," she objects, giving me a gentle slap on the arm.

Meanwhile, Eve and Ariel haven't stopped talking. Emma and I follow them into the kitchen. We raid the fridge—cold chicken, pasta salad, muffins and lemonade. I'm not sure where Lorna is. As I watch Eve and see how happy she is to be with us, I push away the thought that she might have been in on setting us up. I observe her without her noticing, and there is nothing guilty or furtive about her behavior.

We sit in the kitchen, gobbling down our food. Finally, now sure I won't faint from hunger, I say to Eve gently, "How are you feeling?"

She shakes her head. "Sometimes I feel fine. Sometimes I don't."

"And you don't know how sick you are?" Emma asks.

"No," she answers.

"How did you get away?" I ask.

"It wasn't hard," she answers, "once I put my mind to it. I crawled out the window. It was easy to break the lock."

"Why would Dr. Mullen bring you back here?" I ask.

"It seems you escaped pretty easily," Emma adds. "What happened to your nurses?"

"They were both in the kitchen or living room when I got out, I think," she says. "Why?"

"Because we were just at that house looking for you. It was empty. No nurses. And we nearly got killed, or at the very least knocked out, by some very nasty gas."

Eve stares at us. "But that's horrible. Why would they do that? It must have been some sort of accident."

"Have you seen the news?" I say.

"No."

I store that at the back of my mind, remembering the TV still on in the living room. But if her story is true and she had been confined to her room, then she wouldn't have seen it.

"Dr. Mullen's made a new clone. A boy," I explain. "And he's announced it to the world. I think he wants to get rid of the rest of us."

For a moment Eve doesn't speak.

"It's possible," she says reluctantly. "When he found out he had me and not his perfect Ariel, he was very angry."

No one speaks until Emma breaks the silence.

"I really think you need to come forward and tell people," she says to me.

"No!" Eve exclaims.

I stare at her in surprise. That's the most emotion she's shown since we found her.

"Why not?"

She seems to try to force herself to calm down. "Think what would happen to you and Ariel."

"I know, I am thinking about it," I say.

"At least you won't be dead," Emma says, her voice low and

258

intense.

"Maybe we'll wish we were," I retort. "And who knows? All the publicity might ruin our lives and still not protect us."

"But maybe it's not even about that," Emma says. "Maybe it's just about exposing him. He's dangerous. The world should know."

"Before we decide about that," I say, "we'd better decide what to do about Eve."

"In what way?" Eve asks.

"Do we let Mother and Father know you are here?"

"I don't think they liked me very much," Eve says.

"I think they may still be in touch with Dr. Mullen," I add. "I don't trust them. I think we should keep you a secret from them."

"She could come and live with us," Emma suggests. "It would be good because my dad could take care of her if she's sick and we could tell people who ask that she's Ariel. And Mom and Dad already know all about her ..."

"That's a great solution," I say to Emma. "Eve, is that okay with you?"

Before she can answer, the phone rings. I answer. It's Mother.

"We're in New York," she says. "We'll be back late tonight. How are you, dear?"

"I'm fine," I say.

"Miranda, you *couldn't* be fine."

"See you later," I say.

"See you later," she echoes.

"My parents will be home later tonight," I report. "No doubt they'll find a way to make everything worse."

"They always do what they think is best for you," Ariel says

259

in their defense.

"Or what's best for them," I say. "Think about it. Without their money and support Dr. Mullen would never have been able to create any of us. And perhaps be ready to kill us now. And why did they do it? They were selfish. They couldn't deal with Jessica's death. It wasn't about her and her life. It was about *them*. I hate them!" I exclaim suddenly.

The others stare at me. Emma pats my hand. "You couldn't hate them if part of you didn't love them, too," she says softly.

"That's what you think," I say, not wanting to admit that she might be right. "Listen, I'm hot—anyone want to go for a swim?"

"Me!" Ariel exclaims.

"Sure," Emma grins. "Eve?"

"I'll dangle my feet," she says. "My head's hurting a bit."

Emma leaves a suit here for just such occasions. Very soon, we're splashing around trying to forget all we have to deal with, and the fact that someone may be trying to get rid of us!

Mother and Father arrive home just before midnight. Eve is safely over at Emma's. After all the hellos, Father excuses himself and goes into his den. Mother goes to shower. I listen at the door of the den. I have to! They still can't be trusted.

"I demand you meet with us to discuss this," I hear Father saying. "Don't think I can't still hurt you. You'd better find a time and a place to meet. Just remember who bankrolled all of this for you. Adam's family will be making millions: book deals, movie deals, sales to newspapers! And us? We funded your entire research, for heaven's sake, and we're practically broke!"

Dr. Mullen must have replied because Father says, "I know we didn't want it to come out. For one thing, there would be a lot of awkward questions about the other clones, wouldn't there." He listens. "That's true, we didn't want to move. But you owe us."

Another silence. "You can't tell me they aren't sharing some of the money from that book and movie deal with you." He pauses again. "Then don't take it out of their cut. Take it out of yours." Another pause. "Because you don't want all your secrets out, do you?" Pause. "No, we don't either. Fine. Tomorrow." He puts the phone down.

I walk into the room. Father looks at me.

"How much did you hear?"

"All of it. Why are you even negotiating with him? He'll stop at nothing—even murder. You can't trust him!"

I plunk myself down in one of the thick leather chairs.

"I think Dr. Mullen is behind the things I've been accused of doing," I state. "He's trying to discredit me and our whole family."

"I don't suppose there's a better explanation," Father says. "I know you would never spray graffiti or shoplift, Miranda. Unless Ariel did. Or a fourth clone. Or even Eve," he adds.

"No, Eve is sick, remember?" I say. "And Ariel had nothing to do with either incident!"

I'm almost completely positive. Of course she wasn't affected by the gas and we were ... but no, she's the one who saved us! Oh, this is driving me mad! Now I'm even suspecting Ariel!

Father comes over to me and pats me on the shoulder.

"Don't worry, Miranda, we'll take care of this," he says. "And no matter what, we've signed the deal on this new

261

venture, so we should be able to get by."

Mother comes into the room.

"And believe me, Miranda, no one is going to hurt you," she says, her voice grim, pulling her robe tight. "You can be sure of that."

I wish I could believe them.

I hurry off to my room to call Emma.

"So?" I ask.

"Well, my parents were a little surprised to see Eve, to say the least."

"Are they okay with it?"

"They are not too happy about Dr. Mullen resurfacing. I didn't tell them about the whole gas thing. You know them. I'd never be let out again on my own."

"Right," I say. "I get it. Won't mention it around them."

"Uh, listen, Miranda."

"What?"

"My dad definitely thinks you need to go public with this. Even without knowing what Dr. Mullen tried to do to us, he thinks the guy is dangerous." She pauses. I know something is up.

"Spill."

"He says if you won't tell, he might have to."

I feel the heat rising to my cheeks.

"He'd do that? I thought I could trust him! He's the only one I *can* trust! Why would he do that against my wishes?"

"Because he's the adult. And he says sometimes the adult has to make the tough decision, if he knows it's the right one."

I try to think. "Okay, I get that. Ask him to give me just a few more days, all right? I need to think it all through."

"That should be good enough for him for now," she replies.

"I'm sorry, Miranda, I know you don't need more on your plate."

"Hey, this is all part of it, isn't it? Meantime my dad is busy negotiating with Dr. Mullen."

"No!"

"Oh, yes."

"How can he still trust him?"

"My parents refuse to see things as they really are. They have their own version. They make their own reality," I sigh. "And aren't I living proof of that?"

"Too true. I better go make sure Eve is settled. Try to get some sleep."

"You, too. See you in the morning."

I hang up the phone and then sit where I am on my bed for the longest time, staring into space. What else might Dr. Mullen have planned?

Chapter 39

Monday morning and we're back at school. I'm nervous. I'm not sure what's going to happen next. Is someone going to try to frame me? Kill me?

Emma and I sit in English class but I can't concentrate. I keep replaying yesterday's conversation between Father and Dr. Mullen. Even though Father's deal went through, he still wants part of Dr. Mullen's money. Is it just greed, or is he that worried about my future health? Father certainly isn't interested in stopping or exposing Dr. Mullen. But why should he be? He was Dr. Mullen's first supporter. He made all this possible. On the other hand, Emma's dad thinks we need to tell the world because it's the only way to stop Dr. Mullen. But he does admit that since the world now knows about Dr. Mullen, maybe Ariel and Eve and I, and our well-being, are more important. He certainly doesn't want to ruin our lives.

Great! Now it's all as clear as a desert sandstorm. If I tell, my parents could go to prison. I mean, can I live with that? And Ariel and me, well, our lives as we know them are done. So maybe it's best just to let Father get as much money out of Dr. Mullen as he can, start over, and pretend everything is normal. Something inside me says that all sounds very logical—but then no one will ever find out what an evil man Dr. Mullen is and how close Ariel came to being killed, as if she wasn't a human being at all. No one will ever know the

264

problems Eve and I have had, physically for sure—rare genetic diseases and all—but also mentally. I mean, growing up a freak isn't the funnest thing in the entire world. And worrying all the time. Every time you get a headache—is it a brain tumor? First grey hair—premature aging? First depression about something—have you gone nuts? Dr. Mullen makes it all look so, so, perfect. But Eve isn't perfect. And I've already almost died once. And ...

The fire alarm interrupts my thoughts.

Everyone in the class groans. Grumbling is heard everywhere as we all file out, figuring it's some kind of drill and we'll have to stand outside in the hot sun. Until we smell the smoke, that is. Then we hurry.

Once outside, the grapevine works fast. Sue comes over to me and Emma.

"Someone exploded something in chem lab."

I roll my eyes. Honestly. At least once a year someone manages to do that.

"On purpose!" she adds.

"What do you mean?" I ask.

"The lab was empty. Someone went in and did something."

"Let's find Ariel," I say to Emma.

The fire trucks have just pulled up and the firefighters are rushing into the school. We find Ariel hanging out with her friends, chatting, enjoying the break.

"What's up?" she asks.

I have to smile. Only a short time ago she would have said, "What is the problem?" Or, "Why have you searched me out?"

"Nothing," I say. "Just wanted to say hello."

She gives me that little sister look, like, Okay, you've said hello, now stop embarrassing me. Emma and I take the hint and leave. At least I know she's fine. They can't leave us baking in the sun for too long—it's 120 degrees today. As soon as the firefighters have everything under control the bell rings and we're let back in.

I'm not at my desk more than five minutes when: "*Will Miranda Martin please come to the office?*"

I groan. "I didn't do it!" I exclaim to the class.

Everyone laughs. They were all with me the whole time, so that's a pretty safe bet. Funnily enough no one really believes I wrote the graffiti either. Well, a few kids always like to think the worst so I did get *some* grief. But mostly everyone thinks I'm too much of a goody-goody. It almost upsets me to think that they couldn't even *imagine* me doing something bad. Who wants to be that predictable?

Still, when I get to the office the secretary motions me to go straight in to Mrs. Dean. When I get to her office, she shuts the door.

"The cameras show you coming out of the lab just before the explosion."

"Mr. Gordon will tell you differently," I say, heart sinking. There *must* be a fourth clone! "I was in English class the entire time."

"He'll confirm that? No bathroom breaks? Nothing?"

"Nothing."

"Can you explain how you can be in two places at once?"

"No." Well, I could, of course, but I won't.

"Miranda, you must have figured out a way to slip out of Mr. Gordon's class without him noticing. The camera doesn't lie."

"What was I wearing?"

She looks at my clothes. "Not that."

"I rest my case. Can I see the video?"

She loads the file and I watch. Bulky top, overalls—as if I'd ever wear overalls—baseball cap. Very similar to me, but not me.

"Maybe someone has it in for me," I suggest. "Dress like me, you know, set me up."

"Why?" she asks.

I shrug.

Mrs. Dean looks unconvinced. She must think I slipped out of class, changed clothes ...

"Why would I want to do it?" I say.

"You tell me," she answers.

"I wouldn't. And I didn't do the graffiti either. Or the shoplifting."

"Well, this is all very odd, Miranda."

"I know, Mrs. Dean," I say.

"You can go."

At lunch Emma and I try to work out what is going on. But we're interrupted by Josh.

"Hey," he says, "can I join?"

"Sure," I say.

He sits down beside Emma.

Emma looks surprised. "You are gracing us with your presence? To what do we owe this honor?"

"Actually, I thought I should tell you I saw Eve at school today. She was supposed to stay home, wasn't she?"

"Are you sure it was Eve, not Ariel?" Emma asks.

"Pretty sure. She was wearing those overalls of yours I think are so stupid. That's why I noticed."

I gasp. Eve? I'd forgotten Emma had those overalls.

"What would she be doing here?" Josh asks.

267

"Blowing up the chem lab?" I suggest.

Josh smiles. He thinks I'm joking.

"When did you see her?" I ask.

"I was on an errand for Ms. Jimenez during second period, and there she was. She disappeared around the corner before I could call her. I only saw her for a second, but like I said, I couldn't miss the stupid overalls."

Emma and I look at each other. We can't say anything while he's here so we try to chat as if nothing is wrong, but soon the conversation fizzles and Josh leaves. As soon as he is gone, Emma grabs my wrist.

"Maybe there's not a fourth clone," she says quietly. "It makes sense. She's grown as tall as you, just like Ariel."

"Maybe," I agree. "But it *doesn't* make sense. Why would she do *any* of this?"

"We'd better find out, don't you think?"

"Yes, I do," I say. "Let's go now."

"No," Emma says. "You're in enough trouble. Call your mom and ask her if you can come over after school. We'll confront Eve then."

"Maybe we shouldn't confront her," I say. "Maybe she won't admit anything. Maybe we need to spy on her. Catch her in the act."

"You might be right," Emma agrees. "Otherwise she can just deny it all."

I shake my head. "I just don't understand," I say. "Why would she do it?"

"Could she regret her decision to take Ariel's place and go back to Dr. Mullen?"

"Why would she?" I ask. "He was her only hope. Everyone else said she was incurable. And he might have succeeded."

268

"Or not," Emma says grimly. "Her headaches are back. What if she is sick? Really sick. And it's affecting her behavior. Remember when she was first diagnosed with the brain tumor—the doctor said it could cause a personality change."

"We don't know Eve very well," I say. "We don't really know what her personality is."

"She *is* a clone of you," Emma points out.

"So, does that mean her personality will be identical?" I challenge Emma. "Does that mean I'm the same as Jessica? Is Ariel the same as me?"

"We've gone over this before," Emma says. "I don't think so."

"Yet you don't think she could be bad because I'm good."

Emma grimaces. "Oh, I don't know what to think."

"No use speculating," I answer. "We'll have to watch her to find out."

"We may need to clue Josh in," Emma says. "I mean, how do we follow her if he won't drive us around?"

"I don't want Josh to know!" I object.

Her eyebrows rise. "You like him."

"I don't!"

"Otherwise you wouldn't care."

I change the subject. "How did Eve get here all the way from your house?"

"No clue," Emma answers. "Another reason to follow her."

"We'll just tell Josh we suspect her—we don't need to tell him the whole clone story."

"Okay," Emma agrees. "Call your mom and tell her you're coming over. We'll take it from there. What the heck is Eve playing at, I wonder?"

"Let's just hope we can find out," I answer.

269

Chapter 40

We arrive at Emma's to find Eve all sweetness and light. She's wearing shorts, though, not overalls. Why would she try to blow up the chemistry lab? Was she trying to get me in trouble? Or was she trying to blow up the school and kill us all?

Ariel has gone home with Mother. It would look suspicious if Emma and I let her hang out with us. We don't want to raise any red flags with my parents.

I'm getting a little worried about following Eve. What if she does something really dangerous and we can't stop her? On the other hand, I guess there still could be a fourth clone and Eve *might* be completely innocent. Emma and I have devised a plan to see if she'll give herself away.

"Emma and I need to study for a really important exam," I say to Eve. "Do you mind if we close the door and work right through till dinner?"

"No," she answers readily. "You go ahead. By the way, how was your day?"

"Oh, fine," I reply.

"Good," she says.

We've decided not to even mention the fire. Let her stew, if it's her.

"How was yours?" I ask.

"I was bored. I sat inside and watched TV and read."

270

Emma and I go into Emma's room and close the door. Not more than five minutes later, Josh comes in.

"She's snuck out of the house," he says.

He's agreed to spy on her for us—although he's getting more and more suspicious about who she is and what's going on.

"Will you help us follow her?" I ask.

"Sure, come on," he says. "Mom, I'm just driving the girls to the mall," he calls to his mother.

"Be home by six for dinner," she calls back.

We head out in the van. Within a minute we spot Eve. She's on Emma's bike and has gone about three blocks.

"Well, at least we know how she got to school, if it was her," I say. "It's not that far from your house to school, after all."

She turns into one of the many mini-malls. We follow at a discreet distance. She parks the bike in front of a big music store, locks it up, goes in. We hurry out of the van and follow her in. Each of us takes a different direction to track her down. I see her first.

She's looking up at the security camera. Then she takes a couple of CDs and drops them in her knapsack! She's obviously going to make a run for it and have the camera show it was me! I stalk over to her, grab the bag and empty it on the floor. About a dozen CDs fall out. I pick them up and put them back on the shelf. Then I take her wrist and drag her over to the front desk.

"Can I speak to the manager?"

Soon an older man shows up. So do Josh and Emma. Eve stands quietly, not looking surprised to see me or upset that I've got a grip of steel on her wrist.

"May I speak to you privately?" I ask the manager.

271

"Yes."

I loosen my grip on Eve. "Don't move," I order her.

The manager and I walk a little away from the others. I call on all my acting skills.

"Your security camera is going to show my cousin there," I point to Eve, "putting CDs in her knapsack. Please could you ignore it this once? She's here from out of town and trying to make friends. She got in with the wrong crowd and they dared her. I promise it won't happen again."

He stares at me for a moment, thinking.

"She has to be banned from the store," he says, finally.

"Of course."

"All right."

"Thank you!"

I turn away from him and motion to the others that it's time to go. Josh has a firm grip on Eve's arm. We collect Emma's bike, throw it in the back of the van and get in. Josh drives us home.

None of us says a word. He parks in the driveway and Emma and I drag Eve into Emma's room. Josh tries to join us, saying, "Hey, I should get to hear what's going on!"

"We need to talk to her alone. Trust me on this," Emma says, blocking Josh at the door.

Josh looks doubtful, but can tell by the tone of Emma's voice that she means it. He shrugs assent.

"Thanks," she says. "I promise I'll explain later."

"I'll hold you to that," he replies.

I shut the door and turn to Eve. "Why?" I ask.

She flips her hair back and stares at me defiantly. "Why not?"

"Sit down," I order her.

272

"I prefer to stand."

Emma and I are standing too. I have my hands on my hips. I'm tempted to thump her.

"Did you have anything to do with the gas in the house?"

"How could I?"

"I don't know how. I'm asking you."

"Don't you think you found that house very easily?" she asks.

"Dr. Mullen wanted us to find it?" I ask.

"Maybe."

"You didn't warn us? You would have let us die?" I exclaim. "I can't believe it. You wouldn't!"

"Oh, grow up," Eve snarls. "I had a choice to make—me or you. And I chose me."

I am so startled by her reply I have no words. Emma steps in.

"I don't understand," Emma says. "You can't be the same Eve who gave herself up for Ariel."

Emma turns to me. "She's probably not Eve at all! She's the fourth clone and Eve is being kept somewhere by Dr. Mullen."

"You go ahead and think that, if it makes you feel better," Eve says.

"Is it true?" I ask. "Are you a fourth clone?"

"I doubt you'll believe me one way or the other," she answers. "But I am Eve. Dr. Mullen gave me a choice: help him get you in serious trouble, even get rid of you, and he'll put all he's got into curing me. At first I refused. Then I got sick. And sicker. So I agreed. He put me on this new experimental drug. He's going to make sure I'm okay."

"Eve," I say, "he might do the best he can—if you can even trust him to do that. But that doesn't mean he can cure you."

273

"I know," she says. "But it's my only chance. He doesn't want you and Ariel around to ruin his business. You were a mistake he wants to forget."

"You mean Miranda and Ariel are proof of his illegal activities. And what about you?" Emma asks. "You're his worst failure. At least Ariel is as perfect as Adam. Don't you think he'll want to get rid of you first?"

"No!"

"Why not?"

For a moment she can't think of an answer. "Because he promised," she finally says.

"And you grabbed at anything," I mutter, "because you were desperate."

"He was fascinated that I agreed," she says. "He said he didn't think my genetic programming would allow me to hurt you."

"He said that?" I say.

"Yes."

"Don't you get it?" I exclaim. "You're just another of his experiments. He wanted to see how far you'd go, to see if you could be a bad girl, his dark clone."

"That's not it!" she insists. "He's going to help me. I can do it because I'm not programmed like you are to be the perfect good girl. Who wants to live like that?"

"But you are my clone!" I insist. "You are the same as me."

"Well then I've broken free! I'm an individual and you're trapped. You're stupid. You are a sitting duck for him right now."

"So are you!" I say.

"No, because I don't care if I have to live in a lab somewhere and have a secret life. I don't care as long as I can live. Who

274

knows what the future will bring?"

Emma goes to the door. "We need to talk," she says to me. She turns to Eve. "You—you stay here. We can catch up to you in the van, so don't try to take off."

Emma grabs Eve's phone and takes it with her.

She leads me out of her room and into the backyard. "What on earth are we going to do?" she says.

"I don't know! I think we need to tell your dad."

"I'm not so sure," Emma says. "He'll freak. He'll expose Dr. Mullen and your parents before he lets anything happen to me or you or Ariel. And then you won't be able to decide anything."

"I don't think they've left me any choice," I say. "I've been trying to protect Ariel, and my parents and me, of course. But maybe by saying nothing I've put us in more danger. I've let Dr. Mullen get in a position now where even if I say anything they'll say oh, she's just a troubled kid. Blowing up labs, shoplifting, vandalism—you know."

"Eve doesn't care if she hurts us, as long as *she* isn't hurt. She doesn't care at all how we feel," Emma says. "So she's very dangerous."

"But we can't *let* her hurt us," I say.

"How do we stop her? We can't lock her up," Emma points out.

"Maybe it's time to tell my father and mother. They've never cared about her. They'll have no compunction about making sure she can't hurt me or you or Ariel."

"I don't like it. They would hand her right back over to Dr. Mullen even though she trusts him ..."

I add to her thought, "He's capable of anything. What if she is some kind of test for him and now that he has his data he'll

275

just let her die. Or kill her."

I am truly at a loss. I don't know what to do. I feel paralyzed. Eve is not on my side, but I still care about what happens to her. How can I let her die?

"You know what my dad always says," Emma suggests. "Do what you believe is right. Sometimes it works out, sometimes it doesn't. You can't control that."

"But I know that if I come forward and tell the world about Dr. Mullen, our lives as we know them are over. So I do know it won't work out."

"But you also know that not saying anything isn't working out either, is it?"

"It certainly isn't," I agree.

A scream from inside the house stops all conversation. It's Eve.

Chapter 41

Emma's dad reaches Eve before we do. He's just back from work. Eve is holding her head, screaming in pain. Dr. Green talks to her in a soothing voice. He looks in her eyes. Then he says, "She needs to get to the hospital. Come on. I'll drive."

It's only five minutes away to Desert Oasis Hospital, where he has privileges. We pile into Dr. Green's car, Eve in back with me, Emma in front with her dad. Eve is whimpering from the pain. I hold her hand. She squeezes mine so hard it hurts. When we get to the hospital she is whisked away and Emma and I are left to wait. I'm feeling so numb and confused I don't know what to think. Finally Dr. Green comes and finds us. He makes us sit, and he perches on a small table across from us. He clears his throat.

"I'm sorry to have to tell you this, but Eve is a very sick girl. From what she tells me Dr. Mullen did operate on her tumor and had some success with her illness. But now her cancer has returned. We can't operate because of where it's situated in her brain. Has she been behaving normally?"

Emma looks at me.

I nod, giving her permission to tell.

"No," Emma sighs. "Not at all. She's been purposely trying to get Miranda in trouble."

"Well, tumors in the area where hers are located can be associated with behavioral changes."

277

"Is there any hope for her?" I ask.

He shakes his head.

"How long?" Emma asks.

"We can never say," he replies. "But we're talking days or weeks, not months or years."

"Can she come home with us?" Emma asks.

"For a while," he answers. "But soon she'll need more care than we can give her." He puts his hands over ours. "I'm sorry, girls. I know how hard this is."

"Dr. Green," I ask, "is this something that could happen to me, or Ariel?"

"I can't tell you that," he replies. "It may have to do with the cloning, it may not. I'm sure of one thing—you need to be monitored more closely than a ...," he pauses, "well, than most teenagers."

He was going to say normal, I know he was.

"We're stabilizing Eve with some strong drugs. She'll stay overnight."

"Can we see her?" I ask.

"Not now," he says. "You'll see her tomorrow after school. She'll be released then. Come on, let's get home and get some food in you two."

Jewish mothers have nothing on Jewish fathers. Emma and I both exchange a small smile despite ourselves. Food cures everything.

We do feel a bit better after we've eaten. My mother is due to pick me up so Emma and I don't have a lot of time to talk. We go back outside, the stars blanketing the sky now, the moon a beautiful crescent. I sit on a rocker and she lies down in a hammock.

"And she thought she was free!" I say. "Instead her tumor

278

was making her do bad things."

"You're too nice," Emma says.

"What do you mean?"

"Just what I said. Say her tumor did change her. She can still choose! She didn't have to try to destroy you. Come on. We all have free choice."

I stop to think about that. "I'm not so sure. I'm engineered to be smart and strong and according to Dr. Mullen, good. And hey, guess what? I'm all of those things."

"Yeah," Emma says, "and you could be the biggest snob in the entire world, but you aren't. You could be at the top of the school with your looks and smarts. But instead you hang out with normal types like me and Sue. And it's not like your parents exactly set the best example—they've always given you everything you've ever asked for."

"They loved me," I say softly.

"They still do." Emma pauses. "Maybe that makes up for everything. No one has ever loved Eve, have they? I mean, you love Ariel and she knows it and look at what a great kid she's turning into. Since Eve didn't get any love, she goes for ... I don't know, survival?"

"But when she sacrificed herself for Ariel, tricking Mullen into taking her instead ..."

"Yeah," Emma says, "she probably thought we'd love her for that. But then she ends up with Dr. Mullen and he only cares about what she can deliver. For whatever use she can be to him. And if that's all she can get—well, that'll be what she goes for."

"I hate to say it," I admit, "but I think you're right. We may have limits, but within those we can choose. Now I have to make the biggest choice of my life, and Ariel's. I just wish there

279

was a way we could expose Dr. Mullen without also exposing me and Ariel, and my parents."

"Maybe there is," Emma says.

"I don't think so."

"Come on. You're so smart. You must be able to think of something."

"There's nowhere we can hide, though, is there? I mean in the olden days people with secrets would go to Europe or London. But the press is even worse over there. The first clones—we'll be tracked every moment of our lives."

"But that'll calm down after a while, right?"

"Yes, but everyone'll know. All our friends. Any new friends I make. I'll be looked at like some sort of freak."

"I don't look at you that way."

"How many of you are out there?"

"You might be surprised."

Dr. Green comes outside and interrupts us.

"Girls?"

"Yes?" Emma says.

"I have some disturbing news."

Emma sits up. "What?"

"Eve has disappeared. She's not in the hospital."

My heart sinks. Now what?

"Where could she have gone?" I ask. "I thought she was all drugged up."

"She is," Dr. Green says. "I'm worried about her. She could be aggressive. She may not be safe to be around."

"Ariel," I blurt out. Without another word I get up and race to the phone. I call home. Mother answers. "Is Ariel there?" I ask.

"No, she went out with a friend," Mother answers.

280

"Who?"

"I'm not sure."

"What do you mean?" I yell. "How could you not know?"

"She said one of her friends from school was picking her up and that she'd be back soon."

"You'd never let me do that," I accuse. "You still don't care about Ariel, do you, even after all this time!"

"I'm trying, Miranda," Mother says, her voice trembling with anger. "I didn't ask to have Ariel here."

No, I want to say, you were just keeping her for parts. But what's the point? I'd said that many times, and it didn't change anything. I hang up and try Ariel's phone. To my relief she answers right away.

"Ariel!"

"Hi, Miranda!"

"Where are you?"

"I'm with Eve."

My heart is in my throat. In fact my throat goes so dry I can hardly speak.

"Where are you?"

"Oh, I'm not sure. She came and got me in a cab, said you needed us both. We're—where are we anyway?"

Suddenly the line goes dead. "Ariel? Ariel?"

I turn to Emma and Dr. Green. "Eve has Ariel. She's taking her somewhere."

"Why?" Dr. Green asks.

"Yes, why?" Emma echoes.

"She saved Ariel only a few months ago," I say. "She knows that Ariel will trust her absolutely. I don't know why she's gone after her, but somehow as soon as I heard Eve was gone I knew she would. Oh, why didn't I think to warn Ariel?"

281

"None of us thought Eve would be going anywhere," Dr. Green reminded me.

"We all forget how strong Ariel and Eve and I are. Drugs that would knock out a normal kid probably just took away her headache and made her feel well enough to get busy," I say.

"But get busy with what?" Emma says.

"I wish I knew," I say. "We'd better find out soon. If she hurts Ariel, I'll ... I'll ..."

"What?" says Emma. "Kill her? Seems to me she doesn't have much to lose." Emma turns to her dad. "Did you tell her about the cancer?"

"I did. She said not to worry. Dr. Mullen would fix it. She was delirious, of course."

"Fix it. Dr. Mullen *would* fix it or *did* fix it?"

"Would," Dr. Green says.

"She already knew about the new tumor," I say. "And Dr. Mullen had promised to cure her again. As long as she does as he asks. And at the same time he can watch her and see what she's willing to do, to avoid dying."

"That's what I'm worried about," Emma says. "Just how bad is she willing to be?"

Chapter 42

"Why would she take Ariel?" I say, almost to myself.

"Why did Dr. Mullen want Ariel last time?" Dr. Green offers. "Her genetic code."

"Plus," I add, another thought occurring to me, "without Ariel I can't tell the world about me being a clone. She and Eve are the only proof I have."

"That's it!" Emma exclaims. "Without Ariel you are just a nut who shoplifts and writes graffiti on walls."

"So he very well might kill her," I say, suddenly realizing how immediate the danger is for Ariel.

"I think we can't rule it out. We'll have to call the police and put out an Amber Alert," Dr. Green says.

The phone rings and makes us jump a mile. Dr. Green answers. He listens. "Yes Eve, I understand." Pause. "Eve, you are very sick. I really think ..." He stares at the phone. "She hung up."

"What did she say?" Emma asks anxiously.

"She said that Ariel won't be hurt—but if we call the police, she'll be killed. And we'll never find her body." He puts down the phone and we watch him as he thinks.

"This might call for my parents," I say, knowing now that I waited too long to make my decision. Too long. "They are the ones in touch with Dr. Mullen. They're the only ones who might be able to negotiate with him."

"All right," Dr. Green says. "But we can't wait forever Miranda. At some point we will have to take whatever action is best for Eve and especially for Ariel."

"I know," I answer.

My mother is due to fetch me at any moment, so I grab my stuff, say a quick goodbye, and promise to keep Emma and her dad up to date.

Mother starts to quiz me as soon as I get into the car.

"Why all the worry about Ariel?" she asks.

"Let's wait till we get home," I say. "Dad will need to be involved."

"Dad?" she says. "I haven't heard you call him that in months."

She's right. Maybe that talk with Emma has softened me a bit. But just a bit. I still think that they were selfish, creating me so they wouldn't have to deal with their grief. But it's also true what I said—they have loved me.

When we get home, we all sit down in the kitchen. Mother puts on the kettle for tea. I grab a lemonade. Suddenly I start to cry. Ariel loves lemonade. And I might never see her again. Father tentatively puts an arm around my shoulder—I've been so angry with him I haven't so much as let him kiss my cheek. But now I find myself sobbing into his embrace.

"Miranda," he says, his voice soothing, "what it is it? It can't be that bad."

"It is," I say, hiccupping. "It is. Dr. Mullen has Ariel. We're never going to see her again." Then I tell them about Eve and about everything that's happened until now.

"You were right to tell us," Father says.

"You should have told us about Eve right away," Mother exclaims. "Why, you could be dead right now! Oh, I'd like to

284

get my hands on Mullen."

"He'll be here in an hour," Father says.

"What?" I exclaim.

"You're joking," Mother says.

"No. It's what I arranged yesterday. He's agreed to split some of his profits with us in exchange for our silence. We're meeting to iron out the deal."

"You can't trust him," I say. "With all of us out of the way, he'd be free and clear."

"Yes," Father says, "I can see that. And with Ariel gone, there's no proof that you are a clone, and so he doesn't need to pay us anything."

"He won't come," I predict. "He doesn't have to now."

We sit and wait. Emma texts me every few minutes. She is trying to hold her dad back from calling the police, but as the evening drags on it gets harder and harder. By eleven o'clock it's clear that Dr. Mullen won't be coming. No call, no show.

A horrible thought occurs to me. I'm home free. Dr. Mullen will never admit I'm a clone. Ariel is gone. If I agree to keep quiet and can convince Dr. Mullen I'm no threat, I could probably have a totally normal life with no one suspecting anything. Even Josh ...

I finally call Emma.

"My parents can't help," I say. "And I can't let Ariel down. If we're going to find her, you and I will have to do it."

"Then we will," Emma answers. "How? Where do we start?"

"Well, we could start at the house where Eve was living before."

"But why would she go back there?"

"Do you have any better ideas?"

285

"No."

"Will Josh take us?"

"I'll ask. Tomorrow after school?"

"Sure."

"Maybe you should think about it first," Emma suggests. "You realize that you are free and clear now."

"I know," I say. "It has crossed my mind, but I couldn't live with myself. If Ariel hadn't given me half her liver I'd be dead now. I can't just let Dr. Mullen take her. She's my sister now."

"Yeah, I know," Emma sighs. "My dad's calling the police first thing in the morning, so we'll need to act fast."

After we hang up I wash up and get into bed. The whole house feels empty without Ariel. I lie in the dark unable to sleep. Why didn't I speak out sooner? I told myself I was trying to protect Ariel but the truth is, I was scared. I was scared of the circus my life would become. I was scared of being labeled a freak. I was just plain scared. Of course the right thing was to stop Dr. Mullen. Stand up to him. Not so easy when you're scared though, is it? Guess that's how bullies and dictators get so powerful. No one wants to stand up to them. I see why now. The trouble is, what happens later is even scarier.

Tears trickle down my cheeks. Poor Ariel. She didn't deserve any of this. Neither did I. At this moment I wish I'd never been—well—created! But I was, and now I have to deal. *I won't let you go without a fight*, I vow to Ariel before I fall into a troubled sleep.

I don't know what wakes me up, but I am suddenly wide awake. I look at the clock by my bed. It's 1 a.m.

Dr. Mullen was supposed to be here tonight. He didn't show. But why set up a meeting like that if you aren't going to be in town? Maybe he'd made the appointment with dad as an

286

insurance policy. If he couldn't snatch Ariel, he'd make a deal with dad. If he could grab her, no deal needed!

I grab the phone. Emma answers, groggy. "Emma, can you get Josh to drive us?"

"Yes, I said I would."

"No! Now!"

"Now?"

"Yes."

"Why?"

"Think about it. Dr. Mullen has Ariel. Alive, she and Eve are proof that I'm a clone. Eve's going to die soon anyway. I'm not perfect. Maybe he doesn't need Ariel alive. He kills her, uses her tissue to create more clones. He doesn't snatch me because I'm not perfect; I've almost died once already. I'm defective. Without her I can't tell on him. Which means his mission will be to store her DNA. Maybe even tonight. We know he was using that house near the Polo Grounds to keep Eve," I say, the words tumbling out. "He might not have anywhere else to take both of them. I think we need to get over there."

"Okay," Emma says. "I'll get Josh and be there soon as we can." She pauses. "Should we call the police?"

"No way! If we're wrong, it's just one more thing that shows how crazy I am."

Emma hangs up. I throw on a pair of jeans and a sweatshirt and sneakers. I creep down the hallway, only to see my dad sitting in the kitchen drinking a scotch. He looks pretty worried. I wonder where Mother is.

"Miranda?"

Oh great! She's right behind me!

I try to seem casual as I turn around. "Yeah?"

287

"What are you doing?"

"Nothing, just getting some water."

She's in her nightgown and looks like she's about to go to bed. "In your jeans?"

"I couldn't sleep. Thought I'd sit outside for a bit."

She nods.

I go into the kitchen and take a glass and fill it with water from the fridge.

"Can't sleep either?" Father asks.

"No."

"Want some company?" The look of hope in his eyes is sad.

"No thanks, Dad," I answer. "I just need to sit for a while. I'll be on the patio."

He seems a little mollified—at least I called him Dad.

I take my glass and go out onto the patio off the kitchen. I sit on a chair where Dad can see me. I can also see the driveway from here.

Then he comes outside anyway!

"Miranda?" He sits down.

"Yeah?"

"None of this is your fault."

I don't want to fight with him. Or talk to him at all. I can't let him see Emma and Josh!

"I know."

"You do?"

"Yes." I don't, but I need to get rid of him. I didn't do the right thing when I could have. But neither did he. And I am his daughter—sort of.

"Look Dad, I'd just like to sit out here alone for a while. Okay?"

"Sure," he says, uncertainly. "But don't beat yourself up."

288

The words just tumble out despite my resolve not to talk to him. "No, but I should learn to take responsibility when I'm wrong, shouldn't I? Or is that something you'd rather not talk about?"

"It's something I'd like to talk about. But I don't admit I was wrong to make you—look at you. We love you so much. We could never agree with you that it was a mistake."

He stares down into his glass and sounds like he's going to cry.

"Sure, Dad," I say, "I see that."

"You do?"

"Yes. I mean," and to my surprise I think I mean it, "I'm glad I'm alive. Even though a little while ago I felt the opposite. I guess I wouldn't have missed this for the world."

He smiles. "Thank you, Miranda. Thank you."

"Now can I just ..."

"Oh. Right. Don't get cold."

It's about 80 degrees, so that's unlikely. "I won't."

"And don't stay out too long. School tomorrow."

"Sure."

"You're free and clear now, you know," he says. "You can be a normal teenager. No one will ever have to know your secret."

"Yeah. I realized that a while ago."

"How does it make you feel?"

"I'd be so happy."

"You'd be ..."

"If not for Ariel."

He knows this is where it gets dangerous. "I'll go in now."

And just in time—because I can see the van turning into the drive.

289

Chapter 43

I slip into the back of the van and close the door as quietly as I can. Josh pulls out onto the street and stops.

"That's it," he says. "I'm not going any farther until I know what's happening. I have the distinct feeling that Mom and Dad should know about this."

"If we tell you, we'd have to kill you."

He calls me on my lame joke. "Not even close to funny enough—come on now. I'm the big brother. I don't intend to get my little sister into trouble."

Emma twists in her seat to look at me. I shrug. She knows what that means. My heart races. How will he react?

"The thing is," Emma says, "we really weren't joking before. Mom and Dad know about this. Miranda really is a clone. So is Ariel. So is Eve. Dr. Mullen is behind it all. And now he's kidnapped Ariel and we think she's in danger—like he might kill her."

"Emma!" Josh exclaims. "It's late. I've got an English test in the morning. This isn't funny."

"She's telling the truth," I say. "I didn't want you to know. I didn't want you to think of me as a freak."

Something in the tone of my voice must make him reconsider. "You're serious?"

"Deadly," I reply.

"But it's impossible."

290

"Well, you know it isn't. You've seen Dr. Mullen on TV with the new clone. I was his first."

That clinches it.

"Man oh man," he says. He pauses. "So shouldn't we be calling the police?"

"Yes," I agree. "We should call the police if we can find Ariel and Dr. Mullen and Eve. But a wild goose chase won't convince anyone. I've got my phone. The minute we find them we'll call the police. And the newspapers. I've got the number of the *Los Angeles Times* with me. Hopefully, once the secret is out we'll be safe."

"You've decided?" Emma says.

"I should have done it days ago. Now it might be too late to save Ariel," I say, trying to fight back tears. I tap Josh on the shoulder. "Can we go?"

"Where to?" he asks.

We give him directions. As we drive through the night I'm reminded again of the time last year, right around now, when I got sick. I was terrified, sure I was going to die. And now I'm terrified all over again. One way or another, everything is about to change.

The lights of the cars whiz past as they did a year ago. I put my window down and feel the air on my face, breathe in the fragrance of the night flowers and lemon trees. This won't be the last time I'm going to be afraid. But I make a vow to myself—that I won't live in fear. I'll try not to make my decisions based on fear. By doing that I've actually made my worst fear come true. Well, hopefully, not yet. Hopefully, Ariel is still alive, somewhere we can find her. I didn't do a very good job of protecting her.

Josh startles me out of my reverie.

"I just want you to know something, Miranda ..."

"Yes?"

"Well, like, that, you're still who you are. You're not a freak or anything. Not really. I mean so you were made differently. Don't get hung up on it." He almost sounds like he's trying to convince himself. "*Does* it make you different?" he continues.

"Who knows?" I say. "The animals they've cloned suffer from premature aging. I could get diseases that older people get, like osteoporosis, even cancer. I've already nearly died once."

"Yeah, well, it sucks, but kids get cancer all the time. I mean, you'll just have to deal as it comes, but we all do, right?"

"Right," I say. Now the tears do come. Why is he being so nice?

He can tell I'm upset so he turns on the iPod and plays whatever's on it. His mom must have been in the van, because it's a jazz playlist. Kinda soothing, actually.

We have Josh park near the back of the golf course and start out on foot. The moon sheds a weak light, enough at least for us to move slowly toward the streets, and once on the street I can easily remember the way.

"What's the plan?" Josh asks, as we stop near the house.

"We don't exactly have one," I whisper. "We're just going to try to see if they are here."

"We need a plan," he insists. "I should go in, you two stay out here."

"No!" I exclaim. "No way. I can get away with being there—if I'm seen, anyone could assume I'm Eve or Ariel—from a distance at least. I think I should go in alone. I'll set my phone to redial your number out here so I only have to press it. If they're there, I'll do it. Then you call in the cavalry."

292

"It makes sense," Emma says. "One kid who looks like the others gives us a better chance. But how do we get you in?"

"And what if there are some tough guys in there and you never get a chance to call?" Josh asks.

"Well, obviously then you'll also know to get help."

"Fine. Two minutes," Josh says. "If you aren't out here in two, telling us that no one's there, then I'm calling for reinforcements."

"Fair enough," I agree.

I walk up to the front door, expecting it to be locked. Then I figure I'll try all the windows. Then the back door. If that fails—well, I'll just ring the doorbell and see if anyone answers. The place looks dark, but I know that could mean anything—they'd want it to look that way.

Heart pounding, I try the knob. Of course it's locked. I walk around until I get to the back of the house. I notice a sliding door—it must lead to the living room. I try it. No luck. I run back to the front.

"Josh," I say, "there's a sliding door. Can you help me open it?"

"Sure," he says, "but it's probably rigged to an alarm."

"That's okay. So long as I get in—if everyone comes running at least we'll know something is up in there."

"Let's do it," Josh says.

The three of us hurry around to the back. Josh kicks the lock hard a few times until it snaps and we can push the door open. Sure enough an alarm goes off. I push some dark, heavy drapes back. Light floods the room and a nasty looking guy, big, dressed incongruously in a bright red Hawaiian shirt, slams out of one of the back rooms and marches into the dining room.

293

"Get away," I hiss to Josh. "Hey," I call out, "someone was trying to get in here."

He stares at me. "I thought you were ..." He looks over at the operating room.

"That guy just broke in here," I shout at the goon. "Get after him or the whole plan is in danger!"

He hesitates for a moment, then takes off out the back door.

I hope Emma and Josh will be able to handle him. The alarm still ringing, I open the door to the small room.

"Get out of here!" three people yell at once. "You're not sterile. Get out!"

Someone is on the table. They've already started cutting. There's a lot of blood. I race over to look at the face. Ariel! She's got a tube down her throat. I stare down at the incision. Everyone is masked, but I'm pretty sure the short guy is Dr. Mullen.

"You have to stop!" I scream. "Stop!"

"It's too late for that," he says. "We're just finishing. We only have her eyes left." It's him.

"What do you mean?"

"I mean kidneys, heart, lungs, liver. They're all on their way already. On a jet out of here. They're worth good money." My legs suddenly feel like jelly. I stagger.

"Get her out of here," Dr. Mullen orders. Someone grabs my arm and pulls me out into the living room.

I shake them off and sink to the floor, gasping for breath. I feel sick. I put my head between my legs, try to stop shaking.

Tears are streaming down my face. Vaguely, through it all, I hear sirens blaring. Then I realize that Dr. Mullen will hear them. He'll try to escape. *But that will not happen.* I look around. There's a large desk in a corner. With strength I didn't know I had, I push it in front of the door to his operating room. Then I place myself in front of it, ready to fight to keep them there if I need to.

Time seems to slow down. Someone is pushing against the door. Pushing hard. Harder. The desk is being pushed back. Pounding starts on the front door. I run over to it, scramble with the lock and fling open the door. It's the police!

"In there!" I shout, pointing. "Behind the desk!"

They push the desk away. The door flies open and Dr. Mullen, mask off, staggers out of the room, along with the others. I slip past them into the room and move over to Ariel's body. I stare down at her. They've dragged a sheet over her, but it's too horrible and I have to look away. When I do, I see a body on the other table. I walk over slowly, dreading what I'll see. Eve?

"Miranda?" A faint voice says.

"Eve?" I whisper.

"Ariel," she says. "That's Eve. You got here in time. Just like, just like, the cavalry."

I laugh and cry at the same time. She's hooked up to a drip in her arm.

"I was next. He was going to take some samples, and then, well, then I don't think he would have needed me anymore. Eve came to get me and she was laughing about how stupid you were. And then she brought me here. Where is she?"

"She's dead," I answer.

Ariel's eyes close.

"Someone help!" I yell.

A policeman hurries over. He talks into his shoulder piece.

"EMS is on their way," he says.

I hold Ariel's hand.

Within a couple of minutes she's being checked by an EMS attendant, a young woman. "Looks like she's just sedated. It should wear off in a few hours."

From the next room I can hear Dr. Mullen protesting as the police take him away.

Is it over?

Or just beginning?

Chapter 44

Cameras flash and I'm almost blinded. Ariel is holding my hand so tightly I can barely stand the pain.

"Miranda! Miranda!"

"One at a time," Dr. Green says. "Please. We need some order."

"Dr. Green! How long have you known about this?"

"Ladies and gentlemen. Please!"

A young man, in charge of the press conference, tries to establish some kind of order. At the table with Ariel and me are Dr. Green, Mother and Father.

"Now, Dr. Green, if you'd answer the question."

So Dr. Green goes through the sequence of events. I can hardly listen. But I remind myself—I always thought this would be my worst nightmare. But my worst nightmare was actually that moment when I thought Ariel was dead. Of course, I feel terrible about Eve. Terrible. But she was doomed and would have died anyway. At least Dr. Mullen didn't tell her what he intended to do. He told her he was operating on her to save her. So she went peacefully, not in fear, but in hope. If I'd spent that night sleeping instead of looking for her, Ariel would have died too. The police told us that Dr. Mullen had arranged for two bodies to go to the crematorium the next morning. All evidence of Eve and Ariel would have been completely erased, except for the DNA he would have kept in

297

his lab in Belize.

Every once in a while Ariel teases me, pretending to be Eve. But I can tell the difference. First of all, just to be sure, while we waited for Mother and Father to pick us up at the hospital, I gave her a quiz.

"When did Mother and Father leave for their trip?"

"Last Friday."

"Where did they go?"

"Europe."

"What's the name of your best friend?"

"Jen."

"What's the favorite thing of mine you always steal?"

"Your grey shirt."

"What else?"

"Your purple skirt."

Only Ariel would know that!

When my parents took us home, I told them everything. Dad held my hand.

"You won't go through this alone," he said.

"I know."

Then I let him hug me. I even let Mother hug me. And then, miracles of miracles, they both hugged Ariel!

Mother said, "We're lucky to have another wonderful daughter. This won't be easy. But we're a family. And we're going to act like one. We almost lost both of you this week. And if that should ever happen—well, we have no substitutes for you. And there won't be any," she assured me. "Never again. Nobody could ever replace you."

And you know, they've behaved just like real parents over the last week. Protecting me and Ariel however they can. Dad did make a pretty good book deal. But I'm okay with that.

I haven't been back to school yet. Don't know if I'll be able to. That'll be the hard part. I mean, what must Mrs. Dean have thought when she realized I was telling the truth! Heart attack time, no doubt.

"Miranda!" Dad is tapping my hand.

"Yes?"

"There's a question for you."

"How does it feel to be a clone?"

Hah. The big question. I think how best to answer.

"I don't know. Confusing, I guess. I don't know what's me, what's Jessica, what's genetically engineered. I'm not just a clone, remember. I'm also enhanced."

"So how do you tell?" the reporter asks.

"I don't," I reply. "I wonder, but I guess everyone wonders, don't they? You know, was I born with that? Did I get that stubborn streak from Grandma or my artistic ability from Mom or Dad? I guess we're all programmed to a certain extent, right? But then, well, I guess we each have some free will. We can think. We can make choices. Choices that can make things better for other people or choices that will hurt other people. Eve was my clone. She made some very bad choices."

I think about the most shocking thing Ariel told me when she was feeling better. Dr. Mullen had given Eve the job of kidnapping Ariel so he could get rid of both her and Eve— although of course Eve didn't know what he had planned for her. But it was Eve herself who had come up with the idea of getting me in trouble, discrediting me, and making my life miserable. Why? We'll never know, I guess. Maybe she was jealous of me and my friends and my parents and my happiness, and she did it out of pure spite. Dr. Mullen

299

approved, of course, because it had the advantage of making anything I said unbelievable, but it was Eve's idea!

"Does that scare you?"

"What?" My mind has wandered again.

"Does it scare you that Eve made such bad choices?"

"No!" I reply. "It gives me hope that I really can choose for myself."

"But Eve was sick!" another reporter calls out. "Could that happen to you?"

Dr. Green interrupts. "It could happen to you, sir. None of us knows what the future holds."

Suddenly Ariel stands up. "I'd like to say something."

The room becomes quiet.

"I just want to say Miranda is a good sister. You shouldn't be so concerned about her being a clone—you're forgetting that she saved my life. She's a hero. Well, she's my hero."

She sits down. I reach over and give her a big hug.

"Actually Ariel saved my life," I say. "So she's my hero."

I see Emma and Josh at the back of the room. Emma gives me a thumbs up. I grin. I thought I'd never smile again once the news got out. But hey, I'm tough. I can take it.

And Dr. Green is right. Who knows what the future holds?

The End

About the Author

Carol Matas is a renowned internationally best-selling author of over 45 books for children and young adults. She writes in all genres, from historical fiction to fantasy, science fiction to contemporary.

Carol's books have been published all over the world in more than fifteen languages. Her books have garnered over a hundred awards and nominations. *Tucson Jo*, an historical novel for middle grades set in the Wild West, was a 2014 National Jewish Book Awards Finalist. Her other awards include a 2014 Sydney Taylor Honor Book Selection, a 2014 Canadian Jewish Book Award, the inaugural Silver Birch Award, the Geoffrey Bilsen Award for Historical Fiction for Young Readers, a New York Times Notable Book Award, as well as two nominations for Canada's prestigious Governor General's Award.

Carol lives in Winnipeg, Canada, with her husband Per K. Brask, a theatre professor, dramaturge, translator, and poet.

Learn more about Carol at carolmatas.com and on her blog at http://carol-matas.blogspot.ca/.

Made in the USA
Charleston, SC
23 October 2016